BETRAYAL.

Book Two of the Keeper Chronicles

Laura,
Hope you enjoy!

-Ben Meeks

BEN MEEKS

Sidestreet Publishing, LLC
www.authorbenmeeks.com

Cover art © 2020 by Monica Maschke.
All rights reserved.
monicamaschke44@gmail.com

For my biggest fans:

ASHLEY,

LILY

and

ELIZABETH

CHAPTER 1

"Dibs," Holt said, eyeballing Martina.

She was a gray fox shifter and member of the Tortured Occult, a shifter-outlaw motorcycle club. In her human form she was a small but strong Latina. She wore boots, jeans, and a T-shirt. Her leather kutte proudly displayed her allegiance. Though she was young, her hair was silver. Today, like most days, she had it pulled back in a ponytail. It would be a mistake to assume that her small stature or gray hair was an indication of frailty. All members of the T.O. were held to certain standards and there were no concessions made for anyone. Weakness wasn't tolerated.

"She might be more woman than you can handle," I said.

"I hope so." He grinned. "Hey, before I forget, I got you this." He pulled a large black rectangle out of his pocket. "It's a smartphone."

"Pass," I said. "I tried one of those things about twenty years ago. It didn't last a week."

"This is different, it's waterproof. I got this protective case for it, you'll love it. It's called an Otter Box, and look, it's got a little otter floating on the back. See? Isn't he cute?" He held the phone up for me to inspect. "And I can connect it to the Bluetooth on your truck, so you can take calls while you're driving."

I did like it, but I wasn't going to let him know. "All right, I'll try it out. I give it two weeks before it's broke and I get to give out some 'I told you so's.'"

He placed it on the seat beside me. I looked out the windshield at the two other club members standing with Martina. The first was Big Ticket, a wolverine shifter, and the muscle of the Tortured Occult. The second was Chisel. Chisel was all right, but I preferred my bikers a little more refined. He was large and rough around the edges with a perpetually sour disposition. Three bikes and the club's black van were parked in front of a small thatched-roof house. It was a modest home, as most of them are in this area. Straight ahead, a second building sat on the edge of the yard. It looked like a shop. It had a large brick chimney and plain gray walls. It was part of a subdivision, of sorts, for those who can't easily blend into human society. This was one of a few more traditional houses for people too large for the trees or lacking the temperament for underground living. The rest of the homes were camouflaged into the landscape to keep things low-key.

Chisel was leaning against his bike. He had a short scruffy beard and unkempt hair. A streak of grease that he either didn't know or care about on his right cheek stood out in stark contrast to his pale complexion. I pulled my truck up in front of them. Chisel chugged the rest of a beer and tossed the can over his shoulder into the yard. I rolled the window down as he walked over. I saw he had gotten a promotion since I had seen him last. He had a Vice President patch sewn onto his kutte.

"What do we have?" I asked.

Chisel let out a loud belch and blew it in my face. It smelled like cheap beer and unbrushed teeth. "Hank's inside with him. Some weird shit going on."

I pulled the truck in line with van and put it into park. I decided to leave the window down to let the burp air out.

"Why don't you wait out here and keep an eye out," I said to Holt.

He was my apprentice. A Keeper in training. We had been working together three and a half months. If this call turned out to be something demon related, it would be our second job together. He still had a long way to go.

"I'll keep an eye on Martina," he said with a wink.

"If I need you, I'll holler," I said, getting out of the truck.

I crossed the yard toward the house, stopping to pick up Chisel's beer can along the way.

I looked at the bikers and saw Big Ticket looking at me. He was short and stocky, built like a tractor, with the nonchalant bearing of a professional fighter. I lifted my head in a nod. He put an index finger on his temple and pointed it at me in a kind of salute. I pulled the front door open and stepped inside. The room had a kitchen to the left and a large table on the right. A couple of doors led to what I assumed were bedrooms. Hank, leader of the T.O., sat at the table. He was in krasis, the half animal-half human form shifters could take. Werebears were some of the largest of all shifters and Hank was no exception. Black fur added to his bulky frame, stretching his jeans and gray T-shirt to their limits. Over his shirt he wore his cut: A black leather vest with the club's colors and the President patch declaring him its leader.

The orc opposite him was muscular with grayish skin, wearing cutoff jean shorts, a plain green T-shirt, and no shoes. The skin of his face drooped loosely, with two large teeth sticking up from his bottom jaw making him look like a bulldog. He seemed to be in a daze or under a spell, completely unaware of his surroundings. He was bruised and bloody with one eye swollen shut. His clothes were ripped and stained with blood. He wore a silver pendant around his neck. It was a circle with an eye in the center. An arrow was affixed to the circle so that it could be moved to rest above the eye or cross it. A pretty standard magical device used to disguise ultranaturals in public. When the arrow was placed across the eye, it would make him look like a human.

"This is Yarwor," Hank said. "He came into the clubhouse with a hammer and tried to kill one of the patrons. Some of the boys roughed him up pretty good. He put up a fight at first, but after we restrained him it was like the lights turned off and he's been like this ever since."

"You really did a number on him. You sure it's not just that you beat him silly?" I asked, moving over, and waving a hand in front of Yarwor's face.

Hank shook his head. "In our defense, a lotta that blood was already there, but I don't think so. He looked kinda loopy when he came in. All he would say is that he's hungry. His family's missing. We started checking around with the neighbors, but they're all gone too. I think this might be more up your alley."

While the Tortured Occult had done a lot for the ultranatural community, my expertise was in creatures invading from other planes. Humans know them as demons, the ones that make trouble anyway.

I put the beer can on the table and knelt in front of Yarwor. "Can you hear me?"

"Hungry," he mumbled.

"You're hungry?" I asked.

"Always hungry."

"Has he said anything else?" I asked Hank.

Hank shook his head.

"Where's your family?" I continued.

"On the pile," he said.

"And your neighbors?" I asked.

"Always hungry," he replied again as a long ribbon of drool ran out of his mouth and onto his bloody shirt.

I gave the house a quick once over; it appeared to be in order. The only thing that really looked out of place was a large bloodstain on the pillow in the master bedroom. I wouldn't put money on the donor being alive.

"Did you find anything at the neighbors' houses?" I asked Hank, returning from the bedroom.

"Blood, no bodies," Hank said, looking out the door. "I think he killed them all. Regardless, he came into the clubhouse starting trouble. We're going to have to do something about that."

"Let's figure out what happened before we start making plans for justice," I said. "I don't think he ate them. There would be a hell of a mess if he butchered them and the place is pretty clean, considering."

Hank leaned back in his chair. "Unless we haven't found where he did it."

"Hungry," Yarwor mumbled from the bed. "Grubby."

I stood in front of him. "Where are the bodies?"

"The mine," Yarwor said without looking at me. "Grubby."

"The copper mines are a couple miles east through the woods," Hank said. "That could be what he's talking about."

I headed for the door. "I'll check it out."

"Want some help?" Hank asked.

"I have Holt. If there's anything in there, we can handle it. Just keep an eye on things here."

Outside, Holt looked downright chummy with the Tortured Occult. With a beer in his hand, the only thing that made him look out of place was that he wasn't wearing a kutte. They laughed and cut up until I had made it across the yard to the truck. I waved him over as I opened the door and pulled out my gear bag.

"Well, is it true?" Holt asked placing his beer on the hood of my truck.

I pulled a couple flashlights out of the bag. "Is what true?"

"They say he went crazy and killed a bunch of people. What do you think?"

I shrugged. "Looks like the cheese slid off his cracker. We're gonna check the mine."

I handed Holt a flashlight. On the far side of the yard we found a trail leading off in the direction of the mine and followed it.

When we were out of earshot of the bikers Holt asked, "Isn't Hank the leader of the Tortured Occult?"

"You know he is," I said, pushing a low hanging branch out of the trail. "Why are you asking?"

Holt stuck his hand out to keep the branch from whipping him in the face as we passed. "Big Ticket has a patch on his vest that says Pack Leader."

"In the T.O. anyone who's killed for the club gets a Wolfpack patch. B.T. is the pack leader of the wolfpack. He's pretty much the club enforcer."

We walked in silence a couple more minutes before Holt asked, "What do ya think's in the mine?"

"If I had to guess," I said, "a pile of bodies."

I stopped walking when we were in sight of the mine.

"What are you doing?" Holt asked. "We're here."

"Let's just watch for a few minutes. No reason to rush in."

We knelt in the brush. I didn't really expect to see anyone, but if someone, or something, was in there, the sooner we knew about it the better. It's too cold and damp in the mine to be fun for any length of time. It dated back to the early 1900s and until recently was open to the public. Now it's fenced off from the road, discouraging visitors. After a few minutes, I was satisfied, and we moved closer.

It'd been years since I'd been here, but it hadn't changed much. The mine shaft was about thirty feet in diameter and two hundred feet deep. It disappeared into a hillside on the edge of the Chestatee River. A large puddle, taking up almost the entrance, blocked the way. There was a small path on the left just big enough for one person to walk at a time and keep their feet dry. The only sound from the mine was steady dripping. I flipped on my flashlight. It was woefully underpowered for the job. Here the darkness was absolute. Holt clicked on his flashlight and we walked single file into the mine. The light looked out of place, like an intruder the darkness was fighting to push out. The mine's chill, a good twenty degrees cooler than the autumn air, sent goosebumps across my arms.

"Krasis?" Holt whispered from behind me.

I nodded. When we cleared the puddle, we made the change to krasis. After a few centuries, my body had become acclimated to the change. Being bound to the otter, I grew a long tail, light brown fur, sharp claws, and teeth. Holt was much newer at this and his body took longer to make the transformation. He twitched and grunted through the thirty seconds it took for him to make the change. He took on the aspect of a Doberman with short black fur and a long snout and teeth. Both of our bodies grew and added muscle.

"How long till it doesn't hurt anymore?" Holt asked when he had finished.

I shrugged. "Hard to say. I think I stopped noticing any pain around eighty years in."

He scowled, apparently unsatisfied with that answer. I understood why. He had been a Keeper about thirty years. Fifty years of the pain from shifting was nothing to shake a stick at. No doubt, by now, the worst of it was over for him.

"Let's split up. I'll follow the right wall and you take the left," I said.

We continued into the mine. My fur did a good job insulating against the cold and I was glad to have it. Even though I couldn't see anything but darkness around me, I could feel the openness of the cavern in my whiskers. It stretched out all around me. Holt moved off to the left, quickly disappearing except for the beam of his flashlight. It bobbed and shook as he made his way over the rocky floor of the mine. I ran my fingers along the wall as I went. It was slow going over cantaloupe-sized rocks littering the floor of the mine. I passed a refrigerator someone had dumped. I couldn't help but wonder if all the effort to get it this far into the mine was better than disposing of it properly. Either way, it probably had something to do with the fence going up. It's been a theme in the area for a while. Some really wonderful places where people would go to take a dip in a river or explore nature are now blocked and signed off. People afraid of being on the receiving end of a lawsuit, or having their property destroyed, tell everyone to stay away. Rites of passage and pieces of the culture die as a result. It's a shame really.

I followed the wall until I came to a large canvas sack sitting on the ground beside a pick. The sack had some rocks in it. I ran my fingers over some fresh gashes on the wall. It looked like someone had been doing a little mining recently. I shined my flashlight around to find I had hit a dead end. I was in a smaller section of the mine near the back wall with nowhere else to go. There was no sign of any bodies or demons. Maybe Holt was having better luck. As if on cue, he gasped from somewhere on the other side of the mine. His voice echoed, making it hard to tell exactly where he was.

"You okay?" I shouted.

I waited for a reply as the sound of my voice bouncing from the walls died down. No response came. He must have found something, or maybe something found him. I could hear movement from somewhere in the mine. I worked my way back along the opposite wall as quickly as I could manage over the rough terrain.

The sound had stopped by the time I got to the other tunnel. I scanned the area for Holt, bodies, or anything unusual. Nothing turned up. As I moved into the other side of the mine, I began to make out a light about fifty feet in front of me, just a pinprick in the distance. I killed my flashlight, stopped, and listened. The only sound was the steady dripping of the forming stalactites. I approached cautiously, moving slowly over the cold, jagged rocks littering the floor. I couldn't help but think that at any second something would jump out from a shadow or from behind a rock.

CHAPTER 2

I could barely make out a boulder beside where Holt had dropped his light. As I moved down the tunnel it became clear it wasn't a rock at all. Holt's flashlight was in front of a pile of bodies. I turned my flashlight off and slipped it into my back pocket, retrieving Holt's to use instead. It was newer and more powerful than mine. Now that I had more lumens to work with, I inspected the pile of bodies. On the bottom were an orc woman and child. That must be Yarwor's family. Covering them were a variety of ultranaturals I assumed to be the missing neighbors. They all looked to have died hard. Some had stab wounds, others blunt force trauma. It looked like Yarwor had been busy. The bodies on the bottom of the pile had pieces missing with strange circular bite marks. Something had been munching on them. It was hard to tell how long the bodies had been there. The coolness of the cave slowed the decay and muted the stench. A trail of blood led into a hole on the left wall. Something had been coming in and out long enough to leave a smooth trail streaked with dried blood. Holt was nowhere to be found.

I inspected the hole. It looked slimy around the edges. I really didn't want to climb down there. I eyeballed it, trying to come up with any other explanation for where Holt had gone. I just couldn't reason my way out of it. The mouth of the hole was just wide enough to fit though. I opted to go in face first. At least that way I wouldn't be sucked in by some unseen monster like a scene in a horror flick. I got down on my hands and knees and shined the light in the hole. It went down for a couple feet and opened to the left. I crawled in. It was a tight fit squeezing around a rock jutting out from the side. I got to the bottom and quickly rolled to pull my legs though. The opening looked to reach back about fifteen feet with lots of irregular formations. It was about four feet tall and smelled like a demon kennel. A few partially eaten body parts and feces were strewn randomly around the cave.

I leaned forward to look around a stalactite and stuck my hand in a pile of crap I hadn't noticed. It was cold and wet, I picked my hand out, stretching strings of slime between my hand and the floor. I shook my hand, sending much of what had stuck onto the nearby wall with a splat. The rest I wiped off onto the rocks. Moving carefully to avoid any more surprises, I made my way around the cave, searching inch by inch, floor to ceiling. When I got to the back wall without finding anything I stopped and turned around. Where was Holt? I climbed out into the main section of the mine.

None of this made any sense. If he had found the demon or if he left for some reason, then why didn't he let me know? Any why didn't he take his flashlight? Maybe he did find the demon and that's what that yelp was. He could be anywhere in the mine; it was large and would take an hour or more to go over in detail. I would need help. With the Tortured Occult I could do it in a fraction of the time. Reluctantly, I made my way back to the mouth of the mine.

The air felt warm when I made it outside. I changed back to human form and spotted Holt's tracks in the mud at the mouth of the mine. He had walked through the puddle, instead of around it, on his way out. He was still in krasis. He knew better than to run around like that in the open—maybe he was chasing something. The tracks went in the direction of Yarwor's house. I followed at a jog. I came out of the trail to see the three bikers chatting the way they had when we left for the mine.

"Where is he?" I asked.

"Where's who?" Chisel said, turning toward me.

"Holt. Did he not come back?"

They looked at each other, confused.

"You're the only person we've seen," Martina replied.

"Obie," Hank called from the doorway of the house. "You're going to want to hear this."

"Keep an eye out," I said, jogging past the bikers. "Something's wrong."

Inside the house I found Yarwor no longer had the glazed over expression. He wrung his hands with worry and paced around the room. I shot Hank a questioning glance.

"This is Obie," Hank said. "He's looking into what happened to you."

"Don't go in the mine," Yarwor said, taking a few steps toward me.

I held my hand out to keep some distance between us. "Too late, we've already been there and back again."

"Did you find it?" he asked.

"I found signs of demon activity and some chewed up bodies," I said. "Holt was with me but left for some reason. I followed his tracks back this way, but no one's seen him."

Yarwor took a seat and the table. "It has him then. That must be why it let me go."

"You wanna catch me up on what we're talking about?" I asked.

"I'd been doing a little digging in the mine, for copper mostly. A couple weeks ago I was attacked. It came out of nowhere and was on me before I knew what was happening. It looked like an overgrown slug with tentacles. It attached to my head and sort of . . . took over. I knew what was going on around me, but couldn't control myself. Even after it got off my head I was still under its control. I could hear it in my mind . . . and this insatiable hunger. That first night when I came back . . . my family." He choked up as he spoke. "I watched as they were killed, by my own hands. I was used as a weapon against them and there's nothing I could do."

Yarwor buried his face in his hands and began to sob quietly. Hank looked skeptical about the claims of being mind controlled. I couldn't blame him, it was unorthodox. Not impossible though. I gave Hank a shrug to let him know the jury was still out.

"That wasn't enough for it," Yarwor continued with tears streaming down his cheeks. "Then it made me start hunting my neighbors. There was already more than it could eat, but it wanted more, always more."

"So, you're not under its control now?" Hank asked.

"About fifteen minutes ago it just went away, like waking up from a bad dream. If two of you went into the mine and now one's missing then it has to have him."

"And what does it want?" I asked.

"To eat," he said grimly, "That's all."

I heard a commotion outside. Hank looked out the window as I moved to the front door. I saw Holt fighting all three of the T.O. and doing pretty well. Chisel was down and not getting up, Martina had stumbled back, holding her face while blood ran through her fingers, and Big Ticket stood toe to toe swapping punches with Holt. The T.O. were still in their human form, apparently taken by surprise. In krasis Holt had a clear advantage. Humans blend in well but are decidedly lacking in natural weaponry. Despite that fact, Big Ticket seemed to be enjoying the exchange. He had a big grin on his face Holt wasn't wiping off, no matter how many times he was hit.

I changed back into krasis and charged outside. While Big Ticket had him distracted, I ran up behind Holt and spun, delivering a whip with my tail. I heard ribs pop when my tail made contact. The impact sprawled Holt out on the ground. With Big Ticket's help, we pinned him to the ground. I wanted to resolve this with as little damage to him as possible. B.T. didn't seem to feel the same way and took a couple shots while Holt was pinned. Holt struggled, but when he couldn't break free, he lay still. His head was covered in an ooze that matted his fur and had run down his shoulders in strings. I didn't see the demon anywhere.

"Everybody okay?" I shouted.

I turned my head to see Martina had changed to krasis. The gray fur and canid features of the fox shifter did little to hide the fresh claw marks running across her face. It would heal completely, but the scars would linger for a bit. I doubt that helped Holt's chances with her any.

"There it is!" Yarwor shouted.

We all looked up to see what appeared to be the back end of a Chihuahua-sized slug disappearing into the side building.

"I'll get it," Yarwor said, running after it.

Holt thrashed without warning, with an unusual strength, even for him. It caught Big Ticket and me by surprise, and Holt was able to wrestle free. He dashed after Yarwor, both of them disappearing into the building, one after the other.

"Check on Chisel," I said to B.T., running after them.

The building turned out to be a smithy. A large anvil mounted to a stump sat in the middle of the room with a coal forge to the right. The walls were lined with tools and tables with plenty of places for the little demon to hide. Yarwor had managed to catch it. He was doing his best to squeeze the life out of it. It screeched and writhed, tentacles flailing wildly. Yarwor wasn't prepared to defend himself. Holt closed in and punched him in the side of the head with enough force to send Yarwor toppling over the anvil. Yarwor dropped the demon and disappeared behind the anvil. The demon scurried under a table. Holt turned slowly toward me. He had the glazed over expression I had seen on Yarwor earlier.

"Snap out of it already," I said.

Holt walked casually over to the wall of tools and picked up a sling blade. "Grubby's hungry."

"Holt, you can fight this," I said. "That demon can't be stronger than you are."

He took a step toward me, then cringed and rubbed the heel of his hand on his temple. "But it's hungry, Obie", he groaned. "It's so hungry,"

It looked like he was starting to come out of it. If he could hang on just long enough to stay out of the way, I could find and kill the demon. It must have realized that it was losing control of Holt because it came scurrying out from under the table, giving me a good look at it for the first time. Yarwor's description was right. The demon had a white, slug-like body about a foot long with tentacles surrounding a circular ring of teeth. It pulled itself with the tentacles and crawled with its segmented body. It moved surprisingly quick for what could best be described as a land squid. It scurried and climbed up Holt, latching onto his head with a stomach-turning slurping sound. With its tentacles hanging and the demon's body on top, Holt looked like a Rastafarian wannabe.

Physical contact must have reinforced the demon's connection; Holt's eyes glazed over again. He raised the sling blade. I jumped back, avoiding his first swing but tripped over some scrap metal, falling backward. I grabbed a piece of pipe and used it as a shield, blocking blow after blow. There's no way I could get to my feet without taking a hit from the blade. The pipe was bending. It wouldn't last much longer, I had to do something quick before the pipe broke. I raised a leg to kick Holt's knee. He went rigid and stopped swinging. He dropped the blade and fell forward on top of me. I got a face full of tentacles and was suddenly overcome by the fear that the demon would try to make a Rastafarian out of me, too. I pushed Holt off to see Yarwor standing there with rather menacing looking hammer and determination on his face.

The demon thrashed in pain from the blow, but it wasn't dead. It crawled off Holt's head, dragging its way toward some wood stacked in the corner. It appeared to be crippled. It pulled itself with its tentacles and wasn't making good time. Yarwor screamed with the rage and sorrow only a man who watched his family die can understand. He drove the hammer down on the demon. The first strike sent its thick black blood splattering into my face. Yarwor pummeled the demon into the dirt. When it was over, there was little more than paste in a hole with some tentacles beside it. I ran a hand over my face wiping the blood away. Yarwor looked down at the demon puddle, dropped the hammer, and walked quietly out of the smithy.

CHAPTER 3

"He's gotta answer for it," Chisel yelled. "Hell, they both do."

I wiped some spittle from my cheek. "First thing, Yarwor's already even. You kicked the crap out of him remember? Second, Holt's a Keeper of Thera, and you're not gonna touch him."

"Oh yeah?" Chisel sneered. "And what if I do?"

I smiled at him. "Then you'll have to answer for it."

We stared each other in the eye for what seemed like ten minutes before Big Ticket chimed in. "I don't see what the big deal is. It's just a little scrap."

"It's not up to you," Chisel snapped.

"You're right. It's up to me," Hank said. "Chisel's right. We have to send a message if somebody comes into the clubhouse causing trouble."

"How about this," I said. "I won't heal him. You already hurt him and that way he has to live with it. Message sent."

Hank ran his tongue over his teeth and looked off into the woods as he contemplated my proposal. "All right. Let's roll."

"Hold up," Chisel said. "What about Holt?"

Hank stepped up, getting in Chisel's face. "Let's roll," he repeated.

They glared at each other. Chisel turned and headed for his bike with the rest of the T.O.

"You good here?" Hank asked.

"Yeah, I'm gonna load the bodies and get them to Hob," I said.

"Sounds good," Hank said.

Hank, Chisel, and Big Ticket climbed on their motorcycles and cranked the engines. Martina had been looking at her face in the van mirror. The scratches Holt gave her had closed into three noticeable scars running from her forehead, across her nose, and down her cheek. On Hank's order, she got in the van and followed them.

I watched them drive away. When they were gone, Holt and I retrieved all the bodies from the mine. Any ultranatural without immediate family would be taken to the duster. I had organized an agreement between local factions years ago to keep the peace. The agreement established borders between the Tortured Occult and the Elven Nation and put rules in place for the manufacture of pixie dust. Dust, used to power magic, was made from the processed corpses of ultranaturals. Dust was dangerous to manufacture. It took specialized knowledge and equipment to produce. Beyond that, the producer had to have a mastery of magic or be close to mindless. If not, the dust could accidentally be ignited by any hint of anger or frustration. To say it would be an explosive situation would be an understatement.

We had Hob to work as our duster and the Tortured Occult handled local distribution. Any surplus went to the rats in Atlanta. Most of the dust came from demons that I supplied. Unfortunately, this time I had a truck full of innocents. I left Yarwor's wife and daughter behind for him to bury and covered the rest under a tarp in the back of my truck.

~⌒⌐

"What are we even doing here?" Holt asked. "Shouldn't we be getting these corpses to Hob?"

"Just making a little stop. I've been hearing rumors about this place and I wanted to check it out. I won't be long." I opened the door to the truck and got out.

"What if someone comes along and starts poking around? About . . . You know," he said, pointing a thumb toward the back of the truck.

"No one's going to mess around in the back of a truck if someone's in it," I said. "Just wait here. Shouldn't take but ten minutes at most."

I closed the truck door and walked down the street to the Bear Book Market. Dahlonega had been without a bookstore for years before this one opened up. It was in a tiny space just off the square. I had been hearing rumors that it was more than just a bookstore, but hadn't had the chance to look into it yet. The storefront had a large glass window and a single door. The shop looked unattended. A rocking chair was placed beside the window with a desk beside it. The walls were lined with bookshelves packed neatly to the gills. Slips of paper were taped to the front of the shelves, designating the sections. I pulled the door open and stepped inside.

The store smelled like old paper. I caught a whiff of cologne and faint scents of humans and ultras that had come through the store. No one greeted me, so I took a minute to look through the books. I pulled a book off the shelves, *Henderson the Rain King*. It had a lion on the cover and I was just flipping it over the read the blurb when the back door opened, and two people walked out.

The first was wearing dirty jeans and a dingy red flannel. He looked tired. He was rolling his right sleeve down and raised his eyebrows when he saw me. I felt as if I had walked into the middle of something that was supposed to be private. The man headed for the door and walked out without saying a word. He smelled like iodine and sweat.

"Hello, I'm Clay. Welcome to the Bear Book Market," the other man said, walking over to the desk and sitting down.

He was wearing khakis, a blue button-up shirt, and a newsboy cap. He had a few days of scruff and gave off an air of sophistication that was unusual for the area. It was clear he wasn't from around here.

"Thanks," I said. "It's my first time in the shop."

"Well, we deal mostly in used books, except for the section there for local authors," he said, pointing to a shelf across the room. "I have more books in the back. If you're looking for something special, I can probably get it for you."

I had heard rumors that a bat shifter was working out of the Bear Book Market. I couldn't tell if it was true yet. The cologne covered his natural scent. If the rumors were true it could be problematic. The myth of vampires was based on werebats: They drank blood and changed into bats. They didn't *need* to drink blood; they had a special ability to draw power from the blood of those they drank from. The more powerful the victim, the more power werebats gained. They had also figured out how to manufacture Ichor from their blood. It was a highly addictive drug that was responsible for ruining countless lives. Not something to take lightly.

The werebats tended to stay in cities. If one had come to Dahlonega it might bring trouble, such as Ichor, with it. It technically wasn't my responsibility, but I live around here, and I didn't want the town going to hell. First thing to do was figure out if the rumors were true. From the guy smelling of iodine and pulling his sleeve down, I had reason to think they were.

"When you say, 'something special,' what do you mean?" I asked, wishing I was more street savvy.

"I have some first edition, autographed Stephen Kings, if that's your thing," he said.

I looked at the book I was holding. "What about Ichor?"

"I'm not familiar with it," he said. "Who wrote it?"

He had the hint of a smirk, barely perceptible.

My phone rang. I pulled it out and looked at the screen. It was Holt. I hit the button on the side of the phone to silence it. I was almost done, and the truck was a two-minute walk away. He was probably just bored. What kind of trouble could he be getting into in town?

"Come on, you know what I'm talking about," I said.

His nose flexed slightly as he subtly sniffed the air. No doubt he was figuring out who and what I was. My phone rang again. This time it came up as Harlan. I swiped the green phone icon to answer and raised it to my ear.

"Hello?" I said.

There was a lot of background noise. It sounded like Harlan had butt-dialed me. I stepped toward the door, thinking I might have a bad connection. I heard a distinctive screech. I immediately recognized it as a hellhound.

"Harlan?" I shouted into the phone.

Automatic gunfire roared over the phone, drowning out the other sounds. I waited and listened, there was nothing else to I could do.

"Demons at the Southern Outpost," Harlan shouted over gunfire and screams. "They're everywhere!"

I ran out the door toward the truck. It was empty. Holt was nowhere to be found. I didn't have time to wait on him. If the elves were being attacked by demons, I had to get there quick with or without him. I jumped behind the driver's seat and realized I still had the book in my hand. I tossed it onto the seat beside me and turned the key in the ignition. The truck roared to life. I slammed it into gear. The tires screamed as I pulled out.

CHAPTER 4

The Southern Outpost was only a fifteen-minute drive from Dahlonega. I made it in twelve. The outpost sat on top of a mountain in North Georgia with the only access being a poorly maintained road that wound lazily to the top. I went up as fast as I could, swerving to avoid potholes and ruts, sparing my suspension from the worst of it. I stopped at the checkpoint halfway up the mountain. The checkpoint was a small concrete building just big enough for the two guards normally on duty. On any other day one of the guards would come outside as soon as they saw my truck. No one greeted me today. I left the truck idling and got out to see if I could lower the barricade blocking the road. Nothing looked out of place. There were no dead elves, blood pools, or bullet holes to hint at what had happened. The autumn air smelled crisp. I didn't detect the scent gunpowder or the sulfuric stink of demons.

I had never been inside the checkpoint before. It was just a counter, a couple of chairs, and a few monitors. A small fridge and space heater sat in the far corner. A back window had an air conditioning unit mounted to it. All the necessities and none of the comfort. A large red button, the kind you imagine launches nuclear missiles, was mounted to the wall by the counter. That had to be what lowered the barricade. The building seemed to have lost power. The light on the ceiling and the monitors were off. I flipped the light switch a few times. I tried the button, giving it a few slaps, but nothing happened. The place was dead.

I'd have to run the rest of the way. I had just stepped outside when I saw a shadowy reflection in my truck window. An athol, a demon resembling a hairless gorilla with wings and a lot of pointy teeth, hit me. The force of the impact sent me flying back into the building. I crashed to the floor with the athol on top of me.

Covering my head and neck with my arms, I made the change to krasis as the demon bit and scratched me. I pulled the demon close and bit into its throat. Its thick, black blood spilled into my mouth. It tasted bitter, like motor oil. I pulled it over on the ground in front of me. I pinned it on the ground with one hand on its chest and the other on its face. I pushed with my hands, pulled with my neck, and ripped its throat out.

The demon writhed and flapped like a fatally wounded chicken, fruitlessly struggling to cling to life. I spit the flesh and as much of the bitter, viscous blood out of my mouth as I could. I spotted a bottle of water on the counter that had been knocked over in the skirmish and used it to wash out my mouth, spitting onto the floor beside the carcass. I had added Velcro to the back of all my pants to make room for my muscular tail in krasis. I hadn't had time to open it and my tail had ripped the left leg of my shorts.

Bursts of gunfire coming from the top of the mountain got my attention. I ran up uphill, weaving my way through the trees and rocks jutting out of the mountainside. The leaves on the forest floor were dry and brittle, crunching with every step; they made enough noise to alert whatever was up there that I was coming. I stopped my charge before the crest of the hill. I moved up the last few feet as slowly and quietly as I could to get an idea of the situation before I went charging out into the open.

A moving truck was parked in front of the compound. It looked to be about half-full of crates. Bodies of elves and demons littered the ground around it. The demons lay, more or less, in lines where the waves of their attack broke against the elven defenses. The elves were scattered, picked off one by one while trying to get to the safety of the outpost. I couldn't remember the last time I had seen so many demons at one time. A few months ago there had been an incident on the bridge outside Gainesville that I don't like to talk about. There were more than a few demons there, but this... there had to be at least thirty demons, and that's just what I could see. The air was thick with the scent of demon blood and the acidic burn of gunpowder. Spent brass littered the ground among the bodies. If there was a winner in this battle, it wasn't clear which side it was.

The only living thing I could see was a hellhound on the far side of the compound. A shadow passed overhead. Another athol was banking hard. It swooped down to where the hound was chewing on an elf carcass. There was plenty of fresh meat scattered around the area, but the athol decided it wanted to eat the only elf that was already being chewed on. It was testament to the nature of these beasts. The athol landed and flapped its wings in the hound's face. The hound jumped away, letting the athol move in. The hellhound circled as the athol took a bite from the elf's abdomen. The body jostled and shook as pieces were bitten away. The hound screeched at the athol, revealing rows of teeth. The athol didn't mind the noise as long as it was getting to eat.

With both of them distracting each other, it gave me the perfect opportunity for a surprise attack. I moved as quietly as I could to the remains of an elven guard, her body mutilated beyond recognition. Her rifle, however, complete with a grenade launcher, was intact. I detached the sling, which still held the weapon to what was left of the body. I took aim at the demons. Pulling the trigger, a baseball-sized explosive flew toward the unaware demons with a loud metallic *pung*. It passed directly between them, exploding harmlessly on the hillside. The detonation showered the area with dirt and disappointment.

The demons spotted me and charged, ready for some fresh meat. The athol took flight and closed the distance faster than the hellhound, even with all six of its legs pushing as hard as they could.

While I had missed with the grenade it meant I now had an opportunity that doesn't come around often: I could unload with one of these elven guns. I don't have anything against guns, they just aren't my tool of choice. When I get the opportunity to use one, I thoroughly enjoy it. I kept the gun at my hip and took a wide stance. My tail waved back and forth with excitement and I found myself laughing a little more maniacally than I care to admit.

"Eat hot lead, stinkbugs!" I shouted, pulling the trigger while visions of Rambo danced in my head.

The rifle sprang to action but only fired a couple rounds, neither of which found the target. I looked down to find the bolt open and the magazine empty. The athol would be on me in a second. I had no time to reload and nothing to reload with. I flipped the gun around, and held it by the barrel. I sidestepped the athol, using the rifle as a club to strike the demon's left wing. It spun out of control and crashed to the ground behind me.

The hound leapt, but I was ready. I thrust the gun into its mouth and rolled back, pushing my feet into its belly. The hound flipped over me, landing on its back. I got to my feet first, twisting the rifle free of the demon's jaws. I brought it down, striking the creature in the head repeatedly as it tried to get to its feet. By the third hit it wasn't fighting anymore.

The athol lumbered over, one wing sticking out awkwardly, broken. It wasn't as agile on the ground as in the air and it was easy to keep out of the way of its claws. After it over-committed with a swipe of its claws, I struck it in the leg with the rifle. It collapsed and I was able to finish it off quickly.

After a quick check to make sure there weren't any more demons about to attack me, I walked around the dead toward the outpost. Surveying the carnage, I couldn't help but wonder if anyone had survived at all. There had to be at least one: Harlan, the Queen's son, who called me. Of course, that call was about twenty minutes ago. By now everyone could be killed. If there were any survivors, they would be inside the outpost.

I had only made it a few steps when a sound caught my attention. A hellhound lying on the ground to my left was still alive. It had been shot at least four times, and something had nearly blown off its front leg. It didn't appear to have any fight left in it. It just lay there with its belly rising and falling, each labored breath a kind of groaning wheeze. I approached it slowly, ready for it to spring to life and attack.

The rule for Keepers has always been to keep suffering to a minimum. It was never mandated that it applied to demons, as well, but I always figured the way you treat your enemies says more about you than the way you treat your friends. I drove the rifle barrel into the creature's head, giving it as quick a death as I could. I left the gun sticking out of the creature's skull like a flag claiming foreign soil.

I spotted something that made me stop in my tracks. Two of the Queen's three daughters lay dead. Their bodies weren't in good shape, but there was no question that it was them. Patsy, the oldest daughter, had been ripped open from throat to abdomen. What was left of her guts had spilled on the ground; most were missing. Shelly, the middle daughter, was missing her right leg and left arm. It looked like someone, or something, had played tug of war with her. I looked around the courtyard again to see if anyone was watching. My first instinct was to run. Head to the truck, start driving, and never look back. There was going to be hell to pay when the Queen found out, and I didn't want to be anywhere in the vicinity when that happened. If I did run and she found out, she would probably take that as proof I had something to do with the attack. Besides that, there could still be people here that needed my help. I didn't see Harlan among the dead. He had to be here somewhere.

If he was still alive, he had to be in the compound. The Southern Outpost was a huge three-story octagon with porches encircling each level. It looked normal enough from the outside, once you got past the unusual structure and size. What couldn't be seen were reinforced concrete walls over a foot thick and the ballistic-glass windows. It was a fortress. On the lower level I found a door ajar, being held open by a dead elf. Her legs stuck out into the sunshine with torn pants and claw marks visible underneath.

I approached the door cautiously, not wanting any surprises, and peeked inside. The air was hazy and heavy with the smell of demon stench and gunpowder. Bodies of demons and elves littered the floor, but nothing moved. I carefully worked my way down the hallway, stepping over bodies and looking for survivors. There were multiple doors in the hallway, all closed except one on the far end. Light spilled into the hallway and I could make out whispering coming from inside. I had almost made it to the door when a shuffling noise behind me caught my attention. A hellhound had come in behind me and was sniffing around the bodies, apparently unaware of my presence. It must have been in the area and the noise of the fighting brought it back.

I turned as quietly as I could and made my way toward it. The demon began chewing on the elf stuck in the doorway. It pulled the elf inside, the door swinging shut behind them. I was feeling good about my chances of killing this hound before it knew I was there when a loud crash came from the room behind me. It was enough to get the attention of the hound. It spotted me and charged.

I was ready for it. It lunged at me, and I took a step back, intending to jump on top of it. I wanted to control its head and, by extension, its teeth. I slipped in some blood, going down on a knee. This put me at eye level with the demon, the exact vantage point I was trying to avoid. I put my hands on its neck and pushed. I was able to stay out of the demon's mouth, but lost any chance of gaining an advantage.

It lunged again. I had no choice, but to drop to the floor. It wasn't expecting this and it ended up over me. I wrapped my arms around the hound's neck before it could reorient itself to my position. Its six legs pumped powerfully, dragging me down the hallway and through the blood and gore lining the floor. The hound jerked its head erratically and slammed up against the walls, trying to get me loose.

It stopped its charge long enough for me to get my feet under me. I pressed up, lifting its front four legs off the ground, and evening the odds. I swept its back legs, threw it to the ground, and fell on top. Things were finally starting to go my way.

We landed on the ground in front of the open door. Inside I saw Harlan and two soldiers. Their rifles were pointed in our direction. I held my left hand out to them, using my right arm to keep the demon under control.

"Don't—"

Their rifles burst to life with automatic fire.

CHAPTER 5

I opened my eyes to a white light. For a moment I thought I might be dead, but if I was, then I wouldn't feel the tingling in my chest that comes from rapid healing. My body had cooled in the fall air and felt stiff. My eyes adjusted to the light and I became aware of a texture in the light. It was a sheet. I took a deep breath and sat up. The sheet clung to me, refusing to concede that I was alive. I pulled it off my face. I found myself lying in a line of elves that had been killed in the attack.

We had been laid in neat rows with bloodstained sheets covering the bodies. The dead elves numbered twelve in all. Blood soaked in the sheets giving hints to what killed them. Some had red stains and empty spaces where limbs should be; many others had head and chest wounds. While the air had a slight chill, it was still too warm for bodies to be outside for any amount of time; the smell of death was creeping in. My shirt had a number of holes in the front, mostly in a central circle at my heart. I ran a hand over my chest and felt a lump. I pulled up my shirt for a look and found the end of a bullet embedded in my skin under my fur. Whenever I got shot, my body would push out the foreign material. I pried at it with my fingers and was rewarded by a stinging pain and a trickle of blood as I pulled the mushroomed piece of metal free. I was covered in blood, not all of it my own. I had a change of clothes in the truck—I always carried extra clothes for situations like this.

I was suddenly aware of the elf lying beside me. I had inadvertently uncovered her. I couldn't tell what killed her. Much of her abdomen was missing, leaving exposed ribs and an empty cavity. She had been chewed on after she died—at least, I hope she died first. Her head was untouched. Her blank eyes stared at me accusingly. She was pretty; her face held the long and deceivingly soft features of elven kind.

"Sorry," I said, standing up.

I restored the sheet and her dignity. A thud from the direction of the compound got my attention and I looked up to see the two elves who had shot me. They had been carrying a demon corpse, and had dropped it and grabbed their guns when they saw me.

"If you shoot me again, we're going to have a problem," I yelled, pointing a finger in their direction. "Go tell Harlan I'm awake."

They squinted and glared at me with distrust. They walked toward the outpost without relaxing the grip on their rifles. I took the opportunity to look around.

In contrast to the care shown the elves, the demons were piled together. The demon stack was about eight feet in diameter and growing. Wings and legs stuck out haphazardly in all directions. There had to be at least twenty in the pile, with more around the grounds waiting to be stacked. Two bodies had been laid on a table close to the building and covered with sheets. I knew those would be the princesses.

Harlan came out to meet me while I surveyed the corpses. A guard followed behind him. They were back on duty, this time watching me. Harlan's head was shaved and his ears had been removed, his punishment for embarrassing the Queen. As always, he wore a plain black shirt, black pants, and combat boots. His left hand was bandaged and he had blood on his hands and face. He had run this outpost, up until an incident almost three months ago, when he was replaced by his sister, Patsy. Due to a promise by the Queen, he was kept around as a representative of the Elven Nation, but I never got the feeling he was particularly welcome here after his sister took over.

"What the hell, Harlan?" I asked.

"Sorry about that," he said. "Would you believe it was an accident?"

I shook my head. "Not even a little bit."

"I'd like to tell you I could reprimand them or something, but we both know I'm a figurehead here. I'd also like to tell you that I'll make it up to you but . . ." He shrugged.

"There must be thirty demons out here, practically an army. How did this happen?"

Harlan glanced at the guards, and pulled me by the elbow in the other direction, so we could speak privately.

"Nobody's asking my opinion, but I'm telling you, there's something really wrong with this," he said. "The attack was timed perfectly."

"What do you mean?"

"The attack happened when both my sisters were together outside. Patsy was running the outpost and Shelly was overseeing the delivery. It's the only time they could be caught together."

"You think they were the targets?" I asked.

He shrugged. "It makes sense."

"What about you? You're the son of the Queen and here for the attack. Do you think you were a target, too?"

"No one cares about me."

I ran a hand over the scruff on my face. "I understand having a problem with the Queen, but using demons like this . . . Why would someone do that?"

"I'm sure I couldn't say," he answered. "I'm just glad some of us made it out alive."

"How many survivors are there?"

"Me, those two," he said, pointing to the two guards watching us, "and a few more wounded inside. They could use your help."

"That's it? What about the guards from the checkpoint?"

He pointed to a pair of bodies. "It took them a few minutes to get up here. By that time, the attack was well underway. They never stood a chance out in the open like that. Easy pickin's."

"Take me to 'em. I'll see what I can do."

I followed Harlan back through the door on the lower level of the Southern Outpost. The hallway had been cleared of most of the bodies, but the blood remained. Harlan did his best to avoid puddles of demon and elf blood as we went. Since I had already been dragged through it, I didn't see the point.

We stepped around the hound I had been shot with and into the room. Judging by the rows of weapons and ammunition lining the walls, this had to be the armory. This was where they'd made their last stand. The room was littered with bodies, mostly elves but a few demons, still lay just inside the door. Three elven women rested on the far side of the room, two lying unconscious and one standing guard. The guard reached for the pistol at her hip when she saw us walk in.

"I can forgive one," I said, waving my tail with irritation. "But only one, so think about it before you draw."

Harlan moved to stand between us. "Everybody relax. We're all friends here."

She lowered her hand, but didn't relax. I paused momentarily at the sight of the compound's staff, the cook and cleaning crew, all male and all dead. It looked as if they fell at the edge of the demon line. They had bite marks and bullet holes, obviously sacrificed, shoved out front as a wall to protect the guards. They had taken the females out and covered them, they were taking out the demons, which I understood, the smell wasn't pleasant. Apparently, these poor men weren't worth picking up. I passed over them, moving on to someone I might be able to help.

I stepped around the guard to the two unconscious elves. I held my hand over the first and concentrated. The energy started flowing through me, but there was nowhere for it to go; she was dead. I moved to the next elf in line. She had a half-moon shape in blood soaked into one of her pant legs. It looked like a hellhound had gotten a nibble in on her, a good bite could have removed the leg completely. I had seen injuries like this many times before.

"Just the leg," I said, giving her a once over for other injuries.

The guard scowled at me. "Is that not enough? I think it's broken."

I hate it when patients are bitchy. I placed one hand on either side of her leg and concentrated. The blue light synonymous with my abilities began to glow from my eyes and hands. I could feel her wounds closing and the bone mending. I stopped when it was done, but before the energy could spill over to any other injuries or ailments. I only wanted to bring them back to the condition they were in before the attack, though maybe a little worse for wear.

I turned back to the first guard. She looked to have some minor scratches, making out far better than anyone else here, except for Harlan.

"I'm fine," she said, holding a hand out before I could even ask.

"Okay," I said, turning to Harlan. "What about you? Need me to look at that hand?"

"It's just a cut. I don't even know how it happened, but it's not bad. Besides, I don't think the Queen would like you healing me. I'm not sure she got over the last time," he said over the rumble of vehicles. "Speaking of the Queen, that should be her now."

We walked out just as the Queen's SUV and two guard trucks pulled up to the outpost. The Royal Guard, the Queen's personal protection force, poured out of the three vehicles, taking positions to secure the area. After everyone was in place, the back door of the SUV opened. The Queen exited, pausing in front of the door to survey damage. Her long blonde hair was pulled back, revealing her long ears. She wore black jeans over combat boots and a flannel shirt. A pair of Old West-style six-shooters hung lazily from her hips. She spotted the surviving elves with Harlan and me standing by the door and walked toward us. Her youngest daughter, Princess Isabelle, climbed out of the car and followed.

The Queen walked in the direction of the elf and demon bodies with Isabelle close behind. Isabelle looked like a ten-year-old human, but she was probably closer to fifty or sixty. She wore a tiara of flowers and a long, silky, blue dress. It was a different style of dress than the other women of the royal family, but she was young. She hadn't started training for the military yet. She had already received her first gun, a bolt action rifle she wore slung over her shoulder. Weapons in the Nation were a status symbol as much as a tool, and a daughter of the Queen would be expected to carry one and be proficient with it early on. I had no doubt she could already outshoot me.

The Queen and Isabelle passed Harlan and me without acknowledging us. Harlan did a quick check to be sure no one was looking, and stuck his tongue out at Isabelle as she passed. She wasted no time in returning the gesture.

"Isn't that kinda dangerous?" I whispered. "I can't imagine the Queen would approve."

"It's worth it," Harlan replied.

It was the first time I had seen him smile in months. The Queen had the sheet removed to properly review the carnage. When she was done, she walked back to where we were standing.

"Where are Patsy and Shelly?" the Queen demanded.

Harlan motioned toward the table. The lead truck had parked in front of the table and blocked her view of them. She walked over and whipped the sheet off, staring at the mangled bodies for a few seconds. She turned to face us. She didn't appear upset, but when she spoke there was a coldness in her voice akin to rage.

"Report," the Queen commanded.

The elf I had healed spoke up: "It was a surprise attack. I've never even heard of anything like it before. We didn't see any portals; all these demons just came out of the woods. They attacked just as Patsy had come out to inspect the monthly delivery. I think she was the target of the attack. She and Shelly were swarmed. The door was propped open with half the soldiers unloading, so we weren't able to save her."

"Why was the door propped open and why were half the soldiers unloading the truck? They should have been standing guard. These are serious security breaches."

"Patsy ordered the guards to help unload the shipment," the guard said. "I can't speak as to who propped the door open."

The Queen nodded, taking in the information. "Survivors?"

"Just the four of us. Oh and him," the elf said, throwing Harlan a contemptuous look. "We lost fourteen and the help."

"Our sisters will be missed," the Queen said.

The four elves nodded in agreement as the Queen turned and approached Harlan and me. She stopped in front of us, taking stock. "Obie, what are you doing here?"

"I called him," Harlan said. "When it looked like we—"

"You will speak when spoken to," the Queen snapped.

Harlan lowered his head.

After giving him a few seconds for the message to sink in, she turned back to me.

"Harlan called and said the outpost was under attack. I was in Dahlonega at the time, so I wasn't far away," I said.

"Were you injured?" she asked, eyeballing my blood-soaked clothing.

"After I fought my way inside to the survivors, they shot me."

I didn't get the impression she was bothered by her soldiers' actions.

She looked me in the eye. "Did you have a hand in this attack?"

"A demon attack?" I scoffed. "You know I didn't."

"Your truck was blocking the road. Perhaps you left it there on purpose keep help from responding?"

I'd like to tell her that she was being a paranoid and asinine, but in my experience, royalty doesn't take to criticism. "The barricade was raised and there wasn't power to lower it. I had to leave the truck and run."

"The barricade can be lowered in the case of emergencies," the Queen said.

"I believe you," I said. "But I don't know how to do it."

"I assure you, I will find whoever is responsible for this attack and make them pay. If you know anything, it's in your interest to speak up now."

I rested my hands on my hips and tried not to let frustration come through as I spoke. "Hunting demons is kind of my whole reason to exist. I want whoever's responsible found as much as you do."

"Your truck was pushed clear," she said. "In the future, I expect the road to be kept open. Take Harlan to the clubhouse to arrange for the next council meeting to be held there. The situation is under control now, you may go."

I smiled to hide my aggravation at being dismissed like one of her servants.

"A question, my Queen," Harlan asked, without looking up.

"Speak."

"The Tortured Occult will want to know if this incident will affect the upcoming run. What should I tell them?"

The Queen thought it over. "Against my better judgement, the run may proceed."

Harlan bowed, and we walked down the hill toward my truck. When we were out of sight of the outpost, I picked up the pace to a jog. When my old

truck had been wrecked, I'd driven a loaner for a while before settling on a
Nissan Frontier. After I bought it, it spent two months in the shop getting a
number of upgrades that would be helpful for the rough life it would lead. Aes-
thetically, the only changes were a heavy-duty grill guard and some metal cages
to protect the lights. Anything to reduce the chances of a run-in with the law
was worth it. Underneath, there were a number of improvements, including
a nice sturdy suspension, armor around the engine and cab, and bulletproof
glass. Things have been tense for the past few months and I can't afford to be
unprepared.

We found the truck, still idling and resting against a tree off the road below the checkpoint. Harlan waited by the checkpoint while I inspected the
truck. The grill guard seemed to have done its job and prevented any damage.
The bodies in the back were still secure. I put on a change of clothes and de-
posited my old clothes into the bed of the truck to get rid of later. I found the
book I had inadvertently stolen and put it in the glovebox. Then I got in, put
it in four-wheel drive, and backed up the hill onto the road.

It wasn't until Harlan was getting in the truck that I noticed two new
guards already manning the checkpoint, watching our progress. The door
hung off broken hinges and a dead demon lay on the floor, but security first, I
suppose. I gave them a wave and pulled out.

CHAPTER 6

The clubhouse of the Tortured Occult Motorcycle Club sat in the middle of a junkyard. The property belonged to Hank, president of the T.O., and owner of the club's legitimate business, by human standards: Morrison Salvage and Repair. The clubhouse served not only as the headquarters for the motorcycle club but also as a social hotspot for ultranaturals in the area. I found an open spot to park among the wrecked and rusted vehicles.

"Go on in," I said to Harlan. "I need a minute."

Harlan got out and headed for the door. I waited a few seconds to have some privacy before I pulled out my phone and called Holt. The phone rang a few times and went to voicemail.

After the beep, I said, "I'm at the clubhouse. I have to take the bodies to Hob as soon as I'm done here. If you haven't got a ride yet, let me know where you are, and I'll pick you up."

I didn't get the impression he was in any kind of trouble, probably just got bored and wandered off. It wouldn't be the first time.

I put the phone back in my pocket, got out of the truck, and went inside. I stepped through the front door into the changing room, a rectangular room with a door on either end that exited into the bar. Harlan was waiting for me there.

"Everything okay?" I asked.

He nodded. "Yeah, I just figured I'd wait on you."

The walls were lined with coat and shoe racks. The clubhouse was a place where people didn't wear disguises. The changing room was the place where pretense was shed. I pulled my shoes off and added them to the row of shoes already lining the wall. As not to lose another pair of pants today, I pulled open the Velcro stitched in the back to make room for my tail and made the change to krasis.

Elves in this situation would normally have made sure their ears were showing. Harlan, having no ears or hair to hide them with, lived unveiled. When I finished the change, we exited through the door on the left into the clubhouse. While relations were better between the Elven Nation and the T.O., the Queen still forbade elves from leaving the Nation. When we walked in, the few people that were there took notice of Harlan. Everyone had heard what the Queen had done to him. I was the only one outside of the elves to witness it firsthand. If he was self-conscious about his appearance, he didn't show it as the curious patrons turned to get their first look at the Queen's brand of justice.

In many respects, the clubhouse was a typical bar. A pool table and dart board claimed the right side of the room with tables spread around the rest. The bar itself took up most of the back wall with a door to the right that lead to the back. There were only two things that made it stand out from a normal bar. The first was the filing cabinet and a single table tucked into the corner to the right of the pool table. It was a de facto office for Adan, the wererat emissary. The second was the fact that there weren't any humans here. An assortment of different shifters lounged around the tables, as well as a group of goblins and kobolds playing a rather spirited game of darts.

I spotted Hank at the bar, sitting with my wayward apprentice. I led Harlan straight to the conference room. It was devoid of decoration, with a plain round table in its center. I thought it would be more comfortable for him to wait there rather than in the bar being eyeballed by everyone.

"Give me a few minutes to get everyone together," I said.

Harlan took a seat at the table. I went back to the bar.

"What's he doing here?" Hank asked.

"Need an emergency meeting," I said. "We got a problem."

Hank downed the rest of his beer and got up. "All right, I'll get folks together."

I sat down in the newly vacant seat beside Holt. I really wasn't pleased with him at the moment and I took a minute to keep from jumping all over his case.

"You were supposed to stay with the truck," I said.

"I just ran over to the Fudge Factory," he said. "I needed a little something."

"You didn't *need* something. We are sustained by Thera. You don't have to eat or drink."

He took a swig from his beer. "Maybe *you* don't need to eat, but I get hungry. I can't go a day without putting something in my stomach."

"You can if you try," I said. "And I need you to try. I needed you in the truck."

"You're the one that said no one would mess with it."

I was trying to be more patient with him than I had been in the past. He was still learning, after all, and it was my job to teach him. I wouldn't have complained if he were a little less pig-headed at times.

"I said no one would mess with it if someone was in it. You were supposed to be that someone. Look, the long and short of it is, I asked you to do something and you didn't. I need you to do better going forward."

"All right," he said. "I hear what you're sayin'."

That was about as good a reaction as I could hope for from him. At least he wasn't arguing with everything I said anymore. Hank stuck his head through the door and gave me a nod; we were ready for the meeting. I followed Hank into the conference room and we took our seats.

Hank began. "Harlan, I'm more than a little surprised to see you here, not that you aren't welcome, of course. What's so important we had to call an emergency meeting?"

Hambone cleared his throat and stood on his chair. The kobold was about three feet tall with the head and fur of a coyote on a humanoid body. Unlike normal shifters, kobolds could only take two forms, a coyote or krasis. He was the member of the council elected to represent the masses and had gotten fat from the benefit of his position. He wheezed from the effort of standing up and began to speak. "Actually, before we get started with that, I have something to say. This will be our first meeting since the election and I am sure you are all as happy as I am that I was reelected."

Adan cut in. "I think Harlan has something important to talk about."

"Yes, yes," Hambone continued. "This will just take a second. I just wanted to say that I appreciate your support in the election."

"You're welcome, Hambone," I said, giving Harlan a nod to start.

"I mean, there was a lot of competition this year," Hambone continued.

Hank put a hand to his head and rubbed his temples.

"I had two opponents and I won by a very slim margin. I know I have a couple years before the next election, but—"

"Hambone, we have something we really need to talk about," I said. "It's important."

"And this isn't?" he asked. "Elections matter and come to think of it, all of you could have been more supportive through it. I mean, not one of you wore the buttons I gave you."

"The Southern Outpost was attacked!" Harlan blurted out.

Hank removed the hand from his head at this revelation. "What do you mean, attacked?"

"It was attacked by demons," Harlan answered.

"A lot of demons," I added.

"Almost everyone at the outpost was killed," Harlan said.

"If you have something like that to talk about then why are we discussing the elections? Really, Harlan, sometimes I wonder about your priorities," Hambone said, sitting back down.

"Sorry, Hambone," Harlan said. "I'll try to stay on topic better in the future."

"It's okay. You're still new at this. Please tell us about the attack," he said.

"Like I said, pretty much everyone was killed, including Patsy and Shelly," Harlan continued. "I don't know how many demons attacked or how many were killed. They were still pulling the bodies out by the time we left."

Hank tapped a finger on the table as he thought about the news. "What the hell's going on? First that thing at the bridge a few months ago and now this? The world's going to shit. I'm guessing the Queen closed the border, right?"

"No, actually, and the run's still on," Harlan said.

"That doesn't sound like her," Adan said.

Harlan shrugged. "I asked specifically about the run and she said it was still on."

Hank and Adan seemed skeptical and looked at me for confirmation.

I nodded. "It's true. I heard her say it."

They were right to be concerned. I couldn't think of a scenario where the Queen's suspicion and paranoia would allow the run to continue. Then again, maybe these past few months since the elves rejoined the council had had some positive impact. Maybe she was starting to come around to the idea that the Tortured Occult wasn't trying to undermine her at every turn.

"If she's up to something, she didn't tell me," Harlan said. "Not that *that* should surprise anyone. She may think you aren't involved because of the attack. The fact that it was a demon attack means magic is involved. It wasn't a normal demon attack either, it was organized. They attacked at a time when the outpost was most vulnerable. It had to be someone with knowledge of the inner workings of the Southern Outpost."

"How do you think she will handle something like that?" I asked.

"Let's just say it would be a good time for her subjects to keep their heads down and not draw attention. She's going to find someone responsible and punish them. Time will tell if she finds the person who actually did it or not," Harlan said.

"It sounds like we need to find who did it before she comes after us," Hambone said. "The last thing we want is a war."

Adan nodded in agreement. "Who could've done it though?"

"The most likely suspect is a resistance group that wants to restore magic to the Elven Nation. The Queen views them as terrorists and let's just say she doesn't negotiate with terrorists," Harlan said. "You know that's why she distrusts you, right?"

"She thinks I'm an elven terrorist?" Hank asked.

Harlan shook his head. "No, she thinks your dust operation is supplying them, intentionally or not."

"It's not just his operation. We set it up together, with the other groups, too. Everyone here is benefiting from it. Does she think we are all out to get her?" Adan asked.

"She did accuse me of being involved in the attack," I said.

Hambone let out a high-pitched cackle that reminded me of a hyena. "Obie involved in a demon attack, that's a good one."

"I think she mostly blames the T.O. for it," Harlan said.

"The Queen has a resistance group." Hank chuckled. "That's what happens when a dictator rules by fear; people start fighting back. She can't be surprised people want her out."

"She's not surprised; she's resentful and bitter," Harlan said.

"Out of control, is more like it," I added. "Which brings us back to why the run wasn't canceled. Do you think it's smart to still go?"

"I'm glad I won't be there," Adan said.

Hank scratched behind his ear as he thought it over. "I don't know if it's smart, but everyone's been looking forward to it. The T.O. needs this and if we don't show up it might look suspicious. Do you think she would do something at the run?"

"I have learned, when trying to predict the Queen's behavior, to err on the side of cruelty and paranoia. You attend that run at your own risk," Harlan said.

"Regardless of what the Queen believes, if someone's summoning demon hordes, that's something I need to look into. Assuming it isn't that resistance group, who do we know that could pull something like this off?" I asked.

Whoever was doing it had to be skilled magically and have access to a large amount of dust. There were very few people around that could meet that criteria, so few I couldn't really think of any.

"Well," Hank said. "Hob could do it."

"Hob? Really? You can't be serious," I said.

"I didn't say I thought he did do it, just that he *could*. I don't know if you've seen him in action, but Hob is scary good with magic," Hank said.

Adan leaned forward, resting an elbow on the table. "Come to think of it, he never sells his cut of the dust. In the years we've been doing this, he could have more than enough stockpiled by now."

"Fair enough. Who else?" I asked.

The five of us looked at each other for a minute. No one could think of another lead.

CHAPTER 7

With the meeting over, everyone walked out into the bar. I found Holt still sitting at the counter, drinking a beer. Harlan and I joined him.

"Obie, one sec," Hank said, coming out of the back room behind us. "Before I forget, we're getting an early start on the run with a party next Thursday night. You should stop by."

"Who all'll be there?" Holt asked.

"The T.O. and friends of the club," Hank said.

"Asking about anyone specific?" I asked. "Martina, maybe?"

"Nope," Holt answered. "But we should go."

I tapped my fingers on the bar, in thought. "We should be able to make it."

"All right," Hank said. "See you then."

"What are you doing here, anyway?" Holt asked when Hank had walked away.

"Trouble at the Southern Outpost," I said, sitting beside him. "I'll fill you in when we have a little more privacy."

Harlan sat down beside me. Tico, the wereraccoon bartender, came up after a minute with a rag over one shoulder. He leaned an elbow on the bar in front of us.

"What can I get you," he asked.

"Nitro Milk Stout," Harlan said before he leaned over and whispered, "The Queen doesn't allow me to drink, so let's keep this between us."

Tico looked at me, even though he knew I wasn't going to get anything.

"I'm good, thanks," I said.

Tico got a pint glass and filled it from the tap with a dark beer with a frothy head, put it on the counter in front of Harlan, and started wiping down the counter with the rag from his shoulder.

"Aren't you worried about the Queen's spies seeing you drink that beer?" I asked as Harlan took his first swig.

"I think she has more important things to worry about, with what just happened and the run coming up," he said.

"Just be careful. I don't need to tell you how seriously she takes disobedience."

"Did you see who else showed up tonight?" Holt asked, motioning to a table by the door.

"Is that Naylet?" Harlan asked. "Who's the guy?"

Naylet and I were together for a long time until about three months ago when she lost her memory from a demon attack. I was able to save her, and the other victims, but I hadn't spoken to her since. I wanted to give her the space to rediscover who she was without pressure and expectations from me. I looked over to discover she was sitting with a man and appeared to be having a good time. I recognized him, too. His name was Titus, another one of the demon's victims. They chatted and laughed and I found myself focusing on the ambient noise to avoid hearing any part of it. Naylet smiled and brushed her hair back behind her ear. She looked in our direction and caught me looking at her. Our eyes met and I looked back to the bar a little too quickly to be played off as casual.

"A victim of the gorgon, like Naylet. He was a sculptor in ancient Rome, I think," I said.

"You know what they say about those Eye-talians," Harlan said, taking a drink from his beer.

"What do they say?" I asked.

"Hell if I know. I don't think I've ever met one," Harlan said. "Why's she sitting with him and not with you? Have you still not talked to her?"

Holt chuckled. "Not only has he not talked to her, he's still paying all her bills."

"I've been giving her time. I've been told she's been having a rough time," I said.

"Yeah, she looks real torn up with all that laughing and smiling," Holt said. "Looks to me like she doesn't know you exist."

"She's got her diary and pictures of me on the wall, so she has to know who I am," I said. "She'll talk to me when she's ready."

"Looks like she's ready now," Tico said. "She's headed this way."

The three of us turned around to see her walking toward us.

"We'll give you some privacy," Harlan said.

The two of them got up and walked off. Tico, on the other hand, continued to wipe the same spot on the bar in front of me.

"You mind?"

"Oh, I wouldn't miss this for the world," he said with a smile.

Naylet eased up to the bar and leaned against it. She stood, arms crossed, with her long blond curls cascading around her shoulders. I knew the pose, assuming it held the same meaning since before she lost her memories. It was the one she used when she wanted to look confident but wasn't. I waited a few seconds and then looked over at her. We stared at each other without speaking. Seconds seemed like an eternity. My mind raced as I tried to think of what the right thing to say in this situation was; nothing came to mind.

"Hey," she said.

My heart pumped a little faster. "Hey babe, I've been looking forward to spending some quality time with you."

Her face contorted into a scowl. "Never mind."

She turned and walked back the way she came.

"That was real smooth," Tico said.

"Shut up." I scowled, getting up to follow her. "Sorry, I didn't mean that the way it sounded."

She stopped walking and turned around.

"You came over because you wanted to talk, right? I'd like to talk to you if you still want to," I said, motioning toward an empty table. "Why don't you tell me what you wanted?"

She moved to the table slowly, as if she hadn't made her mind up on what to do, before she pulled a chair out and sat down. I sat across from her. After putting my foot in my mouth like that, I wasn't going to risk scaring her off again.

Awkward silence filled up most of a minute before I decided I better say something. "You know, autumn's my favorite season. After all the warm weather I really enjoy things cooling off. I haven't told many people this, but while some people are getting ready to hibernate this time of year, the cooler weather always makes me want to travel. It's like the cool breeze is an invitation from somewhere far away."

I watched her face as I said it, looking for any kind of recognition. She was the only person who knew that about me. If it rang any bells for her, she didn't show it.

"I saw you that day," she said. "When I woke up. You were the first one there. I've seen you at the house a few times, too, when you stopped by to talk to Zaria. I found out about everyone else I met that day except for you. I've been getting vague answers about what happened to me and who you are, so I thought I would ask you while I had the chance."

"What do you mean, 'while you had the chance'?" I asked.

"Zaria says I should stay away from you," she said.

"Does she now?" I was speaking more to myself than Naylet.

Zaria and Naylet had been friends a long time. When Naylet was attacked she needed help. Zaria was my first choice. I arranged for Zaria to move in and I took care of all of Naylet's expenses. Naylet was right that I had been to the house. I stopped by a few times early on to check in on her. Zaria always met me in the yard and said Naylet wasn't having a good day. I didn't know why she would tell Naylet to stay away from me, but it sounded like she had been doing a good job keeping her in the dark.

"What do you know about me?" I asked.

"I'm told you're a Keeper and that you're trouble."

"I see." I said resting my elbow on the table. "Anything else?"

"I don't even know your name," she said.

Zaria definitely had some explaining to do.

"My name is Obie," I said. "I'm really a nice guy, I just don't have any references. They're all dead or in jail." I waited for a reaction to my joke. She just sat across from me looking unsure. "So, you don't recognize me from anywhere? Maybe a picture? Wait, the pictures are of my human form." I changed to my human form, hoping she recognized it. "Ringing any bells?"

She shook her head.

"Where's Zaria at now?" I asked after I changed back to krasis.

"She'll be here soon."

"She may be right, I might be trouble," I said. "But what do you think?"

"I think there's more to it. She's not telling me something. I have good instincts and you don't seem that bad to me. Did I know you?" She cocked her head to one side.

I found myself just looking at her, wondering how to answer that question. Her expression softened and she lowered her arms. I was suddenly aware my answer was taking too long and I wasn't sure what my face was saying, so I looked over at the bar trying to appear casual.

"You did," I said. "I hoped you would remember."

She crossed her arms and looked at the floor. "I wish I could."

"Can I get you a drink?"

I got Tico's attention with a wave and motioned toward Naylet. He gave me a nod. We had done that so many times before it was almost unconscious.

"So, you're Obie?" she asked. "Is that short for something?"

"It was a long time ago, but not anymore," I said. "How have you been?"

Naylet shrugged. "It's been hard. Everyone is acting nice, but it's all fake. I'm tired of being coddled."

Tico put a sangria on the table in front of her. The red beverage with apple and orange slices floating in it had been one of Naylet's favorite afternoon drinks before the attack. She took a sip and stared at the concoction, moving it around in her hands.

"This is what I'm talking about," she said, eyeballing her drink.

"You don't like it?" I asked.

Naylet pushed the drink away from her. "I do like it. That's the problem."

"I'm not following."

"Somebody puts a drink in front of me and tells me I'll like it and I do, or I'm going to order something for myself and I'm told I won't like it. I get it anyway and they were right. Did you know everything I do is paid for?" she asked. "I could make an offer on this bar and the money would just show up. Where's it all coming from?"

I guess she wasn't told I was the one paying her expenses. It wasn't a burden; I had the money with nothing to spend it on and she had simple tastes, although apparently, she didn't know it.

"You don't want this place. Some knockers dug a bunch of tunnels under it a while ago. I say fifty-fifty chance, it falls into a sinkhole," I said.

"Everyone else seems to know what I want more than I do, that's the problem," she said. "It's driving me crazy. Sometimes I just want to run away."

"Where would you go?" I asked.

"I don't know. I don't even know what's out there," she replied.

I didn't like the idea of her leaving, but she didn't seem to be happy where she was. It had to be hard to have lost all your memories, to feel that you had been put in someone else's life.

"Maybe you should go," I said.

She scoffed. "I can't do that."

"Why not? What do you really have keeping you here?" I asked. "If getting away is what you need, then I think you should. It's better than buying this dump."

"I can't afford something like that," she said.

"You don't have to worry about that. If you want to travel the money will be there."

Naylet narrowed her eyes. "Are you the one that's been paying for me?"

I nodded. "It's not a problem."

"Why would you do that?" Naylet asked.

"Have you not read your diary?"

Naylet shook her head. "I don't have a diary."

"Sorry I'm late," Zaria said, walking up to table.

Zaria was a nymph, like Naylet, and shared the slender build and delicate features. They could have passed for sisters; the biggest difference between them was Zaria had long brown hair compared to Naylet's blonde curls.

"I need to borrow Zaria for one second," I said, pushing my chair back and standing up.

I led her by the elbow to the far side of the bar where we could speak privately.

"Well?" I asked.

She jerked her arm out of my hand. "Well what?"

"Why doesn't she know who I am?"

"I'm not going to let you hurt her again. You need to stay away, or I'll make you sorry," she said jabbing a finger into my chest.

"First, I have never hurt her. Second, I'll support whatever she decides," I said. "So you go ahead and make me sorry, if you have it in you, because I'm not going to let you manipulate her. You're going to give her the diary and pictures and answer any questions she has. Honestly."

Zaria crossed her arms and looked away. "Are you done?"

"Yep."

She turned around and headed back to the table where Naylet was sitting.

"Tonight," I called after her.

I met Naylet's gaze from across the room and gave her a half-hearted smile. I was pretty sure Zaria would do the right thing, but I would have to double-check in a few days, just to be safe. I found Adan at his usual table in the corner and sat down.

"I need a woman," I said.

"Obie, I didn't know you had it in you." Adan grinned. "What'd you have in mind?"

CHAPTER 8

The checkpoint door at the Southern Outpost had been boarded up with plywood, making it functional, if not visually appealing. I pulled up to the barricade, intending to drive Harlan all the way to the top of the mountain. A guard stepped out and walked over to the driver's side window.

"No one can enter, on orders of the Queen. He'll have to walk," she said.

"Is the outpost closed or the Nation itself," I asked.

She stared at me, but didn't answer. I guess I didn't have the proper clearance or something.

Harlan and I shared a look. He got out of the truck.

"Let me know if anything's changed," I said.

"I'll be in touch," he said and started walking up the road to the outpost.

Having dropped Harlan off, Holt and I headed to meet Hob. It didn't take us long to get to the farm. We pulled off highway twenty onto the dirt road running between the cornfields that led to the main house. The farmhouse sat in the middle of the property. There was a chicken coop, and a few barns, the largest of which housed the dust facility. It was tucked away on the back of the property beside the Etowah River. I saw Hob sitting on his front porch, enjoying the evening air. I needed to talk to him, but I needed to get rid of the bodies in the back of the truck more. We exchanged a wave as I passed him on the way to the dust barn. When I got there, I backed the truck up to the door. Holt pounded on the door while I removed the tarp from the bodies. The barn door opened, revealing an interior of polished steel and machinery. A large ogre wearing an apron, hairnet, and booties came out and began unloading the truck.

"Hey, Eric, good to see you," I said.

The ogre grunted in recognition, about as warm a greeting you could expect. Tallypo Wilix, the goblin foreman, came out with his clipboard and climbed on the bumper of the truck to get a look.

"Hmmm..." Wilix said, looking over the carnage. "I hope this wasn't your handiwork?"

"I'm just delivering it. The demon that's responsible is in there somewhere," I said. "What's left of it anyway."

Wilix jumped down from the truck. "All right, it'll take us about ten minutes to weigh everything and get the numbers for you."

"We're not going to stick around for all that. Just put it on our accounts," I said. "I trust you."

"That's bad business," Wilix said, shaking his pencil in my general direction.

I shrugged. "Yeah, it really is."

Wilix shook his head and sighed. "We'll have you on your way in a minute."

Holt came over and whispered, "Just had an idea. What if they're skimming dust, considering everything that's going on?"

I shook my head. "If Hob or Wilix wanted to rip us off, we would never know it. They're both a lot smarter than either of us. But they keep records that track the whole process. We could run the numbers. Hob already gets a cut of the dust. I don't why he would need to skim a little more. Either way, I trust 'em."

—————◆—————

With the bodies unloaded and the bed of the truck sprayed out, I drove to the farmhouse and parked. Holt and I walked up the stairs to join Hob on the porch.

"*Guten abend*, please have a seat," he said in his German accent. "If I had known you were coming, I would have a plate ready for you. Tonight, we have *Zwiebelkuchen*, an old recipe from the *Vaterland*. I have grown the onions myself. Would you like some?"

"Thanks, but we just came to drop off some demons," I said.

"I'll take a piece," Holt said, sitting down at the table.

"Excellent," Hob said, standing up and disappearing into the house.

"You couldn't help yourself, could you?" I asked.

Holt shrugged. "You must not be smelling the same zwedible-whatever that I am."

Hob returned a second later with a spare plate and served Holt a large piece of the pie.

"You had many demons today," Hob said, returning to his seat. "It has been a rough day, *Ja*?"

"You don't even know the half of it," Holt said in the middle of chewing his first bite. "Obie, you should try this, it's really good."

"We had two run-ins," I said. "That load was from the first one. Innocents. They'd been in the truck most of the day. I'm afraid they're starting to turn. After I got that cleaned up, the Southern Outpost was attacked by a horde of demons."

Hob put his fork down and wiped his mouth, giving us his full attention. Holt on the other hand, was more focused on the food than the conversation.

I continued. "It was an organized attack, not like anything I've seen before. Someone was controlling the demons and targeted the outpost strategically. We think Patsy was the target, but the Queen had two daughters killed in the attack."

"I feel sorry for my brethren under the Queen's rule," he said. "I have no doubt her response will be harsh."

"We're definitely concerned about how it's all going to play out," I said.

Hob folded his hands in his lap. "Who would do such a thing?"

"We were hoping you could tell us," Holt said through a mouthful of pie.

Hob was sharp as a tack and the subtlety of the statement wasn't lost on him. "Surely you don't think I am the mastermind, hmm? Do we not know each other better than this?"

"I don't know you from Adam," Holt said.

I suddenly became aware of figures out in the cornfield around the house. I couldn't pinpoint exactly how many there were, but enough to surround us. Although I couldn't see them, I knew they were corn demons. Some of the many creatures Hob had helping out around the farm. They were demons in the sense that they were from another place, but unlike the demons I had fought this morning, they were more of sentient plants. Not really a threat, as far as I knew, but there were a bunch of them out there. They blended in with the stalks perfectly and the only hint they were around was that prickly feeling on the back of my neck.

I not so subtly bumped into Holt, knocking his next bite of pie off his fork and onto the plate.

"Of course we do," I said. "We didn't come to accuse you of anything, we're just trying to figure this out. Do you know anyone who has the skill and access to enough dust to pull something like that off?"

The tingly feeling subsided somewhat as he answered. "*Ja*, I know someone. It's me," he said without the least bit of concern in his voice.

"You aren't worried about implicating yourself with two Keepers right in front of you?" Holt asked.

"I do not see two Keepers here, there are only two friends," he said.

I leaned on the porch railing. "Can you think of anyone else that could do it?"

"I know of some, but they are not here. I know of no one with the dust, but with enough time it could be collected. All that is necessary is by buying a little now *und* again *und* saving it."

"It could be a group effort," Holt added. "A few people could put it together pretty fast."

If there was a group working together, it could be very difficult to find them. I was already behind the curve and not feeling any closer to finding our culprit, especially if that culprit was the guerrilla resistance group I had just become aware of.

"Have you ever heard of a magical resistance group inside the Elven Nation?" I asked. "Apparently they're some kind of terrorist group."

"*Ja*, I know of them. They are not the terrorist group," Hob said.

Holt dropped his fork on the empty plate and leaned back in his chair. "Yeah? Well what are they, then?"

"They protect those gifted with magic from the Elven Nation by taking them away to safety. If the Queen wants to do away with magic, then she should love these people," Hob said.

"So, kind of like a magical underground railroad?" I asked.

Hob looked confused. "*Nein*, Obie, they do not use a railroad."

"Right," I said, deciding not to explain the underground railroad. "Anyway, Harlan thinks the Queen is going to go after them first. If there is anything you can tell me about them, I would appreciate it."

"It is a waste of time," Hob said.

"We need to find somebody that could collect a lotta dust and is good with magic. Those people fit the bill," Holt said.

"Regardless of where the dust has come from, there has to be a circle for the portal to function. Find the circle *und* it will lead you to the one that has used it," Hob said.

"The Queen closed the outpost, so I'm not going to be getting in to look around anytime soon," I said. "Since you brought up dust, I have to ask . . . What do you do with your share of the dust?"

Hob sighed. "Let us take a walk. I will show you."

We followed Hob to the barn closest to the farmhouse. He opened the door and we walked inside. He flipped a light switch and the overhead fluorescents came to life. He had a couple tractors, some farm equipment, and toolboxes inside. We followed him to the far side of the barn where stairs tucked away behind the toolboxes went to an upper story. We followed Hob up the stairs and through a door at the top. Inside I found a nice, albeit modest, looking apartment. We stepped into the living room. A group of elves were sitting around the coffee table. Two women, a man, and a couple of kids lounged on a couch and loveseat playing cards. When we came in, one of the women got up and came over to us. Her hair was dyed a peach color and she wore a sweatshirt that almost perfectly matched it.

"This is the Corwin family *und* my assistant, Tiffany. We are helping to relocate them away from the Queen," Hob said.

"What did they do," Holt asked.

"They had the nerve to exist," Tiffany answered before turning to Hob. "Is everything okay?"

"*Ja, ganz gut.* These are friends," Hob said. "I am just checking, are they comfortable?"

"They're nervous, which is to be expected, but overall, yes," she said.

"We will not disturb them any longer," Hob said, ushering us out the door. "We remove those in danger, *und* if necessary protect ourselves. That is where my dust has gone."

CHAPTER 9

We spent most of the next week looking for leads and coming up with nothing. There weren't any more attacks and things seemed to be settling down. At least there weren't attacks that I heard about. The Queen might be keeping an incident secret—it wouldn't surprise me. Regardless, I didn't believe for a second someone had gone to all that trouble only to kill a couple of the Queen's daughters. It was a matter of time before more demons showed up. Having exhausted all other options, I was grasping at straws. I had one straw left, but I didn't want to go anywhere near it.

I pulled up to the house and honked the horn. The blinds on his window raised a moment later and Holt held a finger up in the international symbol of "give me a minute." I put the truck in park and waited. A few minutes later he came out wearing a Hawaiian shirt. It had a black base with leaves all over it. Blue and red flowers dotted the foliage, with multicolored parrots facing every direction filling in the gaps. It almost hurt to look at. He jogged up to the truck and hopped in.

"What are you wearing, and more importantly, why?" I asked.

He looked hopeful. "You like it?"

I put the truck in reverse and backed out onto the road. "I didn't say that."

"I was watching this documentary and it was talking about ornamentation with birds. They glued decorations on birds and the ones that were fancy attracted more mates. This one bird got just a plain stick on a plastic circle glued to its head and boom, mating advantage. I figured a little something extra to get noticed wouldn't hurt."

"Martina's still not talking to you?" I asked.

He shook his head. "Not a word since the incident."

"You did claw her right in the face."

"Under demon mind control! It's healed up, you can't even tell it happened," he protested.

"It doesn't mean it didn't leave a scar," I said. "Maybe you should just give her a little time."

"Like you're doing with Naylet?" he asked.

"That's different. The two of you just started talking. Naylet and I were together for over 150 years. Then her memory was wiped and now she apparently just found out I exist."

He smirked. "That's your own fault."

"She needed security and stability while she recovered. I did what I thought was right," I said.

"She could use your support or something," he said. "Chicks love that stuff."

He could have been right. The truth was, I didn't know how to handle it. There wasn't an amnesia expert in my back pocket I could talk to about it. I must have been lost in thought for a while because Holt started talking again.

"So where are we going?" he asked.

"Bear Book Market," I said. "It's a long shot."

He scoffed. "You think the guy in the bookstore is summoning demons?"

"No, I think he might be able to give me a lead."

"Oh yeah, why's that?" he asked.

I sighed, turned on my blinker and pulled into the turn lane for 400 North. "Have you been in the bookstore?"

"Just once, when you abandoned me in town last week," he said. "I stopped in to ask when you left."

"And what could you tell about the guy running the store?" I asked.

"Clay? He's all right, I guess," Holt said. "A little weird, maybe. We talked for a few minutes and got on the subject of blood somehow. He said he would give me five hundred dollars for a pint of blood. Who jokes like that?"

I rested an elbow on the door and rubbed my forehead. "He wasn't joking."

"What? He'd really give me five hundred for a pint?"

"I'm sure he would, but you'd be getting ripped off."

"Really? What do you think he would pay?" Holt asked.

I shrugged. "I can't say for certain, but I would expect at least five grand."

"Five thousand dollars for a pint of blood," Holt mumbled, looking out the window. "Huh."

"Don't get any ideas. Did you notice how he smelled?"

"Under the cologne?" Holt asked. "I noticed it, but I'm not familiar with it."

"He's a werebat," I said, throwing him a quick glance. "Remember the scent and don't ever turn your back on them."

"Is Clay really all that scary?" Holt asked.

"He may not look it, but he's dangerous. What do you know about the bats?"

"Not much. I don't think I've ever seen one before," he said.

"You probably have and didn't know it," I said. "They hardly change out of their human form. There's some speculation about it, but I think it's because they have wings in krasis. I don't see wings being as useful if there's trouble, unless you're trying to escape. The end result is that they blend in better with humans than anyone else."

"Do they really drink blood?" Holt asked.

"They don't live off it," I said. "They eat the same as anyone else, but they have the ability to pull power from the blood. The stronger the host, the stronger they get from it. The effect's temporary, but if you ever find yourself fighting a bat and they get their teeth into you just run. That's why you never turn your back on them."

Holt chuckled. "Come on, they can't be that bad."

"You can take my word for it, they are," I said. "If a werebat bites you, run, wait about twelve hours, and then find it and cuts its head off, first thing."

We made it to Dahlonega just before sundown. I parked around the corner from the Bear Book Market, and Holt and I walked over. We found Clay standing outside, smoking a cigarette.

He smiled when he saw me. "Look who it is. Returning to the scene of the crime?"

"What's he talking about?" Holt asked.

"Your buddy's a shoplifter," Clay said, taking a puff from his cigarette. "Maybe I should call the cops."

"Shoplifter, huh?" Holt beamed. "And here I thought you didn't have any hobbies."

I had forgotten about the book in my glovebox. I didn't mean to steal it, and I didn't have a problem paying for it, but I would rather Holt not found out about it. Something told me he wasn't going to let me forget about it anytime soon.

"We both know you ain't callin' the cops," I said. "Don't be overdramatic."

Clay took a long drag from his cigarette and tossed the butt into the gutter. "If it was just me, I'd let it go, but I'm part of a community and it's my civic duty to report criminals."

"Look, I'll pay for the book."

"Oh, that we agree on. Come inside, gentlemen," Clay said, crossing the sidewalk and pulling the door open.

He held it for us as Holt and I walked inside. Clay took a seat behind the desk. I took a sawbuck out of my pocket and tossed it on the desk in front of him.

He eyed the twenty-dollar bill, but didn't pick it up. "That's not enough."

"The sticker on the book said eight dollars," I said.

"Sure, that was the price to buy it," Clay said. "You took it. We have to consider fair compensation. We have rental fees for the week you've kept it plus purchase price, plus damages both to my business and mental health."

"Mental health?" I questioned.

"I moved here under the impression that Dahlonega was a quiet mountain town, a safe place to do business. Here I haven't been in business but a few weeks before I'm robbed. I've been up nights, not sleeping. I'm thinking of getting a security system. I've experienced a great deal of mental anguish," he said calmly.

"I have no doubt you've been up nights, not that it has anything to do with me," I said. "I know what you are, and I know you don't really care about these books. They're just a cover for what you've really got going on. So let's cut the crap."

"Right to the point . . . a good trait for Keepers to have," he said.

"You know who we are?" Holt asked.

Clay gave him a smile. "You think you're the only one with a nose? Or that I would set up shop here without doing my research? An otter and a dog sticking their nose in everyone's business, who else could it be? I'm honestly surprised it took you this long to come by."

"Tell me what you're really doing here," I said. "Behind the books."

"Last time you were in the shop, I believe you were inquiring about Ichor? I may be able to get you some," Clay said. "Honestly, I thought Keepers would prefer something a little more natural . . . Weed maybe?"

"You can get us weed?" Holt asked.

I shot him a look.

"Not that I want any," Holt clarified.

"Sure, I can get all kind of things for my friends," Clay said. "And we are going to be friends, aren't we?"

I scratched my chin, thinking how to steer the conversation in the direction I wanted it to go. "What about information?"

"Everything's for sale. Except the heater. My landlord still hasn't turned the heat on in the building," Clay said, pointing to a rickety old heater a few feet away.

"What about dust?" I asked.

Clay tapped his fingers on the desk. "If you need dust, I may be able to locate some for you."

"Did you hear about the attack on the Southern Outpost?" I asked.

"I heard you got shot up," he said. "That's the day you decided to walk off with my merchandise, if I'm not mistaken."

"I've got bigger problems that anything you got going on here. I'm trying to figure out who orchestrated the attack. I'm looking for an elf that's been buying dust. Have you had any customers that fit that description?"

Clay gave me a smile. "Oh no, we've established you're the kind to run off. You're going to have to prepay."

"How much?" I asked.

He opened the drawer in his desk and pulled out an empty vial. "I'll tell you everything I know for one vial."

I shook my head. "Cash. I'm not giving you blood."

"That's the price of information," he said, waving the vial.

"Come on," I said. "You can take cash."

"You think you're some kinda Jedi, with the mind tricks?" Clay asked. "If you want the info, it costs blood."

I sighed. "Have you ever had Keeper blood?"

Clay leaned forward over his desk, with hunger in his eyes. "No, but I'm dying to try it."

I stared at him for a minute, thinking it over. Giving a werebat my blood wasn't something I planned to do, and definitely not an entire vial of it. It was too dangerous. If Clay drank it all at once, he'd be more trouble than Holt and I could handle. If he didn't hoard it all for himself he could sell it off a little here and there. Any werebat that got their hands on it would be hard to handle. There's no telling who would be hurt by it. Even though the effects only last for a short time it's still more risk than I was willing to take.

"Come on," he said, breaking the silence. "I'll even forget about that misunderstanding with the book."

"I'll give you one drop," I said. "I can't let you have enough to keep laying around."

Clay squinted at me, considering my offer. "Deal."

He opened the drawer again and brought out the kind of finger stick used in diabetes tests. He placed it on the desk in front of me.

I picked it up. "Where am I putting the drop?"

"Right in the pie hole," Clay said, pointing toward his mouth. "I want my first taste fresh."

"Open up, buttercup," I said, giving my finger a flurry of sticks, just to make sure I could get a drop out before I healed.

Clay tilted his head back as I raised my finger over his mouth, squeezing the end of it with my other hand to push the blood out. A drop formed on the end of my finger. The anticipation began to show in Clay's eyes. They widened and bulged to unnatural dimensions. As the drop formed his face began to elongate. Fangs grew out of his teeth and thick dark hair sprouted from his cheeks and chin.

"Jesus," Holt whispered under his breath.

His mouth opened wider and wider, much farther than seemed possible. His tongue grew slender and forked, swirling around in his mouth in anticipation. The blood fell from my finger. His jaws slammed shut around it, the momentum bowing him over and knocking the hat from his head onto the floor. I withdrew my hand and wiped my finger on the inside of my pocket. Clay rubbed the top of his head and began to shake it from side to side. He slammed his hands down on his desk and lifted his head to look at me. His face had returned to normal, mostly. I could see the veins in his neck bulging and his eyes had changed from hazel to a deep, almost blood red. Sweat dotted his forehead.

"You feel that," he said. "It's got a kick."

He stood up from the desk, walking over and leaning against a bookcase. He knocked a few books on the floor and didn't seem to notice.

I gave Holt my "get ready" look. He nodded and took a step away from me to put some distance between us.

"Well?" I asked. "What can you tell me?"

"I had an elf come in that wanted some dust. She lives right here in town," he said.

Finally, we were making some progress. This could be the only solid lead I'd had all week.

"Great," I said. "Who is it and where can I find her."

"I'd love to tell you more, but I just can't remember," he said. "Maybe if I had a little more of that finger candy?"

"We had a deal," I said. "I paid and you owe me."

Clay turned back to me with his tongue over his top teeth, sucking them. His eyes were still deep red. "A drop gets you a drop."

"That's it then?" I asked.

Clay stood breathing slow and heavy. He just smiled.

"Come on, Holt," I said, backing toward the door.

Holt followed my lead. He moved over to the desk, grabbed my twenty, and we left.

CHAPTER 10

"So, what now?" Holt asked. "We heading to the party?"

I tapped my fingers on the steering wheel of my truck. If Clay was telling the truth and the elf lived in town, I had one other option, but it was a last resort.

"There's one more thing we can try. I know someone who lives in town that would probably know where this elf is," I said. "Assuming Clay was telling the truth."

"Who's that?" Holt asked.

"Her name's Slagtooth. She comes out some nights and prowls around town. If there's an elf around, she'll know it."

"Well then, let's go talk to her," Holt said.

I shook my head. "It's not that simple. We're going to need a lotta meat first."

We drove over to Walmart to pick up some meat. We ended up with just over fifty pounds of pork shoulder. By the time we made it back to downtown Dahlonega, the shops were just closing. The town began to clear as the tourists and locals headed to their cars. I pulled off the square and parked on the southeast side of Hancock Park. This time of night the back streets were deserted and poorly lit, just what I was looking for. The diving bell sat on the edge of the park, ahead of us on the left. It was a large metal box with a point on one end and what looked like a chimney coming out of the top. Back in the gold mining days it was attached to a barge and floated around the Chestatee. They lowered it into the river and pumped all the water out so they could pan the previously inaccessible riverbed.

"So, where's this contact at?" Holt asked.

"She lives in the diving bell," I said, pointing at the large metal box.

"Anything I need to know before we go?"

"Don't show fear, and don't run," I said, opening the door. "And don't get bit."

I grabbed the bags of meat, and we got out of the truck.

We walked up the sidewalk and under the pavilion that had been built to cover the artifact. It had a triangular roof with stone pillars that turned into large wood beams. A few large mechanical pieces of the contraption were mounted close by for inspection along with a few signs explaining the history of the bell. The bell itself was mounted about three feet off the ground on a wooden frame. I sat down on the stone bench running in a half circle on the opposite side of the pavilion.

"Well? Where is she?" Holt asked.

"Go pound on the bell a few times," I said, starting to open the meat. The plastic covering the meat was thick and tough, and I wished I had a knife, but I managed to get a few of them ripped open.

Holt walked up to the bell, raised a fist, and paused. "What's going to happen?"

"Well, Slagtooth will know we're here," I said.

"And then?"

"And then she'll come out," I answered.

He started to hit the bell again and paused a second time. "What kind of lady is Slagtooth?"

"Oh, she's no lady," I said. "You'll be fine. I'm right over here."

Holt looked from me, sitting fifteen feet away on the bench, to the diving bell and back to me. "You knock and I'll sit over there," he said, moving to take my spot on the bench and jabbing a thumb at the bell.

"Suit yourself," I said, putting the bags of meat on the bench. "Finish opening these up. When she comes out, I want you to give one to her. Only one."

I gave the bell a solid knock. The metal reverberated, rumbling deeply like a drum. The long pipe sticking from the top of the bell had a small porthole, a few inches in diameter, about twelve feet off the ground. I stepped back to get a look at it and after a couple seconds I could hear shuffling from inside the bell. A reptilian eye appeared in the porthole. I gave it a wave. The eye disappeared and a door, disguised as part of the frame the bell sat on, burst open.

A lizard, roughly fifteen feet in length, shot out of the bell. Her body was covered in bony gray scales. She slithered on all fours in between a five-foot-long tubular hatch and an axle with a large gear in the middle. She stopped and eyeballed us with her head poking out from around the hatch. A slender forked tongue over a foot long popped in and out of her mouth. She stood up, stretching about ten feet with her tail trailing behind her and her front claws resting on the hatch. She looked pissed off to me, but I couldn't be sure, I've never known a lizard with a cheerful expression.

"What does the Keeper want?" she asked in a deep rumbling whisper of a voice.

"I need some information," I said, looking up at her. "But before we get into that, I brought you something."

I motioned at Holt to toss her some meat. Slagtooth whipped her head in his direction and with the sight of meat and the smell of blood her base instincts took over. She charged a few steps in his direction. Holt tossed the meat in the air and fell back over the stone bench. Slagtooth snatched the meat out of the air and swallowed it in a single gulp. Holt took off through the bushes, at least he tried to. The movement caught Slagtooth's attention and she pounced.

Holt grabbed her throat with one hand to keep her from biting him and changed to krasis. With the Doberman features and the horrendous shirt he looked like one of the old Egyptian gods on a Hawaiian vacation. He bit her neck, sinking his long teeth in between her scales. While he had her distracted, I grabbed the bags of meat. Holt was able to keep her from biting him. She had him pinned and resorted to the claws on her hind legs. She brought them up and tore them into Holt's belly.

"That's enough," I shouted, pulling her off him by the tail.

Hissing, she reeled around on me. I dropped her tail and punched her in the face. She fell against the stone bench before getting back to her feet and scurried behind one of the pillars.

"Stop," I commanded, holding up a finger.

Holt groaned, and got up, clutching his abdomen. Blood soaked through his tattered shirt. I could see traces of his intestines poking from around his fingers. She had torn him up good and he was going to need a few minutes to recover.

"We just came for some information, not to fight," I said.

"Why would Slagtooth tell you anything?"

"I brought you a snack," I said, shaking the bags of pork.

She peeked from around the pillar, but didn't come out.

"How about if I bring you some more at the beginning of spring when you wake up from hibernation?" I asked.

She eased her way out from behind the pillar. I pulled the meat out of the bags and stacked it on the ground in a big pile. I stepped to the side and held a hand, offering it to her. She charged and attacked them, cramming all fifty pounds into her mouth at once. While she was able to hold it in her mouth at once, she wasn't able to swallow it. She tried to stretch and wiggle her neck to work the meat down. When that didn't work, she moved over to the bench and slammed her mouth onto the corner of the stone, forcing the meat deeper and deeper until large lumps visibly moved down her throat. I noticed blood on her neck where Holt had bitten her.

I waited patiently as this circus of mastication played out. With a hand over his stomach, Holt watched from the safety of bushes. After swallowing the meat, the lizard creature crawled on all fours to the bushes and wiped her mouth on the leaves, pausing for a second for a closer look at Holt. The area looked like something out of a slasher film. Blood was everywhere.

"I was told there's an elf living in town," I said. "I need to find her. Have you smelled any elves around?"

She lowered her head in a posture that reminded me of a cat about to pounce. "Slagtooth didn't eat the elf."

I shook my head. "I'm not accusing you of anything. I just want to know where to find her."

"House on the edge of town," she said, pointing her nose toward the west.

"Okay, that's all I wanted," I said. "Hey, did he hurt you? Let me take a look."

She showed me the place on her neck where Holt had bitten her. She was bleeding, but didn't appear to be seriously injured. I moved my hand slowly, as not to appear threatening, over her injury. When it was in place, I healed her injury. She started making a guttural ticking sound. When her injuries were closed, I ran my hand over her scales. They were smooth and I could feel the power underneath as she moved. She circled around and rubbed up against me. I petted her.

"I'll bring you another snack in spring, okay?" I said softly.

She walked back to the diving bell, pausing for a second to send Holt an icy glare before she disappeared inside, closing the door behind her. I could hear the shuffling as she settled.

"You okay?" I asked when it was quiet.

He groaned. "Is this town full of monsters or what?"

"I wouldn't say *full*," I said. "Need help?"

Holt limped out of the bushes, easing his way to me with one hand on his gut. "I'm all right. She scratched the hell out of me and ruined my shirt."

"She did you a favor."

"But what about Martina?" he asked.

"I think you'd have more luck with a plunger glued to your head," I said. "Seriously though, you don't need gimmicks to get her attention. You did that already when you tried to claw her face off. You just need to let her come around."

He sighed. "And what if she doesn't come around?"

"Then you move on," I replied. "Either way, you can't walk around with bloody clothes. When you're up to it, we'll head to the truck and get you a fresh set."

"I never put new clothes in the car after the last time," he said.

"I'll give you some of mine," I said. "Always make sure to have spare clothes handy."

We went back to the truck and I gave Holt a change of clothes. He was still bloody, but it was dark, and I wasn't planning to be spending time around a lot of people. We walked a few blocks to the edge of town. There were only a couple rows of houses in that direction that the elf could live in. The street bordered woods.

"Let's use our animal forms to sniff around. We can use the woods for cover," I said. "I'll take Hawkins Street and you take Church Street."

We walked into the woods out of sight of the houses. I took the form of an otter and Holt changed into a Doberman. Holt took off down Church Street, zigzagging with his nose to the ground. I headed down the sidewalk of Hawkins, going into yards and onto porches to find our elf. I caught the scent of a number of humans, dogs, cats, squirrels, and even a chipmunk, but no elves.

Holt barked and I abandoned my search to see what he had found. He was sitting in front of a white house on top of a grassy hill. The house looked like it had been built about a hundred years ago. A cozy place that looked like a poster for reminiscing about America's past. The lights were off. I sniffed around a bit and confirmed that there had definitely been an elf here recently. We went back into the woods. I changed back to my human form, and started getting dressed.

"It doesn't look like anyone's home," I said. "Stay in that form and head down to the other end of the street. Find somewhere to keep out of sight. We'll hang out a bit and see if our elf comes back."

Holt barked in recognition and bounded off. I sat on an old brick wall off the edge of the road to wait. It was covered in vines and moss, slowly being reclaimed by the forest. The Tortured Occult's party was probably getting underway. I didn't mind missing it. The T.O. hadn't been the same since Otis's death. They were more crude and vulgar, definitely rougher around the edges. I hadn't realized how tame Otis had kept them. It wasn't the same wholesome bunch of ruffians I was used to. It was an important relationship, however, and Holt was looking forward to the party, so we would go. It would be good for him to blow off some steam.

After waiting close to an hour, a car pulled up to the house. Holt and I closed in. I got there first just as a woman was getting out. She closed the door and turned to see who was walking up her driveway. She reached a hand in a bag she had slung over her shoulder. I didn't know if she was reaching for a gun or dust. She moved her hand deeper into her bag. Holt came up beside me and growled. She froze. If I hadn't recognized her, I would have charged her. It was the elven woman working with Hob.

"Tiffany?"

She took a step back in a defensive posture. "Are you following me?"

"I'm following a lead that led me to you," I said. "Did you try to buy dust from Clay over at the Bear Book Market?"

"How I spend my time's none of your business," she said.

Holt growled a little louder and took a step toward her.

I put my hands out to look as unthreatening as possible. "We're all friends here."

"No, you're friends with Hob," she corrected. "I don't know you."

"Fair enough. If you don't wanna be friends that fine with me. I don't have to be friendly. Now answer the question."

I could see her wheels turning as she weighed her options. "Yeah, I talked to him about dust," she said.

"Was that so hard?" I asked. "Let's go."

I took a few steps back. Holt followed. She didn't take her hand out of the bag as we walked backward out of the driveway.

CHAPTER 11

The property of Morrison Salvage was fenced, but the gates were rarely closed. We pulled up to find the gate not only closed, but guarded by a bored looking man. He was Latino, a little round around the edges, with a scraggly beard. He wore the black leather kutte common to the Tortured Occult, but this one didn't have any patches on the front. It had a single rocker on the back, reading PROSPECT. I had seen him around, but hadn't spoken to him before. He walked over to the open window of the truck.

"Hey, I'm Obie, this is Holt. We were invited," I said.

He sighed. "I been waitin' forever on you two. Lemme get the gate."

He rolled open the chain link fence blocking the road. He stood by while I pulled through.

"It must suck to be a prospect," Holt mused as we passed. "Always having to do the shit jobs."

I shrugged. "It's like any other initiation. Proving your worth to be part of the group can be a powerful thing. Besides, it's not permanent."

"I'm glad the Keepers don't have something like that," Holt said.

"Don't we?" I asked. "You're kinda like my prospect, if you think about it."

"I think partners is more accurate. Hulk and Thor, you know?"

"Batman and Robin?" I suggested.

"Sure, if I'm Batman," he said. "I'm nobody's sidekick."

The prospect swung the gate closed behind us and started walking to the clubhouse.

I threw a thumb toward the bed of the truck out the window. "Jump in the back, I'll give you a ride."

He did and we pulled up the dirt path to the clubhouse. I parked beside a larger row of motorcycles than I had ever seen at the clubhouse. When we got out, the prospect had already changed to krasis. He had the catlike features and tawny yellow fur with black spots of a jaguar. He jumped out of the back of the truck, carrying the work boots he'd been wearing that wouldn't fit his paws.

The lights on the property were off, including the streetlight. The moon was a waxing crescent, not giving enough light to make walking in krasis an issue, even though we were only three hundred feet from the road. Holt and I kicked off our shoes and left them in the truck after making the change to krasis. We followed the prospect to the back of the building.

I found the party in full swing. There were more people there than I'd expected. Everyone was in krasis. All of the Tortured Occult were in attendance along with the people closest to the club. Holt, Adan, and me as well as a few others. What I didn't expect was an entire other motorcycle club. They looked to be all wolves and coyotes and the back of their kuttes had a dog's head engulfed in flames with a caption: WRETCHED DOGS MC, CHARLOTTE SC.

The only light came from a bonfire in the center of the event. There was a slight chill in the air, not anything that facilitated an eight-foot-tall pyre, but I got the impression it was more for ambiance than function. There was a table with an assortment of liquor as well as beer coolers spread out around the party. You could stand anywhere and never be more than a few steps away from booze. Many of the partiers were smoking. Irregular puffs rose up from all around and the air hung heavy with the smell of weed. Empty bottles and cans littered the ground. Whole animals on spits spun on large rotisseries. Bikers would bite pieces directly off the carcasses. Many of the shifters, men and women, weren't wearing clothes, others just wore their kuttes and nothing else. There were a lot of women I didn't recognize. They were all drunk.

"I didn't think you were coming," Tico said.

He was sitting on an overturned five-gallon bucket, with a beer in his hand.

"You would miss me if I weren't here," I replied. "Who are the Wretched Dogs?"

"MC from South Carolina," he said. "They're a bunch of assholes, if you ask me."

He was much too relaxed and downright cheerful to be acting in his official capacity as a bartender. He must have made the list of friends of the club invited, which made sense since he spent so much time with them.

"Do you like anybody?" I asked.

He paused with the bottle in front of his mouth. "I like Naylet. She's a good person, much too good for you," he said, and threw his head back and finished off the beer and tossed the bottle on the ground. "I'm going to get another. You want one?"

I didn't really want one, but this was the best we had gotten along in as long as I could remember. So if he wanted to make a peace offering, I would take it.

"Sure," I said.

He walked toward a cooler. "Then get it yourself."

"What'd you do to him?" Holt asked.

"Why the hell is it that I had to do something to him? Did it ever occur to you, the guy's just a jerk?"

"Nah," Holt answered. "You probably did something. I'm going to get a drink."

Holt walked off toward the table of liquor. A sudden burst of laughter from behind me caught my attention. I turned around to find Cotton, Lug Nut, and Ginsu who were standing with some of the Wretched Dogs. Ginsu, a red wolf, and one of the most colorful members of the T.O., noticed me. He was called Ginsu because he had a thing for knives and was guaranteed to have at least three on him at any given time. The only one I could see was a large Bowie on his belt.

"Obie," Ginsu said. "You gotta hear this. What do you call an elf from France?"

I grinned and shook my head.

"A tree frog." He cackled. "Get it? Tree frog!"

It wasn't the best joke I had ever heard and I was sure the Queen wouldn't find the humor in it. I give him a polite smile and nod.

"What? You think you can do better?" Ginsu asked, the smell of alcohol heavy on his breath.

"No, it's pretty good," I answered.

He didn't seem satisfied and stumbled as he took a step forward. "Let's hear it then. Quiet everybody, the comedian here is going to tell us a joke."

The group looked at me, armed with smirks and judgment. I wasn't going to let him show me up.

"Two guys are walking through the woods and come up on a dog licking his balls. The first guy says, 'I wish I could do that.' The second guy says, 'That dog will bite *youuu!*'"

A hearty round of chuckles ran through the group. Lug Nut, Hank's oldest son, who was always quick to laugh, was in the middle of swig from his beer and proceeded to spit it out all over Ginsu as he erupted in a fit. That set off the rest of the group into hearty fits of laughter. Lug Nut bent forward, slapping his leg as the remainder of the beer ran freely out of his mouth and nose and onto the ground. Ginsu wiped his face with his hands, removing the beer as well as he could from his fur. He didn't find it as funny as the rest of us, who burst out with even louder howls when they saw how sour he was about it. After a few seconds Ginsu started chuckling along with the rest of us.

"All right, pretty good, Obie," he said, shaking the beer off his hands and wiping them on his pants.

As the laughter died down, another sound from the other side of the bonfire overpowered our joviality—pain. Across the yard a fight was taking place. Close to a third of everyone at the party was gathered around watching. Whenever the T.O. had a party they always had a circle for some friendly competition. The rules were simple. A large circle was spray painted on the ground. Two people agree to terms, enter the circle, and fight. It doesn't end until one person leaves the circle, intentionally or not, or is unable to continue. I say the circle was for friendly competition and that's true enough, but things had a way of devolving. Egos get in the way, people start taking liberties with the agreed upon rules, and next thing you know, you end up with exactly what I was looking at now.

Through the legs of the crowd I could see a wolverine had a coyote pinned.

I knew the wolverine was Big Ticket; I didn't recognize the coyote, they all look alike to me. B.T. was sinking his teeth into the coyote's soft belly. The coyote yelped in pain before wiggling free and dragging itself away as quickly as it could. B.T. pounced on the defenseless animal again. The coyote was trying to leave and end the fight—that was clear for anyone to see. Unfortunately, it had been maimed and couldn't move well. If its muzzle reached the edge of the orange circle painted on the ground, Big Ticket would stop attacking it. The coyote was learning the hard way what getting into the circle with B.T. meant. He never ran and he didn't accept it from anyone else either. The coyote succumbed to blood loss before it made it to the edge of the circle. Big Ticket changed to krasis, and walked out of the ring, leaving the coyote motionless behind him. It wasn't a huge deal; as a shifter the coyote would heal pretty quickly. I doubted it would forget his run-in with Big Ticket any time soon.

Cotton stepped in close to not be overheard. "B.T.'s been working his way through the Wretched Dogs all night. They haven't given him any real challenge so far."

Cotton was an artic wolf; one of the oldest members of the Tortured Occult. The light of the bonfire dancing on his thick white fur made him look like some kind of werewolf ghost.

"Maybe you should show 'em how it's done."

Cotton shook his head. "I'd rather stay in one piece tonight, besides we both know you're the one he really wants to fight."

"Yeah, I'll pass," I said.

"What's the matter?" one of the Wretched Dogs said. "You scared?"

Ginsu laughed. "Obie ain't scared. He won last time they got in the circle."

"Bullshit," the biker said.

"I saw it with my own eyes," Ginsu said. "Ever since, B.T.'s been wanting a rematch, but Obie hasn't given it to 'im."

The Wretched Dog chugged the rest of his beer, let out a loud belch, and tossed the bottle over his shoulder out into the junkyard. "That's just bad manners."

It was probably nice for Big Ticket to have some fresh competition. He thrived on fighting and dedicated himself to its perfection, making him possibly the most dangerous member of the T.O. He had long black and tan fur in a distinctive pattern. If you knew B.T., you wouldn't mistake him for any other wolverine you had the misfortune to cross paths with. I spotted Hank sitting at a table at the edge of the party. I excused myself and went over, pulling an empty chair beside him. I saw Holt take a bite out of one of the animals on the spits. I didn't think much of it until I noticed that the animal looked . . . different . . . than the others. It had no head or feet. It was just an abdomen and legs. I recognized it as human or maybe an elf.

"What kind of meat is that, Holt's eating?" I asked.

"Something the Dogs brought," Hank said.

"I'm just curious."

Hank sighed. "Look, Obie, you're doing that thing again where you ask questions you don't really want the answers to. I made sure that everything we got here was sustainably sourced."

His answer confirmed it was some kind of humanoid. I didn't know if sustainably sourced meant they were someone bad or just that no one would miss them. Either way, I decided not to push it.

"Nice party. It smells like a music festival," I said. "I'm surprised to see another club here. You aren't thinking of taking them on the run tomorrow, are you?"

Hank drank straight from a bottle of Jack Daniels. "So what if I am?"

"We both know she wouldn't like it," I said. "If you're asking me, I don't think any of you should go."

"It doesn't matter what she likes, she agreed to it." Hank wiped his mouth on his forearm. "You think she's gonna try something?"

"You know how the Queen is. With the attack on the Southern Outpost, you should probably keep your distance till things cool off."

He ran a hand over the tuft of black fur on the end of his chin that resembled a goatee. "You're probably right, but it's too late to back out now. The club wants to go, so we'll go."

"What's it going to take to change your mind?"

"It's not just my mind you have to change." Hank held a hand out to the club enjoying the party. "You have to change enough of their minds to win a vote."

A rather curvy wereraccoon sat in Hank's lap under his outstretched arm. She, like many of the other ladies at the party, wasn't wearing any clothes and her eyes were glazed from alcohol or possibly something stronger. He rested his hand on her hip and took another swig from the bottle. I had never seen her before. She may have come with the Wretched Dogs. I looked from the girl to Hank and back to the girl.

Hank suddenly looked as if he had offended me. "Sorry, Obie, did you want one? You can have this one."

"No no," I said.

Hank took the girl's hand and directed her to my lap. She wrapped one arm around my neck and began to nuzzle my neck. Her other hand rested on my chest.

"I don't—" I said before Hank interrupted me.

"Okay, I get it," he said. "She's made a couple rounds already. I can get you a fresh one."

I shook my head. "It's not that. I didn't come here looking for companionship."

My body didn't get the memo that my mind was sending. I was suddenly aware of how long it had been since I had had some kind of intimate contact. My heart pumped a little faster with a familiar tingle welling up in my groin from her touch.

"Why the hell didn't you tell me?" Holt asked, walking up to where we were sitting.

"Tell you what?"

"That you beat Big Ticket," Holt said. "Everybody's talking about it."

I shrugged. "It never came up."

"I'm going to fight him. You got some advice? Weaknesses or anything like that?" Holt asked.

"Yeah, I got some advice for you," I said. "Don't fight B.T."

Holt chuckled. "Aw, come on, we're Keepers. He can't be that tough."

Hank leaned forward. "How about a bet? If he can beat B.T. in the circle, I'll try to get the run canceled."

"Hold on," Holt said. "Why do you want to cancel the run?"

I sighed. "I just don't think it's safe."

"No bet then?" Hank asked with a smirk. "It's the only way you have a chance to get the run canceled."

I looked up at Holt. "You shouldn't fight B.T."

He looked a little hurt. "You don't think I can win, do you?"

"I didn't say that."

"You got a bet, Hank," Holt said, turning and walking toward the circle.

I jumped from my seat, put the girl down as quickly and gently as I could, and went after him. "You don't have to do this."

"I'm going to show you I can win." Holt spotted Big Ticket, pointed a finger at him, and shouted, "I got next."

B.T. gave us a nod and walked over to the circle. He still had bites and scratches from his last fight that weren't fully healed, but they didn't seem to bother him.

I grabbed Holt's arm to get his attention. "Listen, I believe you can win, but you're going to have the fight of your life. He doesn't play and he isn't going to go easy on you. You have to go in hard, get the upper hand, and don't let up until he's unconscious. If you give him an inch or make a mistake, you lose."

He pulled free of my grip. "Relax, I got it under control."

I didn't get the impression he was taking what I was telling him seriously. I could see Big Ticket in the circle. As Holt continued to back toward it, Big Ticket moved forward. The match would start as soon as they were both in the circle.

I pointed behind Holt and shouted, "Pay attention."

Holt held up his hands and unknowingly backed into the circle. "Don't worry so—"

Big Ticket popped up behind him and sank his teeth into Holt's right shoulder. Holt was pulled to the ground and the crowd cheered and closed in, blocking my view.

I put my hands on my hips and lowered my head. I knew Holt wasn't going to be able to recover from a start that bad. I walked back to my seat beside Hank.

Hank took a swig from the bottle. "Are you and Holt still joining us tomorrow?"

"We'll be there. In spite of Holt taking your stupid bet, he is looking forward to the run. I think it will be good for him to get out and experience some pack life. I'm not planning on running with you, my legs are too short for me to keep up with a bunch of bears and wolves. If you have a pack swim give me a call."

"You could always run in krasis," he offered. "That's what Skinny Pete does. He wouldn't be able to keep up with us as a rat either."

I looked around the yard at the Tortured Occult and Wretched Dogs drinking, laughing, and cheering on Big Ticket as he mangled Holt, all with a feeling of real comradery. Maybe Holt wasn't the only one who could benefit from some community. I had been lonely without Naylet around; being a Keeper can be isolating, even with a partner.

"What the hell," I said.

After a minute, Big Ticket came out through the crowd. His fur was stained with fresh blood that ran from his mouth to his knees. He must have really done a number on Holt. He walked over to where we were sitting.

"That was fun," he said. "You feeling up to a match?"

I shook my head. "Not tonight."

B.T. leaned forward and looked me in the eye to emphasize his words. "I'm going to get my rematch."

The party wound down, with bikers disappearing or passing out in random places around the yard. I eventually found myself not really feeling like dealing with drunken bikers so I went to my truck. I opened the windows, pulled a book out of the glovebox, and lay down with my feet sticking out the passenger side. I made it through a few chapters of *Henderson the Rain King* before I was interrupted.

"Where'd you get off to?"

I lowered my book and parted my feet to see Holt through the window, wearing a Tortured Occult T-shirt. "I got a little tired of the party. What are you wearing?"

He ran a hand over the shirt. "Yeah, Big Ticket was hard your other one. I didn't want to take another change of clothes from you after Slagtooth. I'm going to have to keep more clothes on hand."

"Probably a good idea," I said, sitting up and sliding over into the driver's seat. "Is the party over?"

"I don't know if this run's going to happen. There's still a couple that haven't passed out yet, but most of them are unconscious. I don't see them getting up for more partying anytime soon."

I started the truck. "They'll be there. Hop in, we'll stop on the way and get you some new clothes. I don't want to show up with you wearing that shirt."

"Where are we going?" Holt asked.

"The Elven Nation. I want to get there early and check things out. I got a bad feeling."

CHAPTER 12

About thirty minutes before the run was scheduled to start, we pulled into a camping area deep inside the Elven Nation. It was just a dirt circle in the middle of the woods with no houses for miles. It spanned roughly fifty feet in diameter and still had the blackened remains of a campfire in the center. Here, the Tortured Occult could party to their hearts' content without worrying about being disturbed. The Queen's SUV and two escort trucks were parked to the right. There was a gray van I hadn't seen before. There was a slight slant of the land here and the Queen has opted to park on the high side. No surprise she took the high ground. I pulled in beside the closest truck and turned the engine off. Harlan got out of the front seat of the SUV and slung a satchel over his shoulder before opening the back door. I expected the Queen, but Isabelle slid out instead and shouldered her rifle.

"That's a good sign. The Queen wouldn't bring Isabelle if she was going to start trouble," Holt said.

I rolled down my window as the pair came to greet us. "You don't know that."

"Mother would like to speak to you," Isabelle said with authority.

"I'll be right there."

The princess was possibly the only person in the Elven Nation that would, or could, speak so informally about the Queen. The two of them walked back to the SUV.

I rolled up the window so Holt and I could have some privacy. "While I'm talking to the Queen, do me a favor and look around the area a little."

"What am I looking for?"

I shrugged. "Elves hiding in the bushes? Anything out of place. I don't want any surprises."

"Do you really think she's gonna to try something?" he asked.

I opened my door. "Do you really think she isn't?"

We got out of the truck. Holt stripped down and changed into a Doberman; I walked over to the SUV. Four elves armed with rifles got out of the vehicles. The closest stepped forward and held a hand out to stop me. I heard the crunching of leaves and looked back to see Holt bounding off into the woods. The Queen got out of her SUV.

"Where's he going?" she asked.

She was dressed as usual: Black combat boots, jeans, a flannel shirt, and two chrome revolvers hanging from a leather belt that sagged from one hip.

"Just stretching his legs," I said. "He's excited about the run."

She crossed her arms. "I wasn't aware you would be joining them."

"I wasn't going to, but I got talked into it last minute."

She motioned for me to join her as she stepped away from her guards. "What have you found out about the attack?"

"I've been working on it, but haven't come up with anything."

She didn't look pleased. "You don't have a lead?"

I shook my head. "Well, no. I've been trying to track the dust. It would take a lot for an attack like that, but I haven't been able to find anyone able to pull it off."

She scowled at me. "Then how are you getting closer?"

"I ruled out some people. I've got a growing list of who it isn't."

"Your attention should be focused on the Tortured Occult. You will find all the connections you need there, if you bother to look."

"I was with them last night and spoke to Hank," I replied.

"As a friend or a suspect?"

I sighed. "Whatever's going on, I am confident Hank isn't part of it."

"You will do a thorough investigation of all members of the Tortured Occult," she commanded.

I was afraid she might try to pull something like this. I don't answer or take orders from her. I was hoping I didn't have to remind her.

"I will find whoever is responsible," I said. "These things take time; they aren't always what they seem on the surface. It's only been a week."

"Exactly, it's been a week. I expect faster results," she said.

I shrugged. "Well, I don't work for you."

I was a little concerned how she would take that and I wasn't alone. The elves within earshot exchanged some sideways glances. I caught the slightest raise of her lip. Expressed completely it would have been a scowl. She was very good at hiding her emotions normally. I wondered if she wasn't trying to hide it or if she was so pissed it slipped through.

"You refuse to take my orders, but you take my help when it suits you," she said. "Have you forgotten that you're in my debt?"

"I have tried to work that out and you refuse anything reasonable," I said. "I think you just want something to hold over my head."

I could hear the rumble of motorcycles coming down the road. They would be here in less than a minute.

"This is your last chance."

"Nothing has changed in the past three seconds."

She walked back to the SUV. "So be it."

Holt came bounding out of the woods and changed to krasis as the motorcycles rolled in. Hank was leading with the Wretched Dogs and the Tortured Occult in two rows behind him. They pulled in and with a precision that comes from practice arranged the bikes in a neat row opposite the elves. The procession was followed by a large moving truck that parked off to the side. No doubt the truck carried everything they would need for three days of debauchery. They killed the engines, got off the bikes, and started congregating in the center. Their excitement was evident. Almost everyone was smiling, except for Chisel, and even he seemed less sour than usual.

"Well?" I asked Holt.

"It's all clear."

I was about to join Hank when the Queen stepped behind her SUV and addressed the group. "The attack on the Southern Outpost last week was unlike anything we have seen before. It was a personal attack on my family, taking the lives of two of my daughters. Despite that, we made an agreement and I keep my word," she said, giving me a sour glance. "However, before the run can begin, I need to know what you can tell me about the attack. Who perpetrated it, where they are hiding, and who the accomplices were. If you volunteer this information freely, I will not consider you all accomplices in the attack."

I gave Harlan, who was standing beside the SUV with Isabelle, a questioning glance. He met my gaze, but didn't give any hint at what was happening. I didn't like where this was going. I didn't need Harlan to tell me it was bad, everyone knew it. A mumble rose from the bikers. Chisel walked a few paces off to the right of the group, putting some space between himself and the rest of the pack, his normal scowl returning to his face.

"There's nothing to tell," Hank said. "We didn't have anything to do with the attack and we don't know anything about it."

The Queen's right hand drifted to the butt of her pistol. "You claim to be a friend that wants to work for mutual benefit. Yet, now that we've been attacked, you keep your mouth shut. Let me put this plainly: Someone here knows something about the attack and they are going to come forward."

The only thing I could tell her that might satiate her paranoia was that I had learned Hob was helping sneak magical adepts and dissenters out of the Nation. Since he worked with us, she would probably blame everyone for it and may do more harm than good. I didn't believe her when she said she wouldn't hold it against the group. Besides, I didn't believe Hob had anything to do with the attack. I wasn't going to be responsible for the Queen sending an assault team over to the farm, assuming she knew where it was. I walked over to put myself between the T.O. and the elves, a place I seemed to be in more and more lately.

"There's no reason for this to get out of hand. We're all friends here."

"Ah yes, Obie, friend to all. Do you think they would still consider you a friend if they knew the truth?" the Queen said with a sneer. "This is your last chance. Anyone with information about the attack, come forward now."

Razor stepped up beside me. "Listen, lady. Hank already told you we don't know nothin' and Obie proved himself repeatedly as a friend of the club. I don't care what you think you know."

"What if I told you I had Otis killed at the bridge and your good friend, Obie, not only knew about it, but kept it from you? I wouldn't think that's a very friendly thing to do, would you?"

"Obie?" Hank said.

I could feel all the eyes of the T.O. on me. There was no way I could explain this here, or maybe at all, tensions were too high. I didn't have the chance to try.

"Since you refuse to cooperate, our alliance is over. Hank, as the leader of this . . . club," she said waving a hand dismissively, "I hold you personally responsible."

With lightning fast reflexes, she drew and fanned the hammer of her revolver, firing a number of shots faster than I could count. The bullets screamed past me to my right. She spun the revolver and returned it to its holster like some gunslinger in a spaghetti Western.

I turned to see Hank collapsing to the ground. The club instantly surrounded him. I couldn't see where he was shot or how bad it was.

"Clean up the rabble," the Queen said with a wave of her hand.

The back doors of the van swung open, revealing one of the M134s. A large gun with six rotating barrels and an insane fire rate. This time it was pointed at me and the T.O.

"*Run!*" I shouted as the barrels began to spin.

A four-foot plume of flame burst from the barrel of the gun. Bullets buzzed all around me as the Queen's guard joined in firing their rifles into the crowd. The bullets slammed into the T.O. with the *thwack* of a hammer on a side of beef. The few lucky enough not to be immediately cut down, scattered. Dust and smoke filled the air, blocking my vision. The acidic smell of gunpowder hung heavy. As quickly as it started, the shooting stopped. Everything was silent for a few seconds. A few moans rose from the scattered bodies. Holt and I were the only ones left untouched. Hank lay on his back with Big Ticket and Lug Nut laying on top of him. Holt and I pulled them off. His kutte had fallen open, revealing his blood-soaked shirt. He had two bullet holes in his upper chest and a half moon across his abdomen. The blood seeping out into his white T-shirt made a gruesome looking smiley face. His chest heaved erratically. It didn't look like he was healing on his own and that meant she had used silver bullets. I put a hand over him and began to channel energy into his wounds.

"Wait, what about the silver?" Holt asked.

"He'll bleed to death before silver toxicity kills him," I said.

I didn't heal him all the way, just enough to stop the bleeding and give him a chance to get help. The blood soaking into the shirt stopped and his breathing eased.

"Start healing people," I said. "Big Ticket first."

I stood up and turned to the Queen. "What the hell?"

She smiled at me. "Relax, we didn't use silver, well, not on everyone. This is just a message."

"This is too much," I said, holding my hand out to the carnage. "You crossed the line."

"No, Obie, this is crossing the line." She motioned to the gun and again the barrels started spinning. "Hit the motorcycles."

Holt and I dove to the ground as the gun opened fire a second time. The ground had become muddy from the blood. I looked back to make sure Holt was alright, but found a dismembered hand instead. It had been shredded about halfway up the forearm. I tossed it away. The bikes were hit by what seemed like a solid stream of lead screaming over my head. They exploded from hundreds of impacts that compounded into complete destruction. Pieces of the motorcycles were scattered, tires exploded, and some burst into flames when the gas tanks were ruptured. After the line of bikes had been demolished the firing stopped.

I stood. Blood and mud clung to my clothes and skin. "You know it's war now," I said. "They aren't going to let this go."

The Queen motioned the air with her index finger. The elves broke ranks and began climbing into the trucks and van. "Obie, when did you become so tedious?"

Harlan had taken Isabelle behind the truck and was peeking out around the side. The Queen started walking for her SUV. I decided enough was enough. Everything I had done with the T.O. and the Elven Nation had been to keep the peace. I could see now there wasn't any peace and wouldn't be with a tyrant in charge. I couldn't look the other way any longer—I wasn't going to let her get away with this.

The elves weren't paying me any mind. Harlan and Isabelle were still behind the truck. I didn't expect any trouble from them. Deciding to take the guards out first before moving on to the Queen. It would be risky. I would probably have to use one of them as a shield to get close enough to kill the Queen. I was about to make my move when a blast of warm air and a familiar sulfuric stench hit me from behind. I looked over my shoulder to see a large portal roughly eight feet in diameter and five feet behind me. I could see the red landscape of the demon world with a large group of demons moving to come through.

CHAPTER 13

I dove to the ground, landing in the blood-soaked ash of the campfire. The elves opened fire as demons poured from the portal. Hounds hit the ground running with athol and winged snakes filling the skies. They seemed to be ignoring me, even though I was the closest; the movement and noise from the elves must have distracted them. I was showered with thick, black demon blood before the first one fell just to my left. The elves, the Queen included, fired as fast as they could. The doors to the van had been closed; it took a few seconds for them to get the doors open and the M134 spun back up before they could start firing. When they managed it, the demons coming through the portal were torn apart, raining down in pieces on top of me and the T.O.

I started my change into krasis as a number of athol landed on top of the gray van that held the M134. The demons grabbed hold of the van wherever they could and flapped their wings, lifting the van off the ground. The M134 kept firing as the van was raised, sending bullets into the ground with dirt and mud exploding into the air. The shooting stopped and a couple of the Queen's guards bailed out. They hit the ground running, heading for the Queen's SUV, but were quickly swarmed. The van fell back to the ground. It landed grill first, accordioning in on itself, before falling onto its side.

The portal slammed shut behind me. The elves were fighting a losing battle to keep the demons away as they closed in on the Queen's SUV. Harlan and Isabelle were cut off and ran into the woods. One of the Queen's guards followed them, shooting approaching demons. There was only one guard left covering the Queen as she climbed into the SUV. The SUV roared to life. The Queen either didn't know or didn't care that the guard was standing directly behind her vehicle. The SUV lurched backward, plowing over the guard. It skidded to a stop as the driver shifted gears. A hellhound bit the bumper and tugged at the vehicle. The tires began spinning, throwing waves of dirt up as the tires struggled to gain traction. After a quick tug of war the bumper broke free of the vehicle. The Queen sped off with a trail of demons chasing after her. One of the survivors hung out the back window, firing at their pursuers. They disappeared down the dirt road into a giant dust cloud with the sounds of gunfire fading into the distance.

When the dust settled, I surveyed the area. Harlan and Isabelle were gone. The air was heavy with the smell of smoke and blood. There were still demons around that hadn't chased the Queen. A few hounds sniffed around the trucks or chewed on the corpses of the Queen's Guard. An athol swooped out of the sky and grabbed the lifeless body of one of the bikers off the ground. It happened so quickly I couldn't tell who it was, but if he were still alive there was no saving him now. I would have expected the demons to attack right away. After all, the Tortured Occult were easy pickin's. Some of the T.O. were starting to wake up, but it would take time before they would be able to defend themselves. Unarmed and in the open, I wouldn't be able to protect them, even with Holt's help. I had a feeling it was just a matter of time before the demons that chased the Queen returned and then we'd really be in trouble.

Holt had finished healing B.T. and Lug Nut, and was moving on to two more. The two bikers changed to krasis and stood up slowly beside me.

"What are they doing?" Lug Nut whispered.

I raised a hand over my mouth to mute the sound of my voice. "Eating. When they realize we're here, they'll come after us."

"What do we do?" Big Ticket asked.

"Hank's been shot with silver," I said. We needed to get him to a doctor quick. The problem was, we couldn't get him into the truck or start it without attracting their attention. "We're gonna have to fight 'em."

Holt had just finished healing Ginsu and a Wretched Dog I didn't know.

That gave us six people to three hounds. That would work, assuming the athol flying around didn't join in.

"Groups of two," I whispered.

I moved as quietly as I could, taking care to step over the recovering bikers and demon bodies the elves had shot down. It was much easier to walk once we were clear of the bodies, not just because of the obstacles, but because the ground wasn't a soppy mess. Everyone paired off and we charged the demons. We hadn't made it a few steps before the closest hound was aware of us. It turned and screeched, alerting the others to our presence. They charged us back, meeting somewhere in the middle. I was the first to a hellhound. It lurched at me and I dodged to the left, moving past it, and grabbing one of its back legs. I pulled, making it twist around to try to bite me. That gave Holt the opportunity to jump on its back and wrap his arms around its neck. It wasn't too difficult for the two of us to flip it on its back. With the softer underbelly exposed, I made quick work of the beast. While Holt held it in place as it bled out, I looked over to see Big Ticket wrestling with the second demon. He had bit it on the side of the throat and the hound screeched in pain as he literally tore it to pieces bit by bit. It would take him a minute to finish it off, but the hound seemed more interested in escaping than fighting. Lug Nut stood watching, clear of the melee, but ready to engage if needed. Behind him Ginsu and the Wretched Dog didn't have it so well.

The hellhound had Ginsu pinned with his arm in the demon's mouth. I knew from firsthand experience that Ginsu's arm would be broken. If we didn't get the hound off of him soon, he might lose it all together. The Wretched Dog punched at the hound as it shook Ginsu. The beast didn't seem to notice. I spotted Ginsu's Bowie knife on the ground. I ran over, picked up the knife and drove it into the neck of the hound. It stopped moving. I twisted the knife. The demon fell dead on top of Ginsu.

"Get Hank loaded in that cargo truck. We need to get him help ASAP," I said, pulling Ginsu from under the hound.

Ginsu pulled his Bowie from the neck of the hound while Lug Nut headed for the van. The rest of the bikers went to get Hank.

Holt started to go with them, but I grabbed his arm. "I'm going to go after

Harlan and Isabelle. Help anyone whose life depends on it, but don't heal everybody. Some of them might be pissed at us and we're already outnumbered. We need things to calm down."

"Pissed at you, you mean," Holt said.

"Same thing."

Holt smiled. "Be careful."

I walked to the place Harlan had been standing with Isabelle during the attack. I easily located their trail leading off into the woods and followed it as fast as I could. Harlan's tracks led in a straight direction through the woods, never turning or shuffling steps, a man with a purpose. Isabelle's tracks weren't as certain. I found multiple places where she stopped and looked back toward the battle. Each time Harlan had pulled her along, leaving lines in the leaves and scuffs in the dirt where he had dragged her. I caught up to them about half a mile into the woods. The guard following them was more erratic in her movements. She moved ahead quickly, then turned back and waited before moving again. I heard shots ahead to my right and took off at a full sprint.

I spotted the elves through the trees. One athol lay motionless on the ground. A second demon wrestled with the guard. She held it back with the rifle, holding it between them to keep enough distance to keep from getting bit. Using it as a shield meant she was unable to bring it to bear on the demon. Isabelle stood between Harlan and an oak tree. Not much protection for her, but the best to be found in the forest.

I charged, grabbed the demon by the head, and pulled it back to the point where it was facing the sky. That left its neck exposed. With my free hand I sank my claws into its throat and squeezed. Thick dark blood ran around my fingers as the beast began to choke on its own blood. I gave it a quick jerk, ripping a handful of flesh away. I pushed the demon, still clinging to life, to my left and tossed the bit of neck to my right. The guard stood up and brought her rifle up in my direction. With a fluid motion I grabbed the barrel and redirected it to my right; she fired two shots that left my ears ringing. I gave the rifle a quick tug. The elf stumbled toward me and I sent a right cross to her face. She collapsed, leaving me holding her rifle by the barrel.

I heard a loud pop followed by a pressure in my gut and pain. I looked up to see Isabelle pointing her rifle at me. Whips of smoke drifted from the barrel. She started to work the bolt to chamber another round when Harlan grabbed the gun and pulled it out of her hands. He put himself between us and held a hand up to me in a defensive posture. The bullet had passed through the soft tissue in my abdomen. I was glad it hadn't hit any bones; those small calibers tended to bounce around inside if they contact bone.

"Relax," I said. "Just a flesh wound. Come on, we need to get you guys out of here."

"Don't shoot him again," Harlan said, handing the rifle back to Isabelle. He pulled me aside for a private word. "I can't go back. I won't."

I shook my head. "I didn't say go back. I said get out of here. There's a bunch of demons that are probably going to find their way back here in a few minutes, not to mention about twenty-five bikers that would love to get their hands on some elves right about now. It's not safe here for any of us."

"I'm going to be straight with you, Obie. I intend to take Isabelle away from the Queen. I won't let her grow up being indoctrinated into her beliefs," Harlan said. "If you aren't going to help us get away, then just leave us alone."

"After this, I'm done with the Queen," I said. "If you don't want to go back I'm not going to make you. I got a friend that doesn't live too far from here. We can stay there while things calm down."

"Okay," Harlan agreed.

I slung the guard over one shoulder and we started walking back toward the campsite.

CHAPTER 14

The van, along with Hank, Lug Nut, and Big Ticket, was gone when we made it back. Ginsu and Martina were sorting the victims of the Queen's attack into rows. No doubt Holt couldn't help himself and had healed her. A number of the bikers had regained consciousness, but not function. A few lay where they had fallen, ignored. They must be the ones that didn't make it. I hustled to my truck to get Isabelle and Harlan inside. I didn't want them exposed to the aftermath of their mother's work. It had been parked to the side out of the way of the gunfire and with no one around it to attract the demon's attention it had made it through the attack without taking any damage. Holt and Ginsu came over when they saw us come out of the woods. Martina stayed behind and tended to the injured.

"You just couldn't help yourself, could ya?" I asked.

Holt shrugged. "We needed one more."

I opened the door for Isabelle and helped her into the back of the truck. "How is everyone?"

"Razor and a couple others are dead. The guns ripped 'em apart," Ginsu said. "Did you set us up?"

"I had nothing to do with this."

"You're a damn liar," Chisel yelled from the line of wounded. "I'm going to gut you like the traitor you are."

He tried to get up, but couldn't make it to his feet. The gaping wounds in his belly hadn't healed. I didn't think he would be gutting anyone in the immediate future. It wouldn't take him too long to heal, though, and I preferred to be gone by then. I'm sure many of the bikers were none too happy with me, but I still had the problem of stray demons running around. If Holt and I left, the club wouldn't be able to defend themselves from that many with only two in fighting shape.

"Here's a peace offering," I said, tossing the guard onto the ground.

Chisel rolled onto his back and grunted, "Shove it up your ass."

I heard the thumping of paws on the ground and turned to see a mass of hellhounds running in our direction. There were maybe nine or ten of them, enough to be a real problem. Considering we had four people able to fight and many more to defend. I found myself wishing for a weapon. I was still holding the guard's rifle, which was better than nothing. I didn't know how many rounds were left. I decided to wait to shoot until they were closer, since I wasn't any kind of crack shot. Ginsu pulled his Bowie knife and gave another blade, pulled from concealment on his belt, to Holt. Martina had her own knife in her boot.

"Get in the truck and stay quiet until this is over," I yelled to Harlan.

I raised the rifle and waited for the pack to come close enough so I wouldn't miss. It took everything I had not to start shooting. I moved my finger to the trigger. The pack slowed and then stopped fifty yards away. I lowered my rifle and exchanged confused looks with everyone. A portal formed beside them on the road. The demons slowed and milled around in front of the portal before going through it one by one. The last gave us a screech before disappearing though.

"That's good news," I said.

"What's good news?" Martina asked.

I tossed the rifle into the ground. "Whoever's doing this isn't interested in us. It's not much, but I'll take it. Tell Hank I'll come see him later to explain everything. We need to go for now."

"What if he doesn't make it?" Ginsu asked.

I shrugged and started walking toward the truck. "Let's not worry about that until we have to."

Holt jogged up beside me. "What if the elves come back? They aren't in any condition to defend themselves."

"If the Queen wanted to kill them, they'd all be dead right now. All she had to do was load those guns with silver bullets. You better believe she has a stockpile of them."

"If she didn't want to kill them, then why do all this?" he asked.

"Who knows why she does what she does? Maybe she just likes hurting people," I said. "If you kill all your enemies, you won't have anyone left to fight."

Martina jabbed a finger on my chest. "Hold on, we need help. The bikes are destroyed and we don't even have the van. We need to get everyone out of here."

I looked around at the injured. She was right, they did need help. I told Harlan to get in the truck and took Holt over to the wounded. Cotton and Fisheye seemed to be the best choice for healing based on injuries and how levelheaded they were. Holt and I each healed one.

Cotton opened his eyes. "Well, that was fucked up."

"We gotta go," I said holding a hand out. "We need to get the injured loaded and get them to safety."

Cotton took my hand and got to his feet.

"Loaded in what?" Fisheye asked, rubbing his face.

I pointed to the trucks the elves had left behind. "The Queen left two trucks that don't look damaged. I'll take some in the back of my truck and drop them at the clubhouse. That should be enough room to get everyone out of here."

I kept my distance from Chisel while we loaded everyone in the trucks. By the time we were finished Chisel was recovered enough to start trouble. Instead of doing so, he grumbled to himself. I dropped the bikers at the clubhouse. When we arrived, they were all able to get out of the trucks under their own power, although some were definitely the worse for wear. I didn't want to stick around any longer than I had to with Harlan and Isabelle in the truck. I had to get them somewhere they could lay low. If it were anyone but the Queen's descendants, I would have gone to Hank for help. That wasn't an option now. There was really only one safe place that came to mind.

The Elven Nation was spider-webbed with not only paved roads but a lot of well-maintained forest service roads. Livy lived off one in the same house she had been living in for over 150 years. I turned onto a small trail leading down-hill into the woods. After about thirty feet we passed through the magical bar-rier that kept her home hidden from the outside world.

The house was built into the hillside, using large, jutting boulders as a roof and walls. The gaps were filled with logs with a dirt mixture to seal it all togeth-er. My old truck, a '41 Ford, had been smashed into the side of it. Rather than have it towed and crushed, Livy decided to keep it where it was and used it as a garden shed and a raised bed to grow some vegetables and medicinal herbs. I was happy to see the truck get a new life. I pulled up beside it and we all piled out.

"Where are we?" Isabelle asked, slinging her rifle over her right shoulder.

"An old friend of mine lives here. You are going to stay with her for a while."

Her face scrunched up. "I want to go home."

"It's not safe for us to go home right now," Harlan said.

I did my best to look reassuring. "Once things calm down a bit."

"Trust me, you'll love it here," Holt chimed in.

She crossed her arms and pouted. "It looks like a dump."

Livy appeared in the doorway, wearing a light blue dress with long sleeves, the kind that went out of fashion at the turn of the last century.

"Spirits alive," Livy said. "I wasn't expecting company. Y'all come on in out of the chill. I'll make you a little something to eat."

"I'll be in in a sec," I said. "Y'all go ahead."

Holt, Isabelle, and Harlan went inside. I walked around to the side of the house to where Livy kept her firewood stacked. It looked like she was in good shape for the winter, but that's not what went there for. I wanted some privacy.

"Thera," I said. "I need to talk to you."

Thera appeared, sitting on the woodpile. Her look changed with the sea-sons, or maybe it was the other way around. Now in autumn, her skin was the smooth gray of a beech tree with fiery red leaves cascading down around her shoulders all the way to the ground. She never wore clothes, but the leaves did a good job of maintaining her modesty.

"You called?"

"I have a problem," I said. "I am hunting someone who is summoning many demons at a time. Today I think there were around twenty in all, so many it was hard to count."

Thera tilted her head to the left. "That is a problem."

"I need a weapon," I continued. "Teeth and claws are great, but don't do much good if we're that outnumbered."

"What did you have in mind?" Thera asked.

I shrugged. "I hadn't thought about it much, to be honest. I liked my old blade, but that was destroyed a few months ago. Something that I can keep concealed, at least in forms besides krasis."

Thera nodded. "This can be done, but there's a cost."

"That's fine," I said. "Can we make something for Holt at the same time?"

"Will you pay the cost for him?" she asked.

"Sure. What do we need?"

"A metalworker," she said. "Call me when you've found one."

She vanished. I couldn't help but feel a little lucky since I had run across a blacksmith a week ago. I wanted to get a jump on this right away. Harlan and Isabelle should be safe here, I just needed to tell them I was leaving. Inside the house I found Livy washing her hands. A trough diverted a stream through the west wall of the kitchen to supply the house with water. Isabelle stood by the door with the rifle still slung over her shoulder. Holt and Harlan sat at the table. Livy dried her hands on a towel she'd knitted and went to sit in her rocking chair.

"It's time for my medicinal," she said, easing onto the chair. She reached for a jug resting on the floor. She took a long swig and, with a puckered mouth, recorked it and held the jug in her lap. She pointed at Isabelle. "Who's this?"

"This is Princess Isabelle," I said.

"Well, I'll be. I've never been visited by a princess before. Come over and let me get a look at you," Livy said, waving a hand.

Isabelle stepped over. "What were you drinking?"

"It's a concoction I made. It's some herbs I foraged from the forest, mixed with some alcohol, and a touch of magic. It's what keeps me young."

With a questioning look, Isabelle put her hands on her hips. "I don't think it's working."

Livy threw her head back and laughed deeply. "Isabelle, do you like to cook?"

"Mother says cooking is servant's work."

"Well, I've never had any servants and I need some help, so set your rifle down and come give us a hand," Livy said.

She set the jug on the floor and rose from the chair, walking slowly to the kitchen. Isabelle looked at Harlan for some kind of reassurance.

"Go on, it will be fun," Harlan said.

She seemed wary as she set the rifle by the door. Livy started a fire in the stove and set the pot of water on top to boil. She reached for a paper bag on a high shelf, barely able to put a finger on it. I got up and pulled it down, handing it to her.

"I had it," she said, taking the bag.

"I never said you didn't."

She gave me a wry smile and passed the bag to Isabelle. "Fill up the pot with these dried apples and keep an eye on them. We need them to be soft. It will take about ten minutes."

Isabelle added a generous amount of the dried apples to the water. Livy and I sat down at the table and watched Isabelle stir and poke at the boiling apples with a wooden spoon.

Eventually Livy broke the silence. "Something serious must have happened if you brought a royal over for a visit. I don't mind the company, of course, but I'm worried what it means. Is there anything I need to know?"

"They just need a safe place to stay. There's nowhere else for them to go," I said.

I filled her in about everything that happened between the Queen, the Tortured Occult, and Harlan. She listened intently. Isabelle could hear us, but didn't show any reaction. She kept her mouth shut and her attention on the pot of simmering apples.

"I'm going to have Holt stay with you just in case there's trouble. There shouldn't be any, though. The Queen doesn't know where they are and the Tortured Occult will be too busy with the elves to worry about her."

Isabelle jabbed the wet spoon in my direction. "Mother will find me, and when she does, you won't be able to keep me here."

I held up my hands defensively. "Isabelle, I don't want you to think or feel like you're a prisoner. That's not it at all. You're here because there's about to be a war and it's not safe for you anywhere else right now. I promise, as soon as it's safe, we will get you home. In the meantime, think of it like a vacation."

She didn't seem to like that answer, but she would come around. There's something magical about living simply and close to the earth, with dirt under your fingernails, in tune with the seasons. I hoped to get Isabelle back to some kind of regular life soon, but with so much uncertainty and instability there's no telling how long it would take.

I turned back to Livy and leaned forward. "I need to run an errand. I'll be back soon."

CHAPTER 15

I pulled up to Yarwor's house a little after sunset. No one was home. A week ago we left Yarwor with his dead wife and child to bury. Looking around the property, I found only one thing to be different. There were two fresh graves on the edge of the yard under a large oak tree. They weren't marked, just mounds of freshly churned earth, roughly body sized.

If Yarwor had been gone a week, he could be anywhere by now. A lot of rumors were circulating about what had happened and what he'd done. Some people dismissed the idea of demon possession, concluding he was some kind of serial killer. Those same people also said the T.O. and I messed up for letting him go. I've never cared for the opinions of the underinformed.

The bad news was, he was gone. The good news was, I had a good chance of finding him. I needed some help. I went back to Livy's. Stepping into her house was like stepping back in time. She used to make apple pocket pies back in the old days, but hadn't in years. They'd been my favorite, before I gave up eating, and the smell of them really sent me back. Everyone sat around the table, with a plate of half eaten pies, playing cards.

"I'm glad you're back, Obie. We need some music for this party. Go get your banjo and play us a little ditty," Livy said, waving to the armoire beside the bed.

"Banjo?" Holt exclaimed.

I shook my head. "Livy, I haven't played in years. You know that."

"Obie, please get your banjo," Holt mocked.

Livy put her cards on the table and looked hard at Holt. "You really are an unlicked cub, ain't ya?"

"Umm . . . I don't know what that means," Holt said.

"At least have the decency to know when you're being insulted," Livy said, before turning back to me. "Do it for me."

I sighed and walked over to the armoire. I found my banjo behind some clothes. When I pulled it out, it had a layer of dust on it, and two of the strings had broken.

I held it up for Livy to see and tried not to sound too pleased when I said, "Couple of the strings broke. I'll have to get some new ones."

"That's too bad. It's your turn, sweetheart," Livy said to Isabelle.

Isabelle drew a card from the deck and looked over the cards in her hand.

"Livy, are you feeling up to a spirit walk?" I asked. "I need some help locating someone."

"Oh, I reckon we can work that out," she said. "Why don't you go build us a fire and I'll be out as soon as we finish this game."

I went outside, assembled a bunch of twigs and sticks, and lit it. I had some larger pieces set aside that I fed into the fire bit by bit. By the time Livy came out, I had a nice little fire popping and crackling away. She brought a foldable camp chair to sit on.

"Tell me who you're looking for," she said as she got settled.

I sat beside her and told her everything I knew about Yarwor.

When I finished, she said, "Why don't you come with me?"

"Come with you? You know I've never done a spirit walk before. I wouldn't even know where to start."

"I can take you," she said, holding a hand out. "Just close your eyes and calm your mind. Focus on your breathing."

I held her hand, closed my eyes, and paid attention to the air moving in and out of my lungs. I sat there for what seemed like twenty minutes, but was probably closer to four. I had concluded that despite my best efforts I just wasn't cut out for a spirit journey. A part of me didn't want to admit failure, but there wasn't any other way around it. Maybe if I had a few months to practice I could manage it. I opened my eyes.

It took a moment for my brain to understand what I was seeing. Everything looked the same except overcast with a gray tint, and kind of wavy around the edges as if nothing understood where it ended. Livy stood beside me. I didn't recognize her at first: She looked to be in her mid-twenties. I hadn't met her until she was in her thirties and that was hundreds of years ago.

"Ready?" she asked, flashing me a smile. "Make sure not to let go of my hand or I'll lose you."

She lead me into the woods. I looked back to see that our bodies were still sitting by the fire. We had our eyes closed as if we were meditating.

I pointed with a questioning finger, making sure not to let go of Livy's hand. "Umm . . . How are we here and there?"

"A spirit journey doesn't rely on a physical body, so we'll leave them here," she said. "Don't worry, they'll be fine without us for a few minutes."

I nodded. "But if we aren't in our bodies, why do I see physical forms?"

"You don't. You perceive physical forms because that's what makes sense to you," she said.

"Okay, but you look younger than you did when I met you, so how am I perceiving you in a way that I've never seen you before? Unless the perception is coming from you instead of me?"

She patted my cheek with her hand. "It's best not to use the logical mind to try to figure out the spirit world."

I looked around with new eyes, like I was seeing everything for the first time. In a sense I was. I looked up and noticed a number of black dots moving through the sky.

"What are those?"

"I'll take you up for a closer look," she said with a smile.

We lifted off the ground and took flight, the Earth falling away from under us. As we flew closer, the dots took shape. They were huge, fish-like animals with stubby leathery wings. We stopped, close enough to get a good look, but far enough away to be what I would consider a safe distance.

"What are they?" I asked.

A voice in my head said, "We are the masters of humanity," followed shortly by, "We are the masters of the Earth."

I swiveled my head and somehow knew which one was speaking to me. It was the closest and off to my right, flying through the blackness of space with a sea of stars behind it.

Livy saw my reaction. "What did they say to you?"

"That they are the masters of the Earth and humanity."

She nodded. "They're always sayin' things like that. You wanna see something really special?"

"More special than the masters of humanity?" I asked.

We turned back toward Earth and I saw just how far up we had come. I could see the curvature of Earth. We descended. I held Livy's hand tighter as North America rushed toward us. We flew back to the yard in front of Livy's house where we'd been two minutes before and touched down. I followed Livy into the house. Holt, Harlan, and Isabelle were still sitting at the table. Holt was shuffling the cards. I followed Livy over to the far side of the house where there was an eight-inch diameter hole dug into the floor. I knew she used it for something shaman related, but we'd never discussed it in detail.

"This is where I normally descend into the earth," she said.

I scratched my head. "I don't think we're going to fit."

"It's just right," she said.

Livy took a step forward. I couldn't tell if the hole grew, or we shrank, but suddenly we were moving into it. We descended into a dark tunnel with the occasional twist and turn. After a minute I saw a pinprick of shimmering light in the tunnel ahead. It grew in size and brightness as we approached. I could just start to see movement in the light when we stopped.

"This is the closest I've been," Livy said, staring absently ahead at the light.

"Closest you've been to what?" I asked. "I thought we were looking for Yarwor."

She barely seemed aware of my presence as she looked ahead at the light. "The Mother."

"Thera?" I asked. "That light is Thera?"

She gave my hand a squeeze. "Yes, come on."

Now we walked. The light grew more intense the closer we got to it. By the time we reached the end of the cave, light was blinding and enormous. More than plain light, it was liquid and churning with formless shadows moving through it, like a ball of lava.

"Isn't it beautiful?" she asked.

I would have found it beautiful, if I was in the headspace to appreciate it. Instead I was overwhelmed by what I was seeing. I had a perception of Thera from the times she had visited me. I looked the same, aside from wearing different clothes, and her appearance looked . . . sort of human, but changing with the seasons. If Livy was correct, and I had no reason to doubt her, then was this Thera's true form? I saw Livy here differently than I usually did, but it wasn't her true form, or was it? Livy started moving forward. I balked, and she ended up pulling me along as we approached the orb. I had a personal relationship with Thera and I knew that while she was beautiful and powerful, she could also be vicious and cold. Not the kind of person you drop in on unannounced.

"I think we're close enough," I said. "We should go back."

Livy continued walking, pulling me along behind her. Her tone was distant when she spoke. "Just a little closer."

I stopped, or tried to, but floated along against my will. I pulled against her, trying to dig my feet into the ground, but it wasn't solid. In the physical world, I could easily overpower Livy, but in this place our roles seemed to be reversed. I was the feeble one.

Livy pulled me up to the ball of light. She reached out her hand and touched the edge. Black streams flowed from where her fingertips touched the light. I saw a shadowy figure with a roughly human outline appear. It moved toward us from inside the ball.

"Livy, let's go back," I said, pulling at her with everything I had.

As the figure approached, I decided I didn't want anything to do with this anymore. I let go of Livy's hand. I was instantly back in my body. I opened my eyes and looked over at Livy. The shimmering light from the fire danced on her face and pushed back the autumn chill. She looked fine. If there was any trouble, I couldn't tell. I lay on my back, peering up at the forest canopy and the numerous stars peeking through the gaps in the leaves that had fallen. We were only thirty feet from her house, but as far into the mountains as we were, there wasn't any light other than the campfire and a bit that spilled from between the boards of the front door of her house. The result was a sky that was filled to the brim with stars. After ten minutes, she spoke.

Her voice was monotone and distant. "The red-eyed orc languishes by goats in the ruins of the city."

The problem with messages from the spirit world was that they were seldom clear. You always got what you were looking for, but it was never as easy as an address or GPS coordinates. I got up and went inside the house, leaving Livy by the campfire alone. If she had found Yarwor, then I doubted I had anything to worry about with her spirit journey. It would take her a bit to come out of her trance.

"Holt, come here a sec," I said, sticking my head in the door.

He stepped outside and closed the door behind him. "Well?"

"We're looking for goats in the ruins of the city," I said. "Whatever that means."

He pulled out his phone and started typing. "Search results don't tell us much. Most promising lead looks like a place in the Yucatan Peninsula."

I scratched at the stubble on my face. "I don't think he got that far. What about Atlanta? Maybe that's the city she's talking about? I hope so anyway."

He went back to typing on his phone. "Atlanta . . . Goats . . . Hmm . . . Atlanta's not exactly in ruins, but let me see what I can find. Looks like we have a string of coffee shops and hello . . . The Goat Farm."

He showed me a picture of industrial-style brick buildings, some of which were in a clear state of disrepair.

"And there are goats there?" I asked.

"Looks that way."

I pulled the phone out of my pocket and called Adan.

"Obie," Adan said. "What did you do?"

I sighed. "It's a long story."

"The club's pissed. I'm on my way back to Atlanta. I don't want to be around when the shooting starts."

"Smart move," I said. "Keep your head down. In the meantime, I have a question. What can you tell me about a place in Atlanta called The Goat Farm?"

"There's not much to tell, really. It's an old industrial complex that worked everything from cotton to mortars over the years. It got taken over by artists. There's a lot of ultras in the area. It's kind of moving back to Thera, if you know what I mean."

"I'm looking for someone I think is there. Is there anything I need to know before I show up?"

"There's a coffee shop at the center of the property that makes a good chai latte," he said. "It's called the Warhorse. You might try asking someone there if you need help."

"All right, thanks Adan. I'll be in touch."

I put the phone back in my pocket and turned to Holt. "I want you to keep an eye on everyone here. I've got to get Yarwor. Thera needs him to make something. After that, we can swing by the clubhouse and try to smooth things out with the T.O. I shouldn't be gone too long."

Holt nodded. "What are the chances they'll just forgive and forget?"

I smiled. "Slim to none, I'd say. One problem at a time, though."

CHAPTER 16

Holt had put directions in my phone. I was still skeptical about having a smartphone, but for navigation, at least, it seemed to be beneficial. I pulled off the interstate, and dutifully followed the directions through unfamiliar city streets. I took my last turn beside an apartment complex to discover a line of trees on the right side of the road. They stood in stark contrast to the concrete, steel, and glass I had been immersed in a moment before. I turned right onto a dirt road running through the trees. It led me to a place that seemed more suited to the mountains where I lived rather than a bustling metropolis.

A few abandoned cars lined the road, slowly being swallowed up by brush. Next, I passed a large fenced-in area. An enormous metal sculpture of a two-headed goat sat a large pile of rubble. A number of goats stood lazily around the strange monument.

"This must be the place," I said to myself.

I pulled into a gravel parking lot in front of a few brick buildings, finding a spot in line with a few other cars. I got out, and surveyed the area. The buildings were run down. Everything looked like it could use a little attention from a handyman. The property had the old industrial vibe down pat. I pretended to tie my shoe, in case someone was watching, and sniffed around for a few seconds. I was met by the scents of goats, humans, dogs, and most interestingly an assortment of ultranaturals, but none of them Yarwor.

I followed a path that ran between the buildings. It led past a large piece of antique machinery—some sort of large press. Years of exposure had taken its toll with rust claiming more of the machine than paint. I continued on toward the center of the property and down some steps beside a small chicken coop. The coop was open and a few of the birds were outside pecking at insects in the grass. They didn't pay any attention to me. At the bottom of the stairs, a single lane road wove its way between the buildings. I took a right and came to a large courtyard.

The building on the left didn't have a roof. All the windows were missing with vines climbing the brick. It was encouraging to see something that I would consider ruins. Between that and the goats I might actually be in the right place. Tables and chairs were set up in front of a building with a sign that read THE WARHORSE. A row of planters lined the wall. All the greenery gave the area a very relaxed and natural vibe. It was reminiscent of what I imagined an Italian café would be like, minus all the Italians.

All the tables were empty, save one, with a woman and a black dog with tan patches on its legs, belly, and face. It looked to be a German Shepard mix. She had brown hair pulled back in a ponytail and wore overalls and a sleeveless shirt. She spared a glance in my direction before returning her full attention to a mug of coffee.

"I hope he doesn't come over here Bhalu," the woman said giving the dogs neck a scratch. "He looks like a real tool."

A human would have been out of earshot. Enhanced senses aren't always an advantage. I didn't want to bother her, but she was the only person I had seen since I arrived. I started to approach her when a man came down some stairs on the far side of the courtyard. He had rich ebony skin, a flat nose, and full lips. He wore jeans, a gray button-up shirt, and flip flops. He said hello to the woman and gave me a smile and a nod as he disappeared into the Warhorse. I gave the air a few quick sniffs and picked up his scent. I couldn't place it. I didn't know what he was, but it wasn't human. He didn't have the stench of demon, so that was good enough for me. Adan had said I could find help at the Warhorse; maybe this was who he was talking about.

I followed the man into an eclectic coffee shop. Antique chairs and sofas with leather and natural fur were arranged around tables made of wood and metal. The back wall was lined with bookshelves that overflowed with old tomes. A piano with an antique typewriter sat under a painting of a man in a North Korean army uniform. Across the room a bright yellow vending machine with the words KICKAPOO JOY JUICE plastered across the front. A few other patrons sat typing away on laptops. The man I followed in took a seat behind simple counter with a red door behind it.

"What can I get you?" the man asked.

I looked over the menu written on chalkboards behind the counter. "What I'd really like is a little information."

His nose flexed subtly as he sniffed the air.

"Turn left in fifty feet," the automated voice of my phone chimed from my pocket.

"Information on how to use maps?" he asked with a smirk.

"Sorry about that," I said, pulling my phone out. The map was still on the screen with a triangle spinning around in the center. I hit the button on the side and the screen turned off. I put it back in my pocket. "I'm looking for someone I heard was here. His name is Yarwor. He's a big guy with umm . . . gray skin," I said a little softer, looking around to make sure we were out of earshot of anyone who might hear.

He didn't look concerned with anyone overhearing his answer. "Yeah, I know who you're talking about, but you might be better off not finding him."

"Why's that?"

"He's getting into some bad things. He keeps to himself and we don't mess with him. A few tried to help him at first, but he didn't seem to want it. Now he's just turning into a problem. If you could get rid of him, you would be doing us a favor."

"So where can I find him?"

He took a sip of coffee. "There's a building by the goat pens with a tree growing out of the wall. He's been staying there."

I thanked him and headed back the way I had come. I looked for the building I was told about. All seemed intact, no noticeable vegetation grew on the brick, let alone a tree. Before I could continue my search something small hit me in the back. I turned around just as another pebble bounced off my chest.

There was a goat standing on the other side of the fence from me chewing on some grass and not seeming to pay me any attention. I spotted a slim face peeking out from behind the rubble pile. It had short curly brown hair, a flat nose ridge ending in a black triangular nose, and two horns sticking up out of the hair, angling away from each other.

A satyr stepped out from behind the rubble pile. The top half of a human with goat legs and hooves, the face being a mix of both. She didn't wear any clothes and wasn't the least bit self-conscious about it. If you had dealings with a satyr, it was best to tread lightly. They could be mischievous or even dangerous if you pissed them off. Best to be polite and get back to looking for Yarwor as quickly as possible. I gave her a wave. She jumped over the fence to join me in the grass.

"Well, hello, handsome," she said batting her eyes. "What's your name?"

"Obie," I said. "Hey, maybe you could help me. I'm looking for someone."

She put her hands on her hips. "Don't you want to know my name?"

I guess this wasn't going to be easy.

"Of course I do, I'm sorry," I said, wishing I hadn't gotten roped into this conversation. "What's your name?"

"Tasha."

"It's very nice to meet you, Tasha. Like I was saying, I am looking for someone. He's an orc—"

"Surely there's time for a little pleasure before business," she said, stepping up and wrapping her arm around mine.

The goat in the pen behind Tasha bleated and she waved her hand in its direction dismissively.

"It's actually really important that I find him so if you wouldn't mind telling me if any orcs have been around lately? The guy at the Warhorse said he was hanging around in a building with a tree in the wall."

"We'll get to that later," she said. "Let's get to know each other a little first."

My phone spoke: "Recalculating."

I grabbed it though the fabric of my pocket and pressed any button I could find.

"I'm with someone, sort of," I said, wishing I had left off the *sort of.*

"You don't sound too sure. A few minutes with me and you'll know exactly where you stand," she said.

She clearly wasn't going to help me find Yarwor, at least not on any kind of timeframe that would work for me. Maybe flattery would make things go a little smoother.

"Tasha, normally I would love to get to know such a pretty girl, but right now I'm on urgent business," I said, pulling my arm away.

She stepped in front of me. "What's more important than making new friends?"

"Unfortunately," I said, stepping past her, "a lot of the things I have to deal with."

I only made it a couple steps when something grabbed my feet. I looked down to see roots had grown up around my ankles.

Tasha's head popped under my arm. "Oh, come on. What could you be doing that's so important?"

"I'm a Keeper of Thera and I'm here on business," I said. "So I'm afraid I have to insist that you let me go."

The goat bleated from behind us.

"Nobody asked you, Deloris!" Tasha screamed. "Are you sure?" she said, returning her attention to me.

"Yes, let me go."

She moved back; the roots retreated from my feet. Tasha pouted, her arms crossed.

"Over there's the building with a tree growing out of the roof that you're looking for," she said, pointing behind the goat pen. "He's been staying there."

I backed away from her. "Thank you."

Once I was a little farther away an argument broke out between Tasha and Deloris. I was glad Tasha's attention was on someone else. Deloris was officially my favorite goat.

CHAPTER 17

I came to a building that seemed, at first glance, to be intact, but covered with plant life. The brick walls had vines drooping down over them; most of the leaves had turned shades of yellow and red. Walking around, I found some yellow caution tape that had been set up to block off the back of the building. A large portion of the back wall had collapsed. A tree that had to be at least twenty years old grew out of the corner of the building. It had pushed what was left of the adjacent wall out about six inches. It didn't look too stable.

Peering around as best I could without stepping over the tape I spotted an old safe that had been built into the wall. The safe was about six feet tall and seemed to be providing the structural support that prevented the building from falling down all together. A path led through the rubble and into the brush on the back side. After a quick look around to make sure no one was watching, I stepped over the tape. I followed the trail through the brush into the back side of the building. It led to a relatively intact room.

It had three standing walls and most of a ceiling with numerous vines hanging down like a natural chandelier. It stank of urine. The rubble had been pushed away to the edges, making a clearing in the center. Yarwor lay face down on the floor with his face on a pile of bricks. It didn't make sense that anyone, including an orc, would use bricks for a pillow. Maybe he had died. He didn't appear to be breathing. I waited for any sign of life. Just when I'd decided he'd kicked the bucket, his chest suddenly heaved and he took in a large wheezing breath. The brick pillow must not be doing his breathing any favors.

Multiple five-gallon buckets were placed around the room. I thought one, or more, of them might've been used as a toilet—it would explain the smell. Only one had anything in it. I gave it a whiff and it turned out to be half full of water. A beetle had fallen into it and kicked its legs in a vain attempt to make it to the edge of the bucket. I scooped it out and held my hand against the wall for it to crawl off. I spotted a small hookah in the corner.

"Oh no," I said, stepping around the bucket for a closer look.

I took a whiff of the hookah. I recognized it right away from the bitter metallic smell: Ichor. A quick look at Yarwor's neck confirmed my suspicions. He had a bitemark that looked to be a few days old. Whoever he was buying from was old school. Werebats like Clay took their victim's blood intravenously. The old bite and suck was an outdated method. Bitemarks were much more conspicuous than track marks. On top of that, taking the blood intravenously allowed it to be stored, to be drunk later or turned into Ichor. Whoever Yarwor had gotten tangled up with was more concerned with pleasure than business.

"Yarwor, what have you done?" I mumbled to myself.

Ichor was dangerous because it didn't just give you a feeling of euphoria. It made people strong, violent, and feeling no pain. Smoking it too much made people a little crazy to boot. It was slightly reassuring to see Yarwor had used a hookah. Passing it through the water filtered it a little, letting it maintain a lot of the euphoria, but taking the edge off the psycho rampage qualities. Now I knew what that fella in the coffee shop meant by "bad things." If Yarwor kept it up, eventually he would hurt someone or himself. He needed help and I was just the guy to give it to him.

"Come on, wake up," I said, giving him a cautious nudge with my foot.

Yarwor let out a low rumble, but didn't move.

I gave him another tap. "Yarwor, I need your help."

He groaned and rolled over on his side. His pillow left indentations on his face, making him look like he'd run face first into a brick wall. One eye opened, just a sliver, and he groaned again before he ran his hands over his arms and started scratching them.

"I'm thirsty," he mumbled absently.

I knelt. "I need your help."

"I can't help you," he said, waving me off and reaching for the bucket with water in it.

He lifted the whole thing and gulped it as fast as he could, only stopping once to take a breath. He only managed to drink about half of it, the rest pouring over him in an impromptu shower. He picked up the other buckets, looking for more water, tossing the empties away.

"I need a blacksmith and you're the only one I know," I said.

"I don't know if you've noticed, but I'm no good to anyone," he said, rechecking the buckets for any drop of water that he'd missed. "Where'd all my water go?"

He became more frantic as the same few buckets were tossed around like there was one hiding somewhere he just hadn't spotted yet. Then he found the hookah. Before I could stop him he grabbed it, pulled the top off, and drank the brown murky water inside it. He doubled over and screamed as if his insides were on fire.

"Yarwor? You okay?"

"Where's my damn water?" he yelled.

He grabbed the buckets again and when they turned up empty this time, he threw them against the wall, shattering them to pieces. I took a step back to get away from the plastic shrapnel flying around the room.

"Where is that rushing coming from?" he said. His chest heaved with rapid breaths and sweat broke out all over his neck and back. No doubt the rushing he was talking about was the blood in his ears. He grabbed bricks and handfuls of dirt and plants and hurled them in every direction.

"Make a U-turn," my pocket announced.

I slapped my hand over my pocket to muffle the sound. Too late. Yarwor stopped his frantic digging and turned his head slowly toward me. His eyes were beyond bloodshot, there didn't seem to be any white left in them. Suddenly what Livy said about the "red-eyed orc" made sense.

Drool ran out of his mouth. "It's coming from you. You're full of water."

The veins in his neck and arms popped as he took a deliberate step toward me.

"Yarwor," I said, taking a step back. "We can get you more water."

It was falling on deaf ears. He lunged at me. I jumped back, but was caught in the brush that had grown up around the room. There was no time to change to krasis. He plowed me into the brush and had me pinned with one hand on my head and another on my legs. I felt his teeth sink into my abdomen, followed by a slurping sound. I have had demons try to eat me many times before, this was the first time someone tried to drink me.

I freed my arms from the brush and punched him. It didn't seem to faze him. Feeling around, I grabbed a brick off the ground and slammed it into his head, shattering it in my hand. This he took note of, but didn't stop, instead biting down harder. If brute force wasn't going to work, I'd have to try something else. I crammed two fingers up his large orc nose. He started gagging and when I wiggled them inside his sinus cavity he let me go and stepped back, rubbing his face frantically with both hands. I took the opportunity to jump on his back. I wrapped one arm around his neck and locked it with my other arm on the back of his head.

With my biceps on one side of his neck and forearm on the other, I was able to squeeze and cut off the blood flow to his brain. No matter how drugged he was, he couldn't stay conscious without oxygen. He grabbed at my arm, but couldn't get a grip with it pressed so tightly into his neck. He started swaying slightly. In a last-ditch effort he charged the brick wall. He passed out just before impact, but the momentum carried us into it.

I woke under a tremendous weight. The wall, or maybe the whole building for all I knew, had come down on top of us. I was still clinging to Yarwor's back with my arm around his neck. He felt cold, but had a pulse. He wasn't moving, which I thought was a considerable improvement. I pulled my arms free and pushed the bricks off until I was able to squeeze my legs out from under Yarwor. I instinctively held my hand out to heal him, but stopped. If I healed him, he would probably wake up. If he woke up he would still be in a drug-induced rage and we would be back to where we started. I didn't want to leave him hurt, especially since I didn't know the extent of the injuries, but

I didn't have any choice. He would need time for the drugs to work their way out of his system.

Most of the building remained standing. We had collided with one of the interior walls which collapsed. The rest of the building seemed to be in decent shape except for one wall that had picked up a slight lean. I couldn't be sure how stable the structure was and didn't want to stick around to find out. I pulled bricks away from Yarwor's head and chest. I would have to carry him to the truck and that meant he needed a disguise. He would normally use an illusion pendant, but I didn't know if he had it or if it was buried under the rubble.

"Where's your necklace? Please don't tell me you lost it," I said, more to myself than him.

I saw the chain around his neck and pulled it out. I flipped the arrow down so that it crossed the eye and waited a few seconds for the illusion to turn this battered and dirty orc into an equally battered and dirty human. Once the illusion had taken hold, I grabbed his arm and hoisted him into a fireman's carry. It was slow going getting out of the brush and uneven ground. Twenty minutes later, I had him at the passenger side of the truck. I felt around for my keys. They weren't in their usual pocket. I patted down all my pockets but couldn't find them. I opened the tailgate and sat Yarwor on it who promptly fell backward into the bed of the truck with his legs dangling off the tailgate.

I tried my pockets for the second time and turned up nothing. If dropped them in the fight before the wall collapsed I could be looking for them all day. Yarwor didn't look as if he was going to run off while I searched. That was fine as long as he didn't wake up and hurt someone while I was gone. It's not like I had a lot of choices. I left him lying in the truck.

When I passed the goat pen, frantic bleating caught my attention. Deloris was standing by the fence, bobbing her head, and stamping at the ground. I hesitated, wondering if it was some kind of trick, but went over to check it out anyway. On the ground in front of her were my keys. I picked them up cautiously and bounced them in my hand. There's no way they should've fallen out there.

"Thanks," I said to the goat.

She bleated a reply I couldn't understand but I assumed it was "You're welcome."

Yarwor was still unconscious when I made it back to the truck. I got him loaded in the passenger seat as quickly as I could. I decided to stop at the first place I passed and buy about ten gallons of water, just in case he woke up on the way back. I drove down the dirt road beside the goat pen. Tasha was standing by the fence. She gave me a mischievous smile with a corresponding wave. I pushed the pedal a little harder.

"You have arrived at your destination," my phone chimed as the tires chirped on the pavement.

CHAPTER 18

I pulled up to the cottage and parked off to the side. Yarwor was still asleep and had only made a few grumbles in the roughly three hours it took to make it back. I had mixed feelings about bringing him here. He'd run away for a reason. Ultimately, how either one of us felt about it didn't matter. This was where the smithy was. I carried the water I had bought inside first, just in case, and returned for Yarwor. I pulled him out into a fireman's carry. I closed the truck door and hit the button to lock it, sliding the keys into my pocket as I walked toward the house.

I still had my reservations about healing Yarwor. I was no expert on Ichor, and didn't know how long it stayed in the system, but I wasn't going to take another detour to Dahlonega to ask my new friend Clay. I put Yarwor on the bed as gently as I could and arranged the gallons of water on the floor in front of the bed. I looked at the jugs, unconvinced that it would be enough to satisfy him if he woke up thirsty again. If it came down to it I could use the kitchen faucet while he worked his way through the jugs on the floor. Maybe the running water would be enough to keep him from attacking me again. Just to be safe, I filled a pitcher, too.

Holding the pitcher in my left hand, I put my right over his chest and channeled energy into him. I could feel it flow, healing his injuries. He groaned as the healing took hold, and opened his eyes. I stopped the flow and pulled my hand back. He wasn't fully healed yet and I was all right with that. Yarwor sat up in the bed and looked around. He spotted me with the water at the ready and reached out a hand. I handed him the pitcher and he promptly dumped it and vomited a black sludge into it. He placed the pitcher on the floor and leaned forward on the edge of the bed to put his head between his knees.

He waved his hand and grunted, "Water," in a hoarse voice.

I was happy to supply it, pulling the lid off one of the gallon jugs and placing it in his hand. I preemptively took the lid off a second jug. Sitting up, he sipped gingerly before tucking it under one arm, clutching the water to his chest like a teddy bear. A little water splashed out as the plastic was compressed but he didn't seem to notice.

"How did I get here?" he asked, looking around.

"I found you squatting in a half-collapsed building in Atlanta and brought you back. You don't remember any of that?"

"No." He rubbed his face with his free hand. "Why does my nose hurt?"

I shook my head. "I sure didn't stick my fingers up there, I'll tell you that much."

He took another sip of water. "I don't want to be here."

"I'm sorry if being here is causing you pain. I wouldn't have brought you back if it wasn't necessary," I said.

He shook his head. "It's not just what happened here, it's everything. You know what they call me now? The butcher. You should see the looks I got last time I went to the clubhouse. This isn't a place I want to be anymore. I didn't mean to hurt anybody."

"I've heard the name and you have to know that Holt and I don't use it. We were here that day. I know you aren't responsible for what you did. How about this, you help me and I'll help you find somewhere where you can have a real life again. Somewhere far away from here."

"I don't deserve a real life," he answered.

I leaned forward and put a hand on his shoulder. "Sometimes people get things they don't deserve. Would it be so bad if it worked out for you?"

He took another drink from the pitcher. "What do you want my help with?"

"I need a weapon. Hell's breaking loose and I'm seriously outgunned and outnumbered. I asked Thera for help and she said I needed to find a black-smith. So here you are."

He was in the middle of another swig of water and choked at my answer, coughing, and wiping his mouth on his arm. "Thera sent you to get me?"

"Not you, specifically," I said. "You're the only blacksmith I know."

"You really know how to make a guy feel special," he said. "If I'm being real honest I'm not exactly sure how much I believe in the whole *Thera* thing."

I smiled. "That's okay. She doesn't require you to believe in her."

"What the hell am I supposed to do?"

"Let's head out to the smithy," I said, pointing a thumb toward the door. "I'll have to call her to figure out what we do after that."

He sighed. "I'll go, but I have to be honest with you. You got the wrong guy."

He got to his feet and I followed him as he made his way slowly out of the house to the smithy. We went inside. Yarwor leaned against the anvil, still clutching the jug of water.

"Well?" he asked. "What now?"

I held up a finger. "Thera. I have the blacksmith."

Yarwor looked around the smithy. After a few seconds, he said, "Well?"

Thera appeared next to a workbench on the left side of the smithy.

"She's here," I said.

"I don't see anything," Yarwor said.

"If you could see her, you wouldn't have any problem believing, would you?"

"Put your hand on his head," Thera said.

"Hold still a second," I said, walking over to him.

"What are you doing?"

"Hold still," I said, resting a hand on the top of his head.

Yarwor crossed his arms. "This is stupid."

I felt an electric charge run up from the ground through my right leg, around my back, and down my left arm into Yarwor's head. He spasmed from the burst of energy and sprawled on the ground, dropping the jug of water. I lowered my arm, shaking my hand. It tingled from the burst of electricity and felt numb. Yarwor set up. He looked dazed, a distant kind of look in his eyes.

"I know what I have to do," he said, getting to his feet. "The first thing is the metal to make the blade from. I think I have something that'll work."

He walked over to a pile of scrap in the corner. He dug through it, tossing bent blades and rusted bars onto the floor behind him, before pulling out what looked like a rock. He turned it over in his hands before returning to the table and setting it down with a loud thud.

"It's a meteor I chanced across years ago," he said. "I've been waiting for something special to do with it. This definitely fits the bill."

He walked over to the hammer on the floor of the smithy. The depression where he had smashed Grubby into the dirt was still black from the demon's blood. He stared at it for a few seconds before sighing and picking it up.

"You're sure about this?" he asked, turning the hammer over in his hands. "It's not too late to call it off."

"Don't get cold feet on me now," I said.

He looked at me with sorrow on his face. "I need you to change to krasis."

I pulled the Velcro on my shorts to make room for my tail and made the change. As soon as I was done I looked up to see the hammer coming down on my head.

I became aware of myself, not of my surroundings, or what had happened to me, only that I again recognized I existed. It was like waking up from a deep sleep when you still linger halfway between dream and reality. The first thing I noticed was a sound. A rhythmic scraping, somewhere off in the distance, that seemed to get closer the more awake I became. The steady tempo seemed to come up from out of the darkness itself. Then another sensation, cold. Dull at first, but growing as I came out of my slumber. Finally, the pain started. Throbbing in my head and a burning sensation all over my body like I was on fire.

I opened my eyes to find myself laid out on the table in the smithy. My body was glossy and red, and the pain intensified through my neck and back from the movement. I couldn't make sense of what was on me, some kind of goo, like an acidic slime. That would account for the burning. Yarwor was seated with his back to me. He had a log resting on a couple of sawhorses with a hide draped over it. He was using a long blade to scrape the flesh and fat from the skin. I had seen the old timers do this with deer skins. As the fog cleared from my head, I realized it wasn't that there was something on me, but that something wasn't—my skin had been removed.

I wasn't going to lie here and be subjected to whatever else was in the works. I went to sit up and only managed to pull myself up on my elbows. The movement sent pain shooting through my body; that didn't subside, but it gave me the vantage point to see the full extent of what had been done. Besides being skinned, my legs had been removed just below the knee. I stared at the stumps where my legs should be, trying to make sense of what I was seeing. The realization sank in slowly that they weren't misplaced or hiding, but just gone.

"You aren't whole. Lie back," Thera said. She stood beside me.

I lay back on the table, sending fresh waves of pain shooting through my body when it made contact. I tried to speak, but couldn't get out anything more than grunts and groans. Thera waved a hand over me and the pain left my body. While I knew it was just the absence of suffering, it felt like bliss and I breathed a sigh of relief to be free of it.

"Your blade is being made," Thera said.

"When you said it would cost me, I didn't know this is what you had in mind," I said.

Now pain-free, I raised my head. Through the back door of the smithy I saw a large dirt oven with wisps of smoke coming out of the top. The heat distorted the air above it. A trashcan full of charcoal sat close by. Yarwor stopped his scraping and bent over to puke into a bucket on the ground beside him. He took a swig of water from a jug, and after swishing it around in his mouth, spit it into the bucket. He looked at me. Our eyes met, and he walked over to where I was lying. He stood there with a long face, wringing his hands for a moment.

"I don't know if you can hear me, but I'm sorry, Obie," he said before going back to his seat and continued scraping my hide.

"I have Holt coming here to watch over you while you heal," Thera said.

My thoughts drifted to my mentor, Cearbhall, and how he'd lost an eye long ago. He had worked with only one for as long as I knew him, but it never grew back. My skin would grow back, I was sure about that. I would probably be horrible scarred for a while. My legs on the other hand, I couldn't work without them.

"Will I get my legs back?" I asked.

"You will, but it will take time to regrow them. You will sleep," she said.

As soon as the words left her lips, my eyelids grew heavy and I fought to stay awake while vines appeared over the edge of the table. They grew up close to my body, weaving together into a dome over me. I was overcome with a warm peaceful feeling as the light of the smithy disappeared between the leaves.

"Holt . . ." I mumbled, trying to remember what I was going to say.

As the vines closed in around me I fell into the first sleep I had had in over two hundred years, since the day I became a Keeper.

CHAPTER 19

I lay still, not wanting to move. I felt warm, comfortable, and protected in a way that I'd never experienced before. I don't know how long it took me to actually open my eyes. I saw the tangled branches that sheltered me from the world. It should have been dark inside my cocoon, but it wasn't. The light was dim and without a distinguishable source, it seemed to come from everything and nothing at the same time. I lay there, not wanting to move, and doing a good job with it, until I heard Thera's voice.

"You're healed," she said. "Get up."

It seemed to me to be as good an idea as anything else, and remembering what had happened last time she pushed me to get up, I decided sooner would be better than later. There wasn't a lot of room to move in the cocoon. I shifted around to make enough space to get my arms above me. I ran my hands along the tangled vines. They were twisted tightly together with barely enough room to wiggle my fingers in between them. They grew thick and tight and didn't want to budge as I began pulling them apart. After a few minutes of pulling and breaking the vines, I was able to make an opening large enough to fit through.

I crawled out enough so I could rest my arms on top of the cocoon. I was alone in the smithy. The doors were closed. It had been cleaned up since the last time I saw it. Everything sat neatly in its place, including the hammer, which rested on the anvil in front of the forge. I pulled myself out onto the floor. My clothes were gone, no surprise there. I ran a hand over my fur. It was softer than normal, not unexpected, considering it was new. I gave my legs a few steps to test them out and my toes a few wiggles; it was as if they had never been gone. There were no scars. A few stomps, kicks, and shakes, and I felt confident they were good to go. The table where I had seen Yarwor at work had been cleaned. On it I found some of my clothes folded beside a cloth with something lumpy under it. I knew Holt had brought them, but I doubted he would have folded them so neatly. Livy had been here as well.

The clothes were gray shorts and a yellow shirt that said BE KIND on the front. I had picked it up at a local school fundraiser a couple of years ago without any real intention of wearing it. Maybe someone wanted to send me a message. I flipped the cloth back. Underneath I found a large blade and a set of knuckle dusters. The blade had a beautiful swirling pattern and an off-white handle. The blade itself was fifteen inches long with a slight curve that came to a dangerous looking point.

I picked it up, feeling the balance. It felt lighter than I thought it would and reacted well when I gave it some test swings. Satisfied, I put it back on the table and picked up the knuckle dusters. I slid my fingers into them. They were shiny steel with aggressive points on the end of each knuckle, nice but not really my thing. I got dressed and went to the door. I undid the latch, pushing it open wide. The sun was shining. No sooner had I swung the door open than a cool breeze blew across my fur. Something strange about the trees caught my attention before I stepped out; they were bare. When I got here they still had leaves, albeit leaves that were about to fall.

I spotted Holt's Honda parked beside my truck as I walked out into the yard. I could tell they had both been parked there for a while from the leaves that had gathered around the windshield wipers. I could hear talking coming from inside the house. I opened the door and stepped in to find Holt, Livy, Harlan, Isabelle, and Yarwor sitting around the kitchen table. Isabelle was sitting in Yarwor's lap. They were in the middle of a game of cards with Isabelle and Yarwor playing together.

"Obie!" Isabelle shouted when I stepped in.

She jumped out of Yarwor's lap in her excitement. I didn't know why she was so thrilled to see me, but the rest of the room had more mixed reactions.

Livy looked relieved, like when she'd been worrying about how a batch of cornbread muffins was going to turn out, even though they always came out perfect.

"You're awake," Holt said with a grin and a nod. "Glad to have you back."

Yarwor stood and walked over to me. "Obie, I'm really sorry. I can explain," he said. "I wasn't myself."

I probably should have been mad. It would be understandable to be angry at anyone who skinned you and cut your legs off, regardless of their good intentions. Maybe it was the time I spent in the cocoon, but I felt at peace.

"You don't have to tell me what can happen when Thera gets in your head," I said.

Yarwor breathed a sigh of relief. "I'm glad to hear you say that. I thought for sure you would be pissed."

I held out my hand and he shook it. "I saw the blade. How could I be mad? It looks awesome. Is it finished?"

"It still has to be bound. Other than that, yes," Yarwor replied.

I nodded. "How do we bind it?"

"That wasn't zapped into my cranium." He shrugged. "You'll have to ask Thera."

"Sounds like someone's a believer," I said.

Yarwor shrugged. "I wouldn't go that far. Something happened that I can't explain. Let's just say, I'm open to the possibility."

I nodded. "I'll take it. You look a lot better than last time I saw you."

"I'm doing my best," he said, looking at the ground. "I was lucky Holt showed up when he did. Livy helped me though the withdrawal with some concoction she made. It tasted like ass but really took the edge off. And Isabelle—let's just say, it's nice having people to care about again."

"I'm glad you're doing better," I said.

"You want to get your blade fitted?"

"I can't wait," I said. "Holt, let's go."

"What do you need me for?" Holt asked.

I looked at Yarwor. "Didn't you tell him?"

Yarwor shook his head. "Didn't seem like my place."

"We have something for you, too," I said.

The three of us walked to the smithy. Yarwor went over to the cloth the weapons were under and flipped the cloth back. He fished around under the table and came up with a belt and sheath for the blade. They were plain leather with only a few runes stamped in them.

Yarwor ran a hand over the smooth leather. "I had to make the buckle out of the same metal as the knife for it to work. It should work the same way as the knife once it's bound. Want to try it on?"

"Before I do, could you explain to me why I was skinned and had my legs cut off?" I asked. "I was surprised by it, to say the least."

"He cut your legs off?" Holt asked.

"The meteorite I used was mostly iron, but to make steel we had to add carbon. The . . . message . . . I got told me the carbon had to come from you. I needed bones." Yarwor shrugged.

"What about the skin?" I asked.

Yarwor looked at the sheath and belt he held. "I had to make leather."

I was hesitant to see how it fit, mostly because the idea of wearing something made from my skin skeeved me out. All I could think about were Nazis making lamp shades out of human skin. What's done was done. I had to have some way to hold the blade. There were no other options, so I was really just delaying the inevitable.

"Yeah, let's try it out," I said, ignoring the chill that ran down my back. I picked up the belt and placed it around my body to find a way to wear it.

I tried to orient the knife, so it rested horizontally across my hips between my shirt and shorts, but it wasn't comfortable. In order for it to change with my body it had to be worn under my clothes. I took my shirt off to find a more comfortable position. I slung it over my left shoulder with the handle down by my right hip. It was the only placement I could think of that would give me access to it without clothing getting in the way. I slid the knife into the sheath, giving it a little adjustment to find a comfortable position.

While I worked getting it in place, Yarwor gave the knuckledusters to Holt. "And these are for you."

"Sweet," Holt said, sliding them onto his fingers. "Thanks, Yarwor."

"Don't thank me," Yarwor said shaking his head. "Thank Obie, he's the one that paid for them."

"They feel great," Holt said. "I could really bust some skulls with these."

"That's the idea," I said.

Holt took a few practice swings to get a feel for them. "What now?"

"That's between you guys and Thera," Yarwor said. "I've had enough close encounters. I'll be in the house."

After Yarwor left, Holt asked, "He cut your legs off?"

"I was surprised as anybody," I said. "Probably more so. How long was I out?"

"Three weeks, two days," Holt said, peering into the cocoon on the table. "But who's counting?"

I wasn't sure I wanted an answer to the next question, but I had to ask. "What'd I miss?"

"Hank's in the hospital," he said. "And Lug Nut's in jail."

"What the hell are they doing there?"

"Well, after we put him in the truck, Lug Nut headed south to take him to Atlanta. He was speeding, of course, and got pulled over. Long story short, when they heard a biker was shot a lot of cops showed up. They ended up getting in a little tussle with Lug Nut. From what I heard he had four of them on him before he remembered he had to let them win. He got arrested and went to jail. The cops found a number of illegal recreational substances in the back of the truck, so I don't see him getting out anytime soon. They took Hank to the hospital.

That was bad news. Normal injuries for shifters didn't require medical attention. Injuries caused by silver wouldn't heal, or they wouldn't heal quickly I should say. The closest place to go for treatment was the wererats hospital in Atlanta. Normal hospitals were great for humans, but not the best place for an injured werebear. What was more concerning was that if he'd spent three weeks in the hospital that meant he had probably been poisoned by the silver the whole time. Otherwise he would have healed up and be out by now. I was surprised to hear he wasn't dead, to be honest.

"So who's leading the T.O.?" I asked.

He paused, knowing I wouldn't like the answer. "Chisel."

I sighed. "We need to get Hank back."

"I don't know if Chisel will give up the reins willingly. It's not the same Tortured Occult as it was when you . . . were indisposed. I think he saw an opportunity to take over the club. They haven't tried to save Hank and haven't posted bail for Lug Nut. A few of the T.O. left the club and are laying low. Chisel recruited some of the Wretched Dogs to fill in the ranks and declared war on the Elven Nation. I haven't had contact with anyone in a couple weeks, but things were heating up then," Holt said. "There's probably been bloodshed by now."

"Okay," I said. "What about everyone here? Harlan and Isabelle holdin' up all right?"

Holt shrugged. "Isabelle's having fun, but I can tell she wants to go home. She's really hit it off with Yarwor. He's become very protective of her in the past month."

"Good," I said. "And Harlan?"

"He disappears a lot. Goes on these long walks by himself for an hour or more at a time. I don't get the impression he wants to be here either, but he definitely don't want to go back to the Queen."

"We'll get 'em both where they need to go, but first things first," I said. "Let's get these weapons done. Then we can worry about Hank and Chisel."

Holt nodded. "Thera," he said, "we need you."

She appeared in the smithy. "Yes?"

"Our weapons are ready," I said, holding up my blade. "What's next?"

"Now we bind them. Fill a large container with the cleanest water you can find. Warming the water to your body temperature will ease the transition," she said. "Call me when it's done."

She vanished again.

"Easy enough," Holt said. "Yarwor's got a bathtub."

We walked back into the house, passing everyone in the living room without answering any of their questioning glances. The house itself was small and the bathroom was no exception. Just a tub, toilet, and sink with enough standing room for one person. Holt turned the hot water all the way and held his hand under it, waiting for it to get warm. When it started to heat up he plugged the tub and made adjustments to keep the water at the right temperature.

"That should just about do it," he said.

"You going first or should I?" I asked.

"I will," he said. "Thera, we're ready."

She appeared in the tub, standing not in the water, but on it. "Holt, in your human form wear your weapon and submerge your hands."

Holt made the change to his human form, put on his knuckledusters, and put his hands under the water. He screamed as the water started to bubble, steam rising from the tub. I waited and watched. Isabelle, Harlan, and Yarwor rushed over to find out what the commotion was. The water continued to boil and steam around Holt's hands for a few seconds and then abruptly stopped. Holt pulled his hands out of the water. The knuckledusters were gone. His hands shook as he held them up. He had scars around his fingers where the metal had been. He turned his hands over to reveal similar scars on his palms. They looked like burns. He flexed his hands.

"Now change to your other forms," Thera said.

He changed to a Doberman first. His front paws had been solid black but now they had brown rings around each of his toes. Then he changed to krasis and the knuckledusters came out of his flesh and into his hands.

"Okay, that's pretty cool," Holt said.

"Obie," Thera said.

I changed to my human form and lowered myself into the tepid water.

Livy poked her head around the corner. "What's all the fuss about?"

"Thera's about to burn a blade into Obie's back," Holt said.

I was going to say, "Let's not be overdramatic," when I was hit with an intense heat. The water in contact with the blade began to boil. Searing pain shot through my body. It focused on the areas the belt and blade touched, but spilled over to the rest of my body. It felt like I was being branded. I didn't scream the way Holt had. I would have liked to, but couldn't get it out. I could feel the blade bending from the center, coming in contact with my back as it burned into my flesh. When the blade had worked its way in and the pain subsided, I stood up. Water poured from my clothes as I raised my shirt to look.

Like Holt, scars were left from the binding. Mine ran around my chest. I could see singed parts on my clothes where they had come into contact with the belt and blade. I changed into an otter to find a khaki discoloration in my normally light brown fur. Finally, I changed to krasis and the blade came out of my body.

I drew the blade and looked at my reflection in it. "All right. Let's get to work."

"What's the plan?" Holt asked.

"We're going to get Hank."

Holt and I changed into our human forms and I put on some dry clothes. We said our goodbyes and went out to my truck. I opened the door and was hit in the face with the scent of rotten fish.

"What the hell is that?" Holt said, with a hand over his nose.

I searched the truck and found something wrapped in paper under the driver's seat. The paper had soaked up some brown liquid and when I unfolded it a fish fell onto the ground.

"Looks like a trout. At least, it was a trout," I said.

There was some writing on the paper that I could barely make out through the fish juice. I pinched the paper between two fingers so I could read it.

Obie,

I didn't realize you were such a cold fish. Hopefully, this will provide companionship more in line with your tastes.

XOXO,

Tasha

CHAPTER 20

I've never cared for the smell of hospitals. Don't get me wrong, there are much worse things to smell, but the smell of a hospital has a quality all its own. I've always found it strange that the smell is uniform across the handful of hospitals I have been in. I shouldn't complain. For most of my life they didn't always have such a sterile, if unnatural, smell to them. They used to smell like death, but that's progress for ya.

I stepped into a normal looking hospital room. Machines with a few too many wires and cables coming off of them were positioned beside the bed in the center of the room. A loveseat sat under a window with a view of roof and sky, not the best view, but it's not as if patients in critical care gaze out for hours on end. There was a TV mounted to the wall opposite the bed. It was off. An I.V., that was almost empty, dripped steadily into Hank's hand.

He didn't look good. His normal java tone was a little more yellow and pallid. His eyes were sunken in and his cheek bones were poking out. He had lost weight, a lotta weight. A good portion of it looked to be muscle. He seemed to be shriveling up right in front of me.

"Hank?" I said, touching his hand.

It was cold. He didn't respond to my voice or touch. I pulled open an eye to find a sickly yellow ball with a dark brown pupil. It was what I was afraid of. The slow wasting away and jaundice, I had seen it before with silver poisoning. It didn't look like he had much time left.

I took a seat, pulled my phone out of my pocket, and dialed a number. It rang a few times before a familiar voice answered.

"This is Rebecca Lin," she said.

"Hey, Doc, it's Obie. Are you in the hospital?"

"I'm in administration. Are *you* in the hospital?" she asked warily.

"Yeah, I'm in 826," I said. "I need to see you when you got a minute."

There was a moment of silence before she spoke again. "Should I be worried?"

"No more than usual."

"Oh no," she said. "I'll be right there."

As I waited for her arrival, I looked at Hank again. This time not as a concerned friend but through a practical lens. My objective from Thera wasn't only to hunt demons, it was to protect life. Granted, there's a lot of interpretation there. That leeway is what caused issues between my mentor Cearbhall and me. A war between the Tortured Occult and the Elven Nation would cost a lot of lives. Not just between the club and the elves, it would spill over to everyone in the area. If there was any hope of restoring peace, I needed Hank to get back to his rightful position as head of the T.O. Between Chisel and the Queen, it would be a war of attrition. With Hank in charge, there might be hope for a solution with minimal loss of life.

Even if we were able to get him back on his feet today, I wasn't sure he would be up to it. Hank always had a presence about him, but now it seemed to be gone. He looked weak and shriveled and fragile. In a perfect world, he would show up and be accepted back with open arms. Chisel clearly made a power play for control of the club. Otherwise Hank would have been out of the hospital already. I wasn't sure Hank was going to be able to do what was necessary to take leadership back. If he wasn't up to it physically, we would have to take a grassroots approach. I sat, pondering the possibilities and alternative scenarios, when Doc Lin walked in and brought me back to reality. She was carrying an assortment of papers and X-rays under her arm and a clipboard in her hand.

"I pulled everything we have on Hank Morrison," she said, putting the documentation on the rolling table at the foot of the bed. "Why's he so important?"

"Kinda jumping the gun a little, aren't you? What if I just picked a room with some guy in a coma so we could talk privately?"

She put a hand on her hip and gave me a look that said she wasn't buying it. "I don't know hardly anything about you, except that you're kind and nothing is ever a coincidence with you."

"It was a coincidence I was there to pull you out of that car wreck," I shot back. "I was just passing by."

"It may have been a coincidence you were passing by, but it wasn't a coincidence you stopped. That's the kind of person you are. So why don't you cut the crap and tell me who this is?"

She had me there and I wasn't going to argue with her. "He's an old friend. I want to help him get better, but I'll need your help."

"Oh, you need help fixing the records? When you healed Ms. Heck a few months ago it was a big deal. They were floating all kinds of theories around. There was even an article in the paper. I see what you were saying about drawing attention. You're right that you can't go around healing everyone without exposing yourself."

"It's not so much about the records, I have another problem. He's being poisoned and until we remove it, he won't get better. I can't do anything about it until the poison's out," I said.

"Let's see," she said, rifling through papers. "Toxicology came back clear."

I shrugged. "I guess it would be closer to an allergy than a poison. I don't really know how to describe it medically."

"It says here he has hemolytic anemia. His red blood cells are being destroyed faster than they can be made. Doesn't look like they've been able to find the cause. He's been kept alive with multiple blood transfusions, but he's continuing to deteriorate."

"What about the gunshots?" I asked.

She returned to the documentation. "He was admitted with six gunshot wounds. Three of the bullets were removed."

"Why only three?" I asked.

"They were the only ones that were life threatening," she said. "We don't remove bullets when they aren't dangerous or if there is a risk of doing more damage getting them out than leaving them in."

"These are dangerous. They're causing his condition. We need to have them taken out."

She looked skeptical. "So, you're saying that the bullets are made out of a toxic metal?"

"Toxic to him," I said. "They're silver."

"Silver bullets?" she questioned.

I nodded.

"Is he a werewolf?" She laughed.

I wasn't sure how to answer. Obviously, Hank wasn't a werewolf, but he wasn't far off. What could I really tell her that wouldn't disclose more of my world than she should be aware of? On the other hand, she had to have an open mind since she knew I could heal people and seemed okay with it. But she didn't know what I was or what else was out there. It was risky to tell her because if she found out and wanted to tell people then I would have to keep her quiet, whatever it took. I liked her and didn't want to do something I would regret.

"Obie," she said after I hadn't answered. "He's not a werewolf . . . is he?"

"Well no, He's not a were*wolf*," I said. "It's complicated."

She dropped the papers on the table and crossed her arms. "Then uncomplicate it. If you want my help, I need to know what's going on."

"What's going on is dangerous and it could get you killed," I said. "The less you know the safer you are. We need to have the bullets removed."

"That's going to be a problem," she said.

"And why's that?"

"Well . . . besides the fact that he might be too weak to survive the surgery, and no one is going to want to perform the operation, take a look at this." She pulled out some X-rays and held them up to the light.

I moved over to get a closer look.

"You see these darker pieces?" she asked, pointing them out with her pinky.

I could see what looked like a leg bone with three darker spots on the X-ray.

"That's all foreign material. One of them is the bullet you're worried about, but which one?"

"How many times was he shot?" I asked.

Doc Lin checked the documentation. "Seven."

The Queen only had six rounds in her revolver. Hank must have picked up another bullet in all the commotion.

"And look at this," she said, pulling up another X-ray.

This one showed ribs and more dark spots. She swapped it for another that showed more.

"See? He's full of metal. I don't even know how he's survived all this. The only option we would have is to remove all the pieces in the areas he was shot to make sure we get the right ones and any fragments they may have broken into. All that's beside the point, because no surgeon is going to operate on him in this condition. He would die on the table and mess up their stats."

I pulled out my phone and called Holt. He had been waiting in the car. We'd come to the hospital in his Civic since my truck had a lingering unpleasant odor.

"I need the dust we stashed in your car," I said.

"That bad, huh?" he said. "I'll be right up."

If surgery wasn't an option, then maybe a little magic would do the trick. We kept a little dust hidden away in case of emergencies. This qualified. Holt walked in a few minutes later and slapped a bag in my hand. I would need his help. What I didn't need was spectators. Doc Lin would have to go.

"What's that?" she asked.

"The answer to my problem," I said. "Thanks for coming by. I appreciate the help, but I can take it from here."

"Unless you packed a surgeon and operating room in that little bag, I don't see how anything has changed," she said.

"I'm just going to do what I do, nothing to worry about," I said. "I have help now, so if you don't mind, a little privacy would be nice."

"You told me you couldn't *do what you do* as long as he had the silver in him." She put her hands on her hips. "I understand why you can't make what you do public, but I expect the truth. If you want to do whatever it is you're planning, then I'm going to be right here for it."

"And you are willing to accept any risks that come from what you will see and learn?" I asked.

"I am."

"Maybe you shouldn't agree too readily to things you don't understand," I offered. "I work pretty hard to keep people in the dark about things going on. There are people that would come after you, if they found out you knew about this stuff."

"Seems to me like there would only be three people that know," she countered. "If I don't tell anyone and you two don't tell anyone . . ."

I wasn't going to stand around and argue with her. Hank didn't have time. Doc Lin's a grown woman. If she's willing to take the risk, who am I to question.

"All right. In that case, there are some things I've got to tell you. All you need to know right now is that magic is real and I'm going to try to use it to pull the silver out of Hank's body. Holt's here to heal Hank and minimize the damage while I work."

"Holt's going to heal him?" Doc Lin asked. "How many of you are out there?"

"Just the two of us close by," I said.

She pointed at the bag in my hand. "What does the bag have to do with it?"

"The thing about magic is anyone can do it, but it has to have a power source," I said. "The fuel for what I'm going to do is in the bag."

She looked skeptical but open. "And where does the fuel come from?"

"If you want to learn more about this kind of stuff, we may be able to make it happen, but for now, baby steps, okay?"

"Hey, Doc," Holt said. "Can you get the door?"

Holt and I took positions on either side of the bed. I put the bag of dust on the table so as to not inadvertently set it off. I don't do magic a lot. I wasn't very comfortable with it, but I knew the process and figured I could make it work. I just needed a couple dry runs to get ready. I held my fists over Hank and visualized all the metal in his body being drawn out as if my hands were magnets pulling it. I ran through this process a few times in my mind before deciding I was ready. I retrieved the bag from the table.

"Okay, let's get started," I said.

Holt held out his hands and began channeling healing energy into Hank. I opened the bag, divided the dust as evenly as I could between my hands, and dropped the bag on the floor, out of the way. I held my fists over Hank the way I had practiced, focusing on the metal in his body being drawn out. I began to feel my hands warm from the dust, and figuring it was now or never, I opened my hands. I was startled when something wet splashed across my face. I didn't have time to worry about it because pain shot through my hands. I pulled them back and looked to find pieces of metal embedded in my palms. Holt was still healing Hank. The holes in Hank's body where the metal had exited were closing up quickly.

The metal came out with enough force to not only imbed itself in my hands, but to splatter Hank's blood all over Holt and me and a good portion of the room around the bed. It looked like Hank had exploded, which I suppose wasn't too far off. Doc Lin had been standing far enough back to avoid the blood spatter. I walked into the bathroom and got a look at myself in the mirror. The blood made me look like a victim in a horror flick. I turned on the sink and held my hands under the cool water. I would need to get the metal out quick, I didn't want it to heal in place.

"Doc, I need your help," I said.

She came in the bathroom. "What the hell was that?"

I gave her a sheepish grin. "Sometimes magic gets a little messy."

"That's a little messy?" she yelled.

"Keep your voice down. If you could pull these out for me I would appreciate it," I said holding my hands over the sink. "Quickly."

She left the room and returned a moment later with what were essentially a fancy looking pair of pliers. She pulled out the shrapnel piece by piece and dropped them into the sink.

She had only gotten one of them out, before I could start to feel the tug created from my flesh healing around the metal. She pulled another piece out and noticed the resistance.

"These things are really in there," she said. "Hold on . . ." She moved my hand under the water to clean off the blood. "Obie, these wounds closed up already, I can even see the one I just pulled closing. How is that even possible?"

"It's a long story," I said. "Just pull harder, they'll come out."

"I can't do that, they're really in there," she said, giving my palm a closer look. "We can take you down to the emergency room. They can take these out cleanly."

"We don't have time for that," I said, pulling my hand away from her.

I looked at my right hand, there were still three pieces of metal embedded in it. The one sticking out the most looked like the tip of a knife. I bit it and yanked it out of my palm, spitting it into the sink. The last two pieces were on the side of my palm and wouldn't get in the way of finishing up on my own.

I took the tool from Rebecca. "Why don't you check on Hank."

I was generally unsatisfied with the way this had gone. I was covered in blood, my hands hurt, and the hospital room was a mess. That was really what was frustrating me. There was always a mess. Whenever there was a mess, it causes more problems that lead to more messes. It would be nice, if for once, something, anything, would go as planned. I pulled the shrapnel out of my hands, one by one, dropping them into the sink. When I was done I took a couple minutes to relocate my center. I stood and breathed, holding my hands under the water as they healed. When they were done, I washed the blood off my face as best I could. The shirt was a lost cause until I could get to a washing machine.

I left the bathroom to find Holt using a wet towel to spot clean blood off the walls and medical equipment. He was almost finished when I came out. What he couldn't clean was the bed. The sheets covering Hank had bloody holes where the metal had been pulled through. I didn't see Rebecca in the room.

"Where did she go?" I asked.

Holt stopped scrubbing. "She's getting fresh sheets and a new gown for

Hank. Think if you gave me a boost I could reach that?" he asked pointing at the ceiling.

A number of spots on the ceiling where blood had made it past my hands. It wasn't a lot, just a few specks here and there.

"Don't worry about it," I said. "No one ever looks up and by the time someone does we'll be long gone. How's Hank?"

Holt leaned against the railing of the bed. "Well, he's not awake, but he ain't dead either."

Rebecca returned with an armload of linens. "I brought you both a scrub top to wear. As long as you don't hang out in the hallways, it should get you out of the building without any trouble. Give me a hand changing the sheets."

We changed Hank's bloody gown and sheets and in few minutes the room was back to normal—as long as no one looked at the ceiling.

"We're going to get out of here," I said. "Can you keep an eye on him and let me know when he wakes up, please?"

"You'll be my first call," Doc Lin said, shoving the bloody sheets into the hazardous waste bin.

Holt and I donned scrubs and headed for the car.

CHAPTER 21

Holt pulled off the road onto the dirt path leading to the clubhouse. He stopped the car before passing through the open gate. "I'm not so sure about this."

"We've got to talk to the T.O. sooner or later," I said. "And if Hank's on the mend some of 'em might like to know."

It's hard to explain how the clubhouse could be empty. Sitting in the middle of a junkyard there were always plenty of cars around, even if most of them had seen better days. It wasn't that the clubhouse looked vacant, after all there seemed to be more motorcycles than normal parked out front. It's more that it felt isolated and empty.

Holt took great care driving his Civic up the dirt road. I knew he was proud of his car, but I'd been trying to get him to get something more practical ever since we started working together. There wasn't any room to transport slain demons, or anything else for that matter. It wasn't suited for the dirt roads we often had to travel. It just didn't make much sense, considering the needs of a Keeper. At the same time, Holt put a lot of work into the Civic. You'd never know it by looking at it; the only thing that hinted that it wasn't a regular car were the wider than normal tires and exhaust. The car crawled up the dirt path, the small bumps that I wouldn't have noticed in my truck were accentuated by the lack of speed and stiff suspension. I was sure I could walk it just as fast as Holt was driving.

"I know you're nervous about seeing the T.O., but this is ridiculous," I said. "Just drive up there already."

Holt shot me a look out the side of his eye. "It's not built for dirt. I don't want to mess anything up."

When we finally made it, we found Cotton standing outside with a biker I didn't recognize. They had been watching us crawl up the dirt path for what felt like the better part of twenty minutes. Holt backed the car up in front of the building to park it. I would have thought he was preparing for a speedy getaway if I didn't just live through the drive from the road to the clubhouse.

"You said you haven't talked to anyone in a couple weeks?" I asked.

"I wasn't sure who to talk with Hank and Lug Nut out of the picture. I got a text message that said to stay away, but I didn't recognize the number. Might be good advice to take."

Cotton said something to the other biker and motioned toward the clubhouse. The second biker walked inside.

"You don't think you should have told me about that before now?" I asked, rolling down my window. "Keep the engine running."

Cotton walked over to the car, leaning forward to rest an elbow on the door. "You shouldn't be here."

"Yeah, that seems to be the consensus," I said.

"Look, I don't know where you've been, but you need to get out of here," Cotton said.

"I healed Hank," I said. "I expect him to be awake soon."

Cotton looked at me for a second before pulling a Sharpie out of his pocket. "Give me your hand."

I held out my hand and he scribbled something on it.

"If you've saved Hank, there may be some hope for us," Cotton said. "There's a number of us that aren't too pleased about the direction Chisel is taking the club, not to mention how he left Hank for dead and Lug Nut in jail."

"If you have a problem about it, why don't you do something?" I asked.

"The club voted," he said. "Some of us don't like it, but we won't go against the club."

"Even if it means the club's destruction?"

Cotton nodded. "Even if."

He put the cap on the Sharpie and stuck it in his pocket. The door to the clubhouse burst open and the Tortured Occult poured out.

"Make it look good," Cotton said.

I was about to ask, "Make what look good," when Cotton reached through the window and grabbed my shirt with one hand. With the other he punched me. I grabbed the hand holding my shirt and twisted, forcing his body to turn awkwardly to the right. I pulled his arm further into the car positioning my shoulder on his elbow. A quick jerk down on his wrist resulted in an audible pop. I pushed Cotton back. He fell to the ground out of sight.

"I'll give you a head start," Chisel shouted. "Then we're gonna hunt you down."

I gave the dash a few quick slaps. "Get us out of here!"

Holt threw it in drive and pulled forward. He drove down the dirt path barely faster than he had come in. Again the car jostled over the bumps. He leaned forward, gripping the wheel like an old woman trying to merge onto the interstate. I looked back to see the T.O. wasn't even bothering to run for their bikes. They looked at the Honda inching its way toward the road in disbelief. Cotton stood up with his harm hanging limply. The other bikers walked to their bikes, put their helmets on, and cranked the bikes at leisure.

I watched the bikers starting to pull out behind us and gaining fast. "If you don't pick up the pace, we're not going to make it out of the parking lot."

"We just have to get to the road," Holt said, white knuckling the wheel.

The scrap cars parked on either side of the road prevented us from being swarmed. One biker pulled up beside the car and started kicking the Honda. Holt swerved in his direction, but the snail's pace we were traveling gave him plenty of time to hit the brakes and avoid being driven into a blue Oldsmobile. The rear window shattered. I turned to see Ginsu on the right side swinging a tire iron. He swung again, this time breaking the right rear window.

"Let's hope they don't get off and run after us, then we would be in real trouble," I said.

"We made it," Holt said, pulling onto the pavement.

The bikes poured out after us as Holt turned to look at me. "You should buckle up."

He pushed the pedal to the floor and the car surged forward with a sudden acceleration that threw me back in my seat and made me scramble for the belt. I looked behind us to see the T.O. falling behind before they realized we were quickly becoming a speck on the horizon, and hit the gas.

"They're sticking with us," I said as I clicked the seatbelt.

"Yeah, bikes are fast," he said. "We can lose them in the curves."

"How?" I asked. "They're outrunning us."

"I put a V6 in my Civic here with a number of other upgrades. Power to weight ratios aren't that far off from a motorcycle. In the curves we have an advantage, another set of wheels. They'll have to slow down or crash," he said. "We have more stability."

"And if you're wrong?" I asked.

"I'm not," Holt said. "Where's the closest curvy road with no stop signs or traffic lights?"

I thought about where we were and said, "About a mile ahead, take a right at the gas station."

Between the traffic in the opposite lane and Holt's driving he was able to keep the T.O. behind us. When we got to the gas station he hit the brakes. The car lurched to the left, tires squealing as Holt made the turn. As soon as we were pointed in the right direction he floored it. I looked back to see the T.O. approaching the turn and slowing way down to make it without crashing. There was a lot less traffic on this road and if the T.O. caught up we might be in serious trouble. They started gaining on us again. The bikers directly behind us drew pistols and began shooting at the car. A few crashed through the already shattered rear window with more thudding into the trunk.

The car's tires screeched around the first turn and I could see what Holt was talking about. Every turn they fell behind, but gained on the straightaways.

"We need to slow them down," I said, looking through the side mirror at bikers gaining on us.

"We got no dust," Holt said.

I did a quick search through the car for anything that I could use. The only thing I came up with were the equipment bags in the back seat.

I grabbed them both. "Anything in here you mind losing?"

"What are you gonna do?"

I opened the bags and pulled everything out, so it was loose and bundled it up in my arms. When I saw a sharp turn ahead I unfastened my seatbelt and rolled down the window.

"Let them catch up for this turn," I said.

Holt let off the gas and the T.O. came up on us quickly. Bullets ricocheted off the car as we entered the turn. The bikers leaned their motorcycles over to make the turn. I hung halfway out the window and dumped our equipment in the road. The harder stuff, like the flashlights, bounced off the road and up into our pursuers. The clothing and bags spread out on the road. Chisel, leading the procession, swerved to avoid the debris and went off the far side of the road. The bikers behind him either hit the clothes or swerved to dodge the obstacles. The result was the same. The club broke ranks into a cluster of screeching tires, crashing bikes, and curses.

We lost sight of them after that. Holt kept our speed up, skillfully winding the car down the two-lane country road. We drove that way for about fifteen minutes without seeing the T.O. before turning off a side road and returning to normal speed. If they were still pursuing us, they never caught back up.

"Where to now?" he asked.

I looked at the writing on my hand. It was a phone number. I pulled the phone out of my pocket. "Let's find out."

A woman's voice answered. "Hello?"

"Hey, Cotton gave me this number," I said. "This is Obie."

"Where the hell have you been?"

"Who am I talking to?' I asked.

"It's Martina."

CHAPTER 22

"This is it," I said.

We pulled up to a two-story, gray house in the middle of a subdivision. It was a nice-looking place in a quiet neighborhood. A blue Acura was parked in front of the garage.

"I don't like this," Holt said, glancing into the rearview.

"It'll be fine. We need to know what's going on," I said.

"What if it's a trap?"

"If they were going to set a trap then why bother to chase us from the clubhouse?" I asked.

"Realism."

I gave him a smile. "Come on, we get to see Martina."

The garage door began to open. When it was three-fourths of the way up it revealed Martina standing in the doorway leading into the house. Hob's truck and two black Harleys were parked in the garage. She was wearing green pajama pants and a loose gray shirt that fell down over one shoulder. Her silver hair was pulled back in a ponytail. I hardly recognized her, and it occurred to me I had never seen her not wearing the T.O.'s colors. She smiled and motioned for us to park in an open spot in front of the motorcycles. Holt pulled the car in and killed the engine. The garage door closed behind us as we got out of the car.

"It's good to see you, I'm glad you came," Martina said. "We're in the living room."

We followed her inside and down a hallway.

"Whose house is this?" I asked.

"It's mine. You didn't think I lived at the clubhouse did you? It smells funny."

"Of course not. It's a nice house," I said. "One question though, if you can afford a place like this, what were you doing hanging around a bunch of dirty bikers?"

"A girl's gotta have hobbies," she said as we rounded the corner into the living room.

Fisheye and Hob were sitting on the couch, each with a beer in their hand. They both stood up when we came in. Fisheye gave us a big hug.

"By the Earth Mother, I've missed you," he said. "Where have you been?"

"Down, boy," I said.

He jumped back, blushing, embarrassed by his show of affection. I shook Hob's hand and we took a seat. Holt and I changed to krasis. It was a strange sensation to feel the blade pull out of my back. I drew it from its sheath and put it in front of me on the coffee table, taking a second to stretch my lower back before sitting down.

"Considering the number of demons we've been seeing lately and the trouble between the T.O. and the Elven Nation . . . We needed some weapons. I spoke to Thera and we had these made. It was more of an ordeal than I intended," I said. "If I could have been here sooner, I would have."

"That's a mean lookin' blade," Fisheye said. "Mind if I check it out?"

I turned it around to hand it to Fisheye by the handle. He took it, turning it over in his hands, inspecting the craftsmanship. I could feel him touching it. I couldn't put a finger exactly where I felt it, everywhere and nowhere at the same time, like a stranger's hands that were a little too comfortable. Chills ran down my back and I could feel my left eye start to twitch involuntarily.

"Sorry, this is a look with your eyes and not your hands kind of thing. I didn't know it until just now," I said, taking the blade from him.

The anxiety that was welling up inside subsided as soon as I had the blade back in my hands. I let out a sigh of relief and sat down.

"You got a blade, too?" Fisheye asked turning to Holt.

Holt held up his hands with his knuckledusters. "I got these."

"You think I could get something like that made?" Fisheye asked.

I shook my head. "I wouldn't recommend it. Let's just say, it was too expensive. Tell me what's been happening while I was away."

"The world's gone to hell," Fisheye said. "With Hank gone, Chisel took over the T.O. He declared war on the Elven Nation. They've been hunting inside the Nation, picking up any elf they run across."

I shot a questioning look at Hob. "Any elf?"

"*Ja*," Hob confirmed. "I am no longer working with the Tortured Occult. They came to the farm making demands. I took the dust *und* left."

Martina leaned back putting her feet on the coffee table. "I had already left the club by then, but the farm was burned down. I don't know if it was the T.O. or the Queen."

"I wouldn't put it past either one of 'em," Fisheye agreed.

Holt took a seat on the couch beside Martina. "Did a lot of the T.O. leave?"

"Hank's sons and us. Some that stayed aren't happy with the direction of things, but aren't willing to leave," Martina said. "Chisel's new recruitment policy seems to focus on hating elves almost exclusively. With Otis, the club was always focused on positive things. Now it's negative and toxic."

"I think the Queen is going to roll up to the clubhouse and open fire with those big guns," Fisheye said. "But then again, the T.O. salvaged one of them from the wreckage when the demons attacked, so that might make her think twice."

I shook my head. "I think the Queen would sacrifice everyone in her kingdom if she thought it would get her what she wanted. She's cruel and reckless enough to attack the Tortured Occult in the open. I have no doubt of that. Something else must be keeping her away."

"*Ja*, she heard rumors the princess is alive," Hob added. "She will not attack if it could hurt the princess."

I shook my head. "That didn't come from any of us. The Tortured Occult were the only ones who knew. Someone's been talking."

Fisheye leaned forward in his chair. "I think Chisel did that on purpose. The idea was the Queen wouldn't attack if she thought they had the princess."

"But he doesn't," Holt said.

"The Queen does not know that," Hob said. "How are Isabelle *und* Harlan?"

"Still safe and bored, like I promised," I said. "They're going to stay that way until I get all this sorted out."

Hob nodded. "I need to know how you will handle Chisel *und* the Queen."

"It's simple, really," I said, leaning back in my chair. "I'm going to get Hank running the T.O. again."

Everyone stared at me silently. I could see the disbelief on their faces, no one wanted to state the obvious. Finally, Fisheye spoke with pain in his voice. "Obie, Hank's not going to make it. The club has been keeping an eye on him. I was at the hospital a couple days ago myself. He's going to check out any day now. I'm surprised he made it this long."

"We went to see him earlier today. We took the silver out and should have him on the mend," I said. "Right, Holt?"

Holt chimed in with a level of eloquence I had come to expect from him: "He looks like ass."

"Assuming he wakes up, that will give us another problem," Martina said. "Chisel isn't going to give up being club president willingly. If he gets word Hank is waking up, he might go finish the job," Martina said. "Even if he doesn't, Hank might be too weak to actually lead."

"The charter says to be in the club, much less run it, you have to ride. If he can't ride, he can't rule," Fisheye said.

"Let me worry about that," I said. "Do we know what Chisel's planning next?"

"Just hunting elves," Fisheye said. "There's not a lot of strategy going on."

The conversation was cut short by the sound of motorcycles on the street. Martina disappeared to the front door to check it out.

"They're here," she said. "Stay quiet and I'll get rid of them."

I gave Holt a nod and we got our weapons ready. I was anxious to see how my new blade performed. We went to the end of the hallway, as close as we could get to the front door without being seen.

The door hinges squeaked as Martina opened it. "What do you want?"

"This guy, Obie, came by the clubhouse earlier today. Chisel wants him and says you know him," the biker said.

"Yeah, I know him, but I haven't seen him in months," she said.

"We're checking around with everyone that knows him," the second biker said.

"I'm here alone," Martina said.

I could hear the bikers sniffing the air. We hadn't had any direct contact with Martina or been by the front door so they probably wouldn't pick up our scent.

"We're going to have to come in and check," the first biker said.

"You're not coming in my house," Martina said.

The second biker spoke up: "While we're checking things, we should make sure she inked over her T.O. tats. Strip search should do it."

"Chisel would want us to be thorough." The first one chuckled.

Holt took a step toward the door and I put a hand on his chest and signaled him to be quiet. We moved up to the edge of the hallway, my hand tightening around my blade. I wanted to see how it cut, but I wasn't going to make a move unless Martina needed me to.

"Before you get any ideas," Martina said, walking down the hall and opening the door to the coat closet beside where I was positioned. She pulled a shotgun out of the closet and pumped it before pointing it in their direction, aiming from the hip. "You're not coming in my house or putting your hands on me."

"Whoa, this is getting interesting," the second biker said. "I bet she doesn't even know how to use it."

"You willing to bet your life on that?" she asked.

"You know that ain't gonna stop us," the first one said.

"That's where you're wrong. See, I loaded these shells with sixteen Mercury dimes, which, in case you dimwits didn't know, are made of silver," Martina said. "So, the real question is: Would I spend twenty dollars to send your sorry asses straight to hell? If either of you want to find out, take a step forward."

It was quiet as the bikers made up their minds. The second biker chimed in, "There's nobody here. This is a waste of time."

"We'll see you later," the first one said as their footsteps retreated off the porch.

"Looking forward to it," Martina yelled after them and slammed the door.

We stayed quiet until we heard the bikes crank up and drive away.

"I can't believe guys in the T.O. are acting like that," Holt said. "There's no excuse for it."

"The club isn't what it used to be," Fisheye said.

I nodded. "Come on, let's finish our talk."

We all went back to the living room and sat down. Martina brought her shotgun.

"What are you thinking?" Hob asked.

I sighed. "As much as I hate the idea of regime change, I don't think the Queen should be running the Nation anymore. She's paranoid and ruthless. The problem is, Isabelle is her only heir. Hob, do you know any other royalty that the people might accept that we could bring in?"

"In my experience, elves are very reluctant to accept outsiders," he answered. "Especially these elves. The Queen has isolated them; they are mistrustful of nearly everyone."

"Could you do it?" I asked.

"Me? Be a king? *Nein*, Obie, you need the royal bloodline," he said.

"Okay, let's come back to that. We'll start with the T.O. That's easier and will give us some time to figure out how to handle the elves. Maybe that's enough, if the Queen will go back to isolating the kingdom. It's not a solution, but it's close," I said.

"So what do we have to do, just kill Chisel?" Holt asked.

"When he took over the club, he changed its dynamic. It's not enough just to take him out, if whoever takes over is the same," Fisheye said. "We need to make sure Hank is back in charge. For that we need enough members that support him. There are some that support him in the Tortured Occult, but I don't know if a majority do. Chisel's recruited a lot and we can't expect any of the new patches to support Hank."

"We can get back anyone that left," Martina said.

"Membership is voted on," Fisheye replied. "Even if we have enough members to vote everyone back in, there's not enough time to go through that process."

"So, we just have to make sure we take out anyone that doesn't support Hank," Martina said, resting the shotgun on her right shoulder.

Martina's phone rang.

She answered it. I turned to Fisheye and said, "Get everyone that you can. When we have everyone together, we'll figure out the best plan of attack."

"We have a problem," Martina said, hanging up the phone. "That was Cotton. Chisel has the princess."

Holt and I looked at each other with the same thought.

"We gotta go," I said. "Friends could be hurt."

"Okay, those guys are probably watching the house. I'll go first and lead them away. Give me five minutes," Martina said, returning the shotgun to the closet and grabbing her keys out of a bowl of change in the hallway.

"I'll start making calls," Fisheye said. "I'll let you know."

After Martina left, we watched the clock for what seemed like an hour until the five minutes passed and we pulled out.

"Holt," I said as we backed out of the garage.

"Yeah?"

"Show me how fast this car can go."

He shifted into first and said, "Hold on."

CHAPTER 23

To say we made it to Yarwor's house in record time would be an understatement. Though I was in the car and witnessed the trip, it still didn't seem possible. One thing was clear, Holt was going to drive from then on out. He had offered to drive a few times before, but I hadn't let him. I could see he put a lot of time into driving and he could handle a vehicle better than I could. With that in mind, it only made sense that he should be the one behind the wheel. I hadn't taken him that seriously, to be honest, at least at first. The more I got to know him, the more I could see the untapped potential in him. Why Cedric had chosen him to be a Keeper was making more and more sense.

We skidded to a stop in front of the house. I had the door open and was stepping out before the car had come to rest. I ran inside, going from room to room, throwing the doors open and shouting names only to come up empty handed. The house was empty.

"Obie," Holt called from outside. "You'll want to see this."

I ran out of the house to find him standing in the doorway of the smithy. Inside was the body of a werecoyote wearing the T.O.'s colors sprawled out on the floor. I stepped into the building to see he had been beheaded. The dead body aside, I could tell from the footprints and scuff marks on the dirt floor that there had been a group of people engaged in a fight in the room. Multiple tracks surrounded the body, but I couldn't tell exactly how many had been here.

"Do you recognize him?" Holt asked, holding up the severed head.

I looked. Its eyes were rolled back and the tongue hung out limply. All I could think was: *This is why you don't mess with orcs.*

"Never seen him before," I said.

Holt dropped the head back to the ground with a melon-esque *thump* and wiped his hand on his pants. I found some tracks from the fight and a blood trail leading out the back door.

"Looks like they went that way," I said, pointing to the back door. "The area's trampled pretty well, but there were at least five or six of them, maybe more."

By the time I finished my sentence, Holt had taken the form of a Doberman and dashed past me into the woods behind the building. He had his nose to the ground, moving back and forth in a zigzag pattern. He disappeared into the underbrush and I set out after him.

By the time I made it through the bushes, I had lost him. I peered through the woods looking for any sign of him. I had decided to go back and follow the scent myself when barking erupted from off to my right. I took off like a shot.

The barking stopped for a few seconds and was replaced by Holt's yelling, "I found them! They're over here."

I crashed through a patch of blackberries, the thorns catching my clothes and scratching my flesh. Livy and Yarwor lay near the center of a small clearing surrounded on a couple of sides by the thorny bushes. Yarwor lay on his back with his head resting on Livy's lap. His body was covered in bites, scratches, and tears. He looked as if a pack of wild dogs had had their way with him. I slid on my knees in the leaves beside them.

"He's still alive, but barely," Holt said, holding his hands over his battered body. His eyes and hands glowed green as he began healing Yarwor's injuries.

I saw claw marks on Livy's face and neck. Tear tracks that hadn't quite dried ran down her face and over the cuts on her cheek. I turned her head to the side to see her injury. Four deep gashes ran down her cheek and neck, cutting deep. The blood that had spilled out had soaked into her shirt and started to dry around the edges. I began channeling energy to heal her wounds. The claw marks promptly closed up and when I felt the energy pouring over her, I stopped. She didn't open her eyes.

I gave her a little shake. "Livy?"

Yarwor groaned, slowly regaining consciousness. Yarwor looked dazed at first then sat straight up and grimaced in pain.

"Go easy," Holt said. "You aren't completely healed yet. They really did a number on you."

"Where's Isabelle?" he asked.

"I was going to ask you," I said, pulling Livy up into a sitting position. "We haven't found her yet,"

"They took her," he growled.

"What about Harlan?" I asked.

"He wasn't here," Yarwor said. "He was out on one of his walks."

"How long has he been gone?" I asked.

Yarwor shook his head. "I don't know exactly. I don't know how long he was gone before we were attacked. I was unconscious for a while, too. We have to get Isabelle back."

I motioned for him to relax. "We'll get her back."

"You're damn right we will," he said, pushing Holt away and getting slowly to his feet with a grunt.

"She's not waking up," I said, scooping Livy up in my arms. "I'm taking her back to the house."

I moved as gently and quickly as I could back to the house. I took her to Yarwor's bed and laid her down. I adjusted the pillow under her head and pulled the sheet over her. I rested a hand against her cheek and forehead. She didn't feel warm. I decided there really wasn't anything else I could do for her at the moment. My energy would be better spent coming up with a game plan to get Isabelle back. I wasn't doing any good for anyone standing around. I walked to the bedroom door, looking out into the kitchen. It was empty. I wasn't sure what was holding Holt and Yarwor up, but they should have been back by now.

"Obie?" a fragile voice said from behind me.

I turned to see Livy with her eyes barely opened.

I knelt beside her. "Hey, you're awake. I was starting to get worried."

"How's Yarwor?" she asked.

"He's fine, Holt's healing him up."

"And Isabelle?"

"They took her," I said.

"It's all my fault. I slowed them down. Yarwor could have gotten away with Isabelle, but he wouldn't leave me behind. He fought them the whole way, keeping them away from us until we got trapped by the briars and got surrounded. I tried to stop them. After they got her they turned on Yarwor. They said they were going to teach him a lesson. They were hurting him just to do it. They thought it was fun," she said with tears flowing down her cheeks. "When they were done, I went over to try to help him and that's when one of them hit me. I tried to take him back to the house, but I couldn't even move him an inch. I passed out right after that. I'm too old and useless to be any good to anybody."

"What did the one that hit you look like?" I asked.

"He had a red shirt and a mohawk," she said.

"Listen to me," I said, taking her hand. "It's not your fault, it's my fault. I shouldn't have put you in a dangerous situation to begin with. I'm going to get you squared away, and I'm going to get Isabelle back. This is all going to be okay."

She turned her head away and didn't say anything else.

"I'll make you some tea," I said.

I went to the kitchen and put a pot of water on to boil. Yarwor came storming in the house a minute later with Holt right behind him.

"What's going on?" I asked.

Holt shrugged. "He said he needed to get something."

Yarwor headed into the bedroom. I heard something heavy being dragged across the floor. Holt and I went into the bedroom to find Yarwor had pulled the dresser away from the wall. A large sword was attached to the back of the dresser. Yarwor pulled a dusty scimitar in a leather scabbard off some hooks. The sword reached to his chest with the tip on the ground. He slid it out a few inches and looked at the blade. The metal was red; not rusted, but the color of Georgia clay.

"What kind of blade is that?" I asked.

Yarwor looked down at the blade in his hands. "I don't know exactly. I was told my great-grandfather brought it through the portal with him from the homeland. They say it's a weapon of honor among my people, not that it means anything here. Just an heirloom without a family. Whatever it's made of, it's a different metal than anything I've seen on Earth."

He stepped past us and headed outside.

"Where's he going?" I asked.

Holt shrugged. We followed him outside. Yarwor walked to Holt's Honda. He opened the passenger side door, flipped up the seat, and crawled into the back. He was so large, he sat knees to chest, leaving less than a foot on either side of the back seat clear. The tip of his scimitar rested on the floor to his right with the pommel touching the ceiling to his left. He cradled it in his arms and sat quietly waiting for Holt and me to get in the car. I opened the passenger door and leaned in to speak to him.

"I need you to stay here," I said, giving it a second to sink in before continuing. "Livy's hurt. We can't leave her here alone. Harlan's still out there somewhere. I know you want to help. The way you can do that is to keep Livy safe while Holt and I get Isabelle."

He looked away as he thought about it. I knew he wasn't going to refuse, he was just that kind of orc, but he needed a minute to remember that about himself.

He climbed out of the car. Standing inches in front of my face he said, "I can't lose any more kids."

He wasn't speaking from a place of anger so much as desperation.

"We'll get her back," I said. "I swear by Thera."

He went back toward the house. Holt and I got in the car, but he didn't crank it.

"Something wrong?" I asked.

"Obie, I don't know if I can do this."

I fastened my seatbelt. "What are we talking about?"

"We're about to go to war with a bunch of people who a month ago were friends. It just doesn't seem right," he said.

"There's a lot of new members in the Tortured Occult. We aren't friends with them and from what I've seen, I don't want to be. The guys that were our friends in the club still are," I said. "Plus some of the people you're thinking about left the club. They'll either not be there or be on our side."

He put his hands on the wheel and looked out the window. "I don't want to hurt my friends."

I knew the uncertainty he was wrestling with. I had felt it, too. "Look," I said. "You're going to do fine. Try not to think too far ahead. All we have to do now is go to the clubhouse and get the princess back. Just do what you need to do. One step at a time. "

He nodded and started the car.

CHAPTER 24

River Park was little more than a parking lot, a couple of picnic tables, and some steps leading down into the Etowah River. It was used by kayakers in Dawsonville to put in or take out, depending on what section of the river they were boating that day. Sometimes families would come there to swim in the river. Today it was the meeting place for our clandestine mission. I had chosen it because it was only about a mile away from the clubhouse, but in a place where we wouldn't attract a lot of attention. Holt drove us in a lap around the parking lot before parking out of sight of the road. There were a few cars in the lot but no people. It's true it was fall and the water would be cold, but diehard kayakers were still out on the rivers; they just wore wetsuits.

"Looks like they're not here yet," Holt said, rolling down the windows before killing the engine. "You want to get out."

"Sure," I said, opening the door.

We got out and leaned against the back of the Civic in silence. After a few minutes, Hob's old pickup pulled in. He parked beside us and Hob and Martina got out of the truck. Hob had a satchel slung over one shoulder. It looked like it had some bulk to it, but didn't seem to be too heavy. No doubt the dust he had brought for our raid.

"How far behind you is everyone else?" I asked.

Martina shrugged. "We're it."

"There's no one else from the Tortured Occult coming?" Holt asked. "Like, no one?"

"There are people that will support Hank, but Hank's not here," she said. "For the time being, what you see is what you get."

"What about Fisheye?" I asked.

Martina shrugged. "He's looking for Torch. Last I heard, he hadn't found him. It'll be fine though. Big Ticket called and said they were headed to the Elven Nation."

"What're they doing there?" Holt asked.

"Probably going to let the Queen know they have Isabelle and make some demands," I postulated. "At least, we won't have everyone to contend with."

"As long as we stick together we will be fine," Hob said.

Martina pulled a box of shotgun shells from the truck and shoved them into her pockets. "Let's get this over with."

Holt went to the Civic and opened the door.

I intercepted him before he could get in. "We should take the truck. We can't get everyone in and out quick with only two doors."

"We're going to leave my car here?" he asked.

I nodded "Yeah, it'll be fine. We'll be back in twenty minutes."

Hob and Martina got in the cab of the truck while Holt and I jumped in the back. Hob drove us about a mile over to the clubhouse and up the dirt path, parking in front of the door. I was sure they would hear the truck engine. A single engine in the middle of the day might not attract any suspicion, it would probably be construed as a customer headed to the shop. We all piled out of the truck. Martina pulled her shotgun from behind the seat. Hob slung the bag of dust over his shoulder. We stood so the truck was between us and the road to keep us out of sight of passersby and made the change to krasis.

"Ready?" I whispered.

Everyone nodded. I drew my new blade and led the group in. We moved in fast, going straight through the changing room into the bar. Inside I found a prospect mopping a bloody spot on the floor. When he saw us, he dropped the mop and moved away, holding his hands up. I ignored him, opting to confront the bikers sitting at the bar. I recognized Skinny Pete, a wererat. He was one of the original members of the Tortured Occult before the mess with Chisel started. He was sitting with Ginsu and a werewolf I didn't recognize. Must be a new patch. The werewolf jumped up and came toward me, baring teeth for the attack. I sidestepped him, slashing with my blade. I felt little resistance in the blade as I passed him. What I did feel was a sensation like dipping my hand in warm water, although not in my hand. It was a similar sensation to when Fisheye had handled my blade. It was going to take some getting used to, but the middle of a fight wasn't the time to figure it out.

I assumed from the ease of the swing the blade had only grazed the were-wolf. I spun, expecting to see fangs chomping at my neck, but he wasn't there. I looked down to see the wolf had been cut in half cleanly at the belly. The sword passed through so smoothly I didn't think it possible to have done that kind of damage. He dragged himself away with trembling hands, leaving a bloody streak behind him. Martina stepped forward and smashed his head with the butt of her shotgun, rendering him unconscious. He wouldn't wake up.

My phone buzzed in my pocket. I looked down by reflex, distracted by the vibration, not really intending to answer it. Martina shouted my name in warning and a shooting pain exploded in my back. I could feel something for-eign and pointy had found itself a home in my belly. I looked down to see the tip of a knife sticking through the front of my shirt. Blood began soaking into my shirt, making a ring around the tip of the blade. I could tell from the color that the knife was silver, which could have been a deadly injury if I had been a normal shifter. Being a Keeper, I lacked the vulnerability to silver. I tuned to find Ginsu with his hand on the blade. He let go of the knife as I turned to face him, the look of certainty draining from his face. I raised my blade to his neck. He didn't move back, but raised his head away from it.

I could feel it scratch him. "You can go sit down with Skinny Pete or you can die."

"Sure, Obie," he said, backing slowly, sheepishly scratching his neck. "Hey, you can't blame a fella for trying, right?"

"Sit," I commanded, pointing to the bar with my blade. "Hob, give me a hand with this."

He inspected the blade running through my back. He opened his bag and pulled out a hockey puck–sized piece of dust. He had pressed the dust with a binder into a mold. It was much easier to use these pucks over powder that could spill, or get blown away. Hob prepared to use magic to remove it.

"Just yank it," I said.

He put the dust puck back in his bag. Placing one hand on my back for support, with the other he took the handle of the knife, giving it a quick tug. I cringed at the feeling of the metal sliding out of my body. I would need a couple minutes to recover. Not a huge deal with three people backing me up.

"I don't want no trouble," the prospect said.

"You can drop the kutte and go, or you can stay and take your chances," I said.

It was a little dramatic, I'll admit, but it would be a good indication of how dedicated he was to the club.

He peeled off the kutte like it was made of lava before throwing it on the floor. He moved toward the door slowly, at first, giving us a wide berth. When he got halfway there, he broke into a run. He disappeared through the door never to be seen again.

"Where's the princess?" I asked, turning back to the bikers at the bar.

"In the conference room," Skinny Pete said. "But you don't wanna go back there."

"Why's that?" I asked.

Ginsu smiled. "Big Ticket's watching her."

"Yeah, yeah." I waved a hand dismissively in his direction as I walked toward the door leading to the princess. "Keep an eye on them, I'll be right back."

I stepped through the door into the back hallway. The kitchen was to my right with the conference room the first door on my left. I caught the smell of meat coming from the kitchen. I stuck my head in and saw a patch I didn't recognize. A werewolf with headphones, bobbing his head to some heavy metal. He had an apron tied around his waist that was smeared with a red sauce. He wore a red shirt under his kutte and his hair was trimmed into a mohawk. This was the guy that hurt Livy. If he knew I was there, he didn't turn around. Instead he put a hand on the door of a large, restaurant-style smoker normally reserved for whole pigs, goats, and the occasional slab of beef. He opened the door revealing an elf. I didn't know her. That didn't mean much, her skin had darkened and distorted from the cooking. She had been gutted with her arms and legs tied close to her body. The cook dabbed a sauce mop in a bucket. He basted the elf, dabbing the red liquid around her body. He put the mop down in the bucket and reached in the smoker to pull off a bit of meat. He blew on it a few times to cool it off before putting it in his mouth and closing the door.

"It's coming along real nice," he said, becoming aware someone was standing behind him. He wiped his hands on the apron and turned around. "When everyone gets back tonight—"

He stopped short when he saw I wasn't there to check on dinner. He pulled the headphones down around his neck.

"Earlier today you hurt a friend of mine," I said.

He smirked. "You come here to rough me up or somethin'?"

"Or something," I said, stabbing my blade into his belly.

He grunted and grabbed the blade. I twisted it and drew it back quickly. I pushed him. He fell back, leaning against the smoker and holding his stomach. I gave him a slash above his left knee, severing his leg. He screamed and fell to the floor, catching himself with his hands. He looked up as I brought the blade down on his neck. His body fell to the floor and his head rolled out in the hallway. I wiped my blade off on his clothes before going after his head. Kicking it back into the kitchen, I closed the door. I moved back down the hallway to the door of the conference room. I waited outside the door and listened.

"This time I'm going to get what I want. I'm not putting up with any more of your tricks," Big Ticket said.

I took a deep breath, testing how my injury had come along. I was almost healed; now I just had a dull ache in my lower back. I paused, not because I was injured, but because I really didn't want to have a go at B.T. one on one, even with my new blade. It wasn't that I was afraid to fight him, or that I thought I would lose, so much as that I considered him a friend. I don't like slicing up my friends. I could get Holt, but that would leave Hob and Martina outnumbered. I would have to do this alone. I could imagine myself charging in and getting drop kicked right back into the hallway. Big Ticket was capable in that way. I decided to open the door and stay in the hall, so I wasn't taken by surprise.

"Do you have," Big Ticket said, as I turned the handle and pushed the door open. "Any fours?"

The door swung wide, revealing B.T. and Isabelle sitting at the table opposite each other, with cards in their hands. There was a large pile of snacks on the table. Open bags of chips and candy spilled out onto the table for easy access.

"Obie," Isabelle shouted when she saw me.

I stepped into the room. "I have to take—"

"Hold on a second," Big Ticket said, holding up a finger. "Fours," he said turning back to Isabelle.

She looked down at her cards and then back up at him with a grin from ear to ear. "Go fish."

He took a card from the deck, added it to his hand, and placed his cards on the table before turning back to me. "Nice blade. Is that why you went M.I.A.?"

I looked down at the blade and turned it to the side, so he could see it. "Yeah, it's a little something from Thera that kept me . . . busy."

"I didn't expect to see you here," B.T. said.

"I came for Isabelle."

"And that scream a minute ago means my brothers are dead?" he asked.

"Two of the new guys," I said. "The first one attacked me. The second almost killed Livy, so he had it coming."

Big Ticket nodded. "Okay. What about the rest of us? Do we have it coming, too?"

"Ginsu put a knife through my back and I didn't hurt him so I'm showing restraint. I've got Holt, Martina, and Hob keeping an eye on them in the bar," I said. "We're putting an end to this war and getting things back to normal. We could really use you on our side."

"You want me to betray my club?" he asked, squinting suspiciously at me.

"Not at all. I want you to stay true to your club," I said. "From what I hear the club abandoned Hank and left Lugnut in jail . . . sounds like the club isn't taking care of its members."

"I don't like leaving Lugnut in jail, but that's what the club decided to do," B.T. said. "And Hank, there's no reason to think he would survive."

I grinned. "I wouldn't be so sure. I paid a visit to the hospital earlier today. Hank was in bad shape, I'll admit, but I was able to get the silver out."

This got his interest. His ears, that had been droopy, perked up a little. "He's okay?"

"He's still unconscious, but I think he'll be all right," I said.

"So, you think he'll be all right, but he could be too far gone to recover," he said.

Isabelle picked up a handful of gummy bears from the table as she quietly watched the exchange.

I leaned against the door frame and shrugged. "Don't be so negative. Everybody looks up to you. I need you on my side."

"You don't have a side," Big Ticket said. "The problems between us and the elves are between us. It's none of your concern, really."

"That may have been true before someone started bringing demon armies through to attack the elves," I said. "That's not good for anyone."

B.T. gave Isabelle a sideways glance and I knew what he was thinking, but not saying. He was thinking that demons eating elves worked out for the Tortured Occult. With the war going on, he was right. The most likely suspect was someone in the T.O. I didn't really think any of them was doing it though. Let's just say, they lacked interest in magic. The Tortured Occult wasn't the kind of group that would outsource its dirty work either.

Big Ticket leaned back in his chair. "You busted in here with your fancy knife to get Isabelle, so go ahead."

"Come on," I sighed. "I'm not gonna cut you up."

"You don't have a choice," Big Ticket said. "If Hank was awake, it might be different, but as it stands, you want Isabelle and I can't let you take her."

I scratched my chin. "How about this . . . I'll give you that fight you've been asking for. If I win, you hand over Isabelle and help us get rid of Chisel."

"And if you don't win?" he asked.

"Then I lose."

It was a vague answer to be sure. The worst-case scenario was that I lost the fight. If I did, Holt, Martina, and Hob would be right there to take care of B.T. Aside from taking the time for the fight, there wasn't really a downside to it.

"In the circle?" he asked.

"Yeah," I said. "No weapons, standard rules."

B.T. nodded. "All right, you got a deal."

The princess followed us out to the bar where Holt and Martina stood guard over the members of the Tortured Occult we had rounded up.

"We're taking this party outside," I said, walking to the door and holding it open for everyone.

Big Ticket walked through first, followed by the rest of the T.O., Martina, and Hob. Holt was last and stopped beside me before going outside.

"What's happening here?" Holt asked.

"B.T. and I are going into the circle," I answered. "If I win, he's going to help us out."

"And what happens if you don't win?" Holt asked.

I shrugged. "Tell Martina to shoot him first."

Holt put his hands on his hips and shook his head. "This is crazy. There has to be a better option."

"Well, we could kill 'em all," I offered.

He looked over at Big Ticket who was stretching his neck and back, getting loosened up for the fight. The bikers took a seat on a picnic table.

"Okay, good luck," he said. "And, Obie?"

"Yeah?"

"For the Mother's sake, bob and weave," he said. "That guy's no joke."

I walked over to a different picnic table with Holt. "Watch this stuff for me," I said putting my phone on the table.

I stabbed my blade into the wood, so it was standing on its own, and moved to the edge of the circle across from Big Ticket. "You ready?"

Big Ticket nodded and motioned toward the circle with his hand in a kind of half-salute, half-invitation. As if on cue, we both charged, colliding in the center. Our claws dug into the ground as we grappled on our feet, struggling to gain the advantage, neither one claiming any territory. I sank my claws into the tender flesh of his lower back. My fingers broke the skin. He screamed as his leg buckled. He pushed me back and tried to bite my neck, but I moved an arm in the way.

I clenched my jaw from the pain of his teeth sinking into my forearm and landed two elbow strikes into the side of his head before he brought his arm up to block. He countered with a few shots to my ribs that lifted me off my feet and made a popping sound that sent pain shooting through my side. I pushed him back to get some space and spun, delivering a tail whip that struck his face. I used the momentum from the spin to deliver a right cross that I was sure would put him back on his heels. He must have known it was coming; at the last second he dropped his head. Instead of landing in his face, my fist contacted with the front of his skull. Pain shot through my hand and I was sure it was broken as well. We paused for a second, I gave my hand a little shake and he did the same with his head. With less than a minute in, I had two broken bones and, aside from being a little dazed, it didn't appear B.T. was slowing down. It was becoming a real possibility that I wasn't going to win this fight if I continued breaking bones. I needed to get myself a little time to heal.

Big Ticket came in swinging his claws. I dodged the first few, but the pain in my side slowed me down. When it was clear I wasn't going to dodge the next one, I ducked, putting my arms around my head to protect myself. I could feel my back being torn to shreds from his claws. I charged in and wrapped my arms around his waist, lifting him off the ground. I could have thrown him out of the circle, but that was winning on a technicality. I respected B.T. too much to do that to him, so I slammed him on the ground instead. The back of his head hit the ground with a *thump*. He wasn't knocked unconscious from the impact, but he clearly was going to need a minute to recover.

I took a step back and put a hand on my ribs. I could feel the warm tingling as they healed. The pain eased. I was about to go over and stomp Big Ticket's head into the ground until I had officially won the fight when Holt entered the circle.

"Two on one?" Big Ticket asked, his eyes hazy.

Holt held my phone out to me. "You need to take this. It's Doc Lin. She says she's been calling you."

"I'm kind of in the middle of something."

"It's Hank," Holt said. "He's awake."

CHAPTER 25

I looked at Big Ticket, still laying on his back. Our eyes met, and I asked, "We done?"

"For now," he said, holding out a hand.

I pulled him to his feet. I took the phone from Holt and stepped away from everyone for some privacy.

"This is Obie," I said into the phone.

"He's awake," Doc Lin said. "He woke up about twenty minutes ago."

"How is he?"

"Weak, grumpy, and refusing treatment," she answered. "Someone needs to come get him."

"I'll be there soon," I said.

I hung up and walked back to the group. "Hank's awake. We need to go get him. It's decision time. Are you going to support Hank or Chisel?"

"We're going to need a minute," Skinny Pete said. "As a club."

I nodded. "No problem."

The bikers huddled and we moved away to respect their privacy.

"Do you think it is wise to let them speak alone?" Hob asked.

I grabbed my blade out of the picnic table. "I think it will be fine. If they want to try something, we still have them outnumbered and outgunned."

After speaking for a few minutes, Ginsu looked over and said, "Martina, come talk to us a sec."

Martina, with her shotgun, joined the conversation. They talked for a few minutes more before breaking the huddle.

"We're in," Skinny Pete said. "But I don't know how we're going to pull this off. Chisel has one of the new guys watching the hospital. There's no way we are going to get him out of there without being seen. He probably already saw you the other day and told Chisel something's up."

I smiled. "Don't be so paranoid. The new members probably wouldn't recognize us. Besides, we have Hob," I said, putting a hand on Hob's shoulder for emphasis. "When we get to the hospital, let's do a lap around the parking lot and find this lookout. We'll figure out a plan from there."

"If you say so," he mumbled. "Whatever voodoo he's going to do, he needs to do it fast. We're supposed to be bringing Isabelle up to meet Chisel. He called right before you showed up. I'm not sure what he has planned."

"One of you tell him there was a problem with the van to give us a little time."

"I'll do it," Big Ticket said.

B.T. made the call. Big Ticket and Ginsu rode their motorcycles while Skinny Pete drove the van. The rest of us piled in the back for the trip to the hospital. I didn't blame them for having doubts; anyone in their position would. Going against Chisel was a high stakes gamble. I had complete faith in Hob's abilities and he had enough dust on hand to work some serious magic. Once they saw what he could do, they wouldn't be concerned anymore.

We drove in silence and I found my thoughts drifting to my own doubts. Doc Lin had said Hank was weak. The last time I saw him he looked close to death. I wasn't sure how the club would feel if they saw him lying in the hospital bed the way Holt and I had. His condition didn't inspire confidence. I wasn't even sure he would be strong enough to assert his authority if it came down to it. We could cross that bridge when we got to it. For now, we just needed to get Hank and get him to where the T.O. was meeting. The plan was to get Hank and catch them by surprise. It's the only way we could get him in a position to talk to the club without Chisel interfering. I didn't believe Chisel would risk losing control of the club under any circumstances, even if it meant murdering club members.

Big Ticket and Ginsu pulled into a shopping center close to the hospital. Their bikes would be too high profile for what we were going for. We pulled into the hospital parking lot and Skinny Pete did a lap while we scanned the cars for the lookout. We spotted him parked up front. I recognized him right way; one of the Dogs that was at the clubhouse when Ginsu told his tree frog joke. I was afraid he was going to spot us, but his attention was focused on his phone instead of anything going on outside of the car he was in.

"Drive to the back on the lot," I said, pulling my phone out of my pocket. "I'll give Doc Lin a call."

I found her number in my contacts and called. She picked up on the second ring. "We're here. Is he ready?"

"Thank God," she said. "I'll have him right out."

We waited for a few minutes before Doc Lin came out the front of the hospital, rolling Hank in a wheelchair.

"Let's go," I said, turning to look at Hob. "Can you keep an eye on the lookout and if he spots us, break his phone?"

"*Ja*," Hob said, retrieving one of the pucks from the box. "It will not be a problem."

Skinny Pete drove the van around, pulling up in front of Hank. I got out of the passenger seat and held the door open for him. Hank looked like hell; his face was still sunken in and his color was off. He was wearing scrubs Doc Lin must have given him, and held a clear plastic bag with his belongings in it. He still looked better than he did when I saw him in the hospital bed.

"Good to see you awake," I said.

He gave me an angry-looking side-eye. I didn't know how much of it was him being upset with me, versus recovering from almost dying and still being on the mend. He put his hands on the arms of the wheelchair and grunted as he pushed himself into a standing position. He climbed into the passenger seat of the van and dropped the bag onto the floorboard. I closed the door.

"Really appreciate it," I said to Doc Lin.

She rolled the wheelchair out of the way and stepped closer to me. "I have some more questions that I want to have answered."

"After I get this sorted, I'll give you a call."

I climbed into the back and closed the door. Hob was holding the dust puck in his hand and staring out the tinted back windows. The puck was slowly dissolving into smoke as he concentrated, consuming the latent power in it. I noticed some powder falling from the puck unconsumed onto the leg of his pants. It must be whatever he used to bind the dust together into shape. I looked through the window to where the lookout was sitting in his car. He was fiddling with his phone in a way that told me he was having trouble with it.

Hob tossed what was left of the puck back in the box. "He will not be making any calls."

"Shouldn't we take care of him?" Holt asked. "What if he goes inside and makes a call? Just magic him to death."

"A dead body in the parking lot will draw too much attention," Hank said. "Pull out and see if he follows. If he does, we can take care of him somewhere more private."

"And if he doesn't?" I asked.

Hank looked back at us. "Then we'll have to draw some attention."

Hank's voice was gruffer that usual and he sounded tired, but I was glad to see he was thinking clearly and in the mood to take charge. Both would be critical if he was going to win confidence from the club. Skinny Pete pulled out of the hospital and we watched to see how the lookout would react. Sure enough, he pulled out behind us, keeping what he thought was a safe distance. The Tortured Occult was meeting in the Chattahoochee National Forest, inside the Queen's territory. It was over an hour drive. At some point along the way we had to take care of our tail. We were followed deep into the mountains where we came to an area secluded enough to deal with him. We still hadn't talked about how we were going to handle our tail.

"Do we have a plan for our shadow?" I asked.

"Hob, do you have enough dust to take care of him quickly?" Hank asked.

Hob lifted the bag of dust. "*Ja*, there is plenty."

"Pull over up here by the cliff," Hank said. "Hob, when he comes around the corner take care of him."

"When you say, 'take care of him,' how do you mean?" Hob asked.

"Just get rid of him quickly and don't leave a mess to draw attention," Hank answered.

I knew the cliff he was talking about. It was the largest pull-off on the winding mountain road between Dahlonega and Suches. A rock face fifty or sixty feet long and forty feet high bordered the right side of the road. It was one of the only places in the area where there was graffiti. Sometimes people used the rockface to climb or rappel, but when we got there it was empty. The other side of the road had a railing to keep cars from plummeting off the mountain side. I heard a rumor that a woman was driving with her granddaughter when she saw a black bear in the pull-off. She wanted to get a picture of it with her daughter so she put some honey on the girl's hand to draw the bear close. The bear ended up taking the girl's arm off. I understand people are going to do stupid things from time to time; I would just prefer innocent people not get hurt by it. Skinny Pete pulled the van over and put it in park. Hob grabbed a few pucks in each hand and jumped out of the back of the van.

A few seconds later the car came around the bend. Hob raised his left hand and the pucks began to disintegrate. The car lifted off the road, tires screamed and then were quiet as they lost their connection with the pavement. The car drifted through the air toward the railing. The biker behind the wheel saw what was coming and tried to open the door. It wouldn't budge. He became more frantic as the car floated over the railing. The biker slammed his body into the driver's door, trying in vain to force it open. As the car drifted out into the open air, the biker changed tactics and kicked the window. It took him a few kicks to clear the window from the passenger side. He stuck his head out and looked down into the landscape dropping away below him. Hob threw the pucks in his right hand. They ignited in midair. A massive fireball slammed into the side of the car with enough force to crush it. The car burned and spun from the impact as it dropped out of view.

For a second there was silence, then the car crashed far below. I jumped out of the van and jogged over to the railing. The only sign of the car was a smoke trail working its way up through the trees around 150 feet below. Hob wiped some sweat from his forehead with his shirtsleeve. It was one of the most impressive displays of magic I had ever seen, and it clearly took some serious effort on his part to pull it off.

I jogged back to the van. "I thought you said it was better to be more subtle with magic?"

"*Ja*, it is," Hob said. "But we are in a hurry *und* this is more fun."

We climbed back into the van and continued on to meet the Tortured Occult.

CHAPTER 26

During the drive, Skinny Pete filled Hank in about what he had missed while he was in the hospital. Hank took particular interest in why no one had bailed Lugnut out of jail or gone through the normal channels to get him a lawyer. Hank's other son, Torch, had disappeared. No one knew what had happened to him, but it was assumed he went into hiding.

"We're getting close," Skinny Pete said.

I stuck my head between the seats. "When we get there, position the van so the back doors are facing everyone. I don't want anyone getting hung up trying to go out one door or running around the van. Hank, you should probably climb in the back with the rest of us."

Hank undid his seatbelt. He grabbed the bag at his feet and moved between the seats to the back of the van. He sat down behind Skinny Pete with Hob in the middle and Holt by the door. I moved to the back across from Holt with Martina between Isabelle and me.

"How long till we get there?" I asked.

"A few minutes, just around the corner up here," Skinny Pete said.

"Let's get ready," I said, sitting down.

We all made the change to krasis. When we had finished, Isabelle sat wide-eyed and quiet.

"What's the matter?" I asked.

"I knew you could do that, but I had never seen it before," she answered.

"Really? Not even at the clubhouse?" I asked. "I thought for sure you would have."

She shook her head. "This is my first time out of the Nation. I've never been around shifters before."

"And? What do you think?" Martina asked.

"Some of you seem nice," Isabelle said. "Some not so nice."

Martina nodded in agreement. "Are we what you expected?"

"Not really. Mother says that shifters are savages and that Hank is the biggest savage of them all," she said.

"Hank's a good man," I said.

Her face scrunched up as she replied. "Mother says there's no such thing."

"You got to spend some time with us, what do you say?" Holt asked.

"I don't know," she said. "Can I ask you a question?"

I nodded. "Sure."

"Does it hurt? When you do that?" she asked, rolling her index fingers around each other.

"I can't speak for anyone else," I said, "but for me the first time was the worst pain I have ever experienced. It was like getting ripped apart and someone used salt to glue you back together with everything out of place. That was over two hundred years ago now. It hurt a little less every time and now I actually like it. It feels like a good stretch to me. It might be a different experience, though, since I was born human."

"That's pretty much the way it was for me," Hank said. "For those of us born into it, the first change happens around puberty and it's hell, but it gets better with time."

"I have another question," Isabelle said.

"Shoot," I said, no elf pun intended.

Isabelle looked up into my eyes. "Are you going to hurt my mother?"

I try not to lie, if I can help it, especially to kids, so this was a difficult answer. "I don't want to hurt her, but she is hurting a lot of other people right now and we have to stop her. If I can stop her without hurting her, I will."

I could see the answer didn't reassure her, but it's all I had. No one else in the van could step up with a more comforting answer. Isabelle turned her head toward the front of the van. She couldn't see out any windows from where she was sitting, but I think it was only important that she was looking away from us. I looked at Martina and she shrugged; she didn't have a better answer than I did.

After a minute Isabelle put her arms on her knees and put her head down to hide her face.

"All right, let's get our plan straight," I said.

Hank let out a heavy sigh. "Ginsu and Big Ticket will pull in with the club. They can get some of our people out of the way. Skinny Pete will get us into position. Y'all'll rush out and catch them by surprise. We need everybody to stay put long enough for me to get out of the van and sort things out. You shouldn't have to subdue everyone, but keep an eye on the new folks especially. There's a chance it could get a little hairy."

"And if things go sideways?" I asked. "What do we do then?"

"Do what you have to, and we'll figure it out later," Hank said.

It surprised me to hear him say that. I would have expected him to advise us against hurting the club if possible. Then again, the club hadn't exactly been living up to expectations lately.

"We're here," Skinny Pete said.

We had Isabelle hide in the footwell of the passenger seat. She could stay there unseen. I debated having Holt or Martina stay in the van with her, but I decided we needed everyone to keep things from getting out of hand. I pulled my blade and put a hand on the door handle as Skinny Pete circled around to get in position. I looked back at everyone as the van stopped. The group exchanged nods, we pushed the doors open, and rushed out.

I was out of the van first with Martina right behind me. Big Ticket grabbed Cotton and Fisheye and backed them away, keeping them out of the conflict. The startled expressions of the rest of the bikers as we poured out of the van confirmed we had caught them by surprise. The first biker I came to had his back to me. He spun around to see what the commotion was. I didn't have time to explain myself, so I crouched, and body-checked him over his motorcycle. The patch next to him reached for a knife he had strapped to his leg. I stepped forward with my right and pivoted, sending my blade up to his throat, stopping short of a fatal blow. I shook my head to impress upon him the urgency that he stayed still. He raised his chin away from the blade and I saw a trickle of blood roll down his neck. I didn't mean to cut him, but the blade and I were still new to each other and I lacked finesse. Either way, the message was sent.

A biker in the back starting drawing a pistol from under his kutte. Ginsu grabbed his arm to stop him. Martina stepped up beside me, firing her shotgun. Both of them were hit and fell to the ground.

I looked over at Hob, standing on the other side of Martina. He was holding his hands up, reminiscent of a boxing stance. His hands were on fire. I'm not ashamed to say it, but Hob scared me a little. With enough dust that guy could probably blow up the world.

Chisel was in the center of the group and didn't look happy to see us. "What the hell is this?" he screamed.

Hank climbed out of the van slowly, grunting as he stepped gingerly to the ground. He looked much better in krasis than he did in human form. His fur covered his pale complexion. He looked a little thinner than normal and had droopy eyes, other than that, he looked all right. He had put his kutte on over the scrubs. The scrubs were stretched to their limit, barely able to accommodate the additional fur and bulk that came with krasis. It was a strange sight, but his kutte was a symbol of his authority—it didn't matter what he wore under it.

To say the situation was tense would be an understatement. When Hank stepped out of the van, his presence seemed to chill the vibe, if only a little. The original members of the Tortured Occult swapped glances as if they were children busted by a parent. The newer members seemed more confused than anything.

Hank put his hands on his hips, looking around the group. "Somebody want to tell me what's going on?"

"I'm glad you're back on your feet," Chisel said. "But you're not up to this. I got it under control, so why don't you go back to the clubhouse and I'll catch you up when we're done here."

"You're going to catch me up on how I have one son missing and another in jail you aren't helping?" Hank asked. "Or how when I got shot up you left me to die, so you could take over the club?"

Chisel shrugged. "It's complicated."

Hank took a step forward. "It's not complicated at all. Lugnut and Torch are part of this club, so besides being my sons, they're also your brothers. You turned your back on them. If we aren't looking out for each other, then none of this means anything. I'm calling a meeting. Everybody get to the clubhouse. We're going to sort this shit out."

Chisel took a step up to Hank. "We're in the middle of something. You need to go, and I'll deal with you when we get back."

Hank tapped a finger on the President patch sewn to the front of his kutte. "I give the orders in this club.

"You *did* give the orders," Chisel said putting a thumb under the President patch on his kutte and pushing it forward. "Not anymore."

Hank looked down at the patch and pulled a loose thread from it. He held it up. "Let's let the club decide. Most of you know me and how I lead. From what I hear, there's been nothing but trouble under Chisel's leadership. Not surprising, since he's new enough to still have loose threads on his patch."

"They're not going to decide." Chisel sneered. "This is my club now. They do what I tell 'em to do."

"The club has always been bigger than one person. You should of learned that by now," Hank said, stepping back. "Martina."

On cue, Martina fired her shotgun into Chisel's chest. He collapsed but he wasn't dead. His chest rose and fell with labored breathing.

"Everyone here has a choice," Hank said. "You can drop your kuttes and you can go, or you can head back to the clubhouse and we can sort this thing out. If you go, I don't want to see you around anymore. Otherwise, mandatory meeting now."

Three of the new members took off their leather vests, dropped them on the ground, and picked up their friend that had been shot. Stopping only long enough to remove his kutte and add it to the pile. They got on their bikes and drove away.

"Do you think it was smart to let them go?" Cotton asked.

Hank avoided the question completely. "Let's check out Ginsu," he said.

He was still alive and writhing in pain on the ground, which I didn't expect, knowing that the shotgun was loaded with silver.

"Lay still," I said.

He hadn't taken the brunt of the blast the way Chisel had. I put my blade back in its sheath and ripped his shirt open, exposing his injuries. I could see numerous entry points where the coins had slammed into his body.

"Turns out, coins aren't a very good shotgun load," Martina said, walking up behind me and eyeballing the injuries. "They don't penetrate deep enough to kill, at least not quickly, so they hurt like hell."

"What the hell did you shoot me for?" Ginsu groaned.

"Friendly fire," Martina answered.

"Next time I think about helpin' somebody, remind me not to," he said.

Martina shrugged. "Why don't you grow a pair and stop whining."

"He needs a doctor," I said.

"What now?" Fisheye asked.

"We get Ginsu some help, then figure out a plan of attack for the Queen," Hank answered.

"She's on the way now," Cotton said. "Chisel set this meeting to discuss terms for Isabelle's return. We could just put an end to all this now."

"No," Hank replied. "We're likely to get attacked by demons again or the Queen will just shoot us up as soon as she sees us."

"What about him?" Cotton asked, motioning toward Chisel.

"He went to a lotta trouble to set a meeting with the Queen. I'd hate for him to miss it. Let's leave him here."

"I know a doctor we can go to," I said.

"All right. Load Ginsu in the van and grab the bikes. We'll follow you," Hank said.

Ginsu was loaded in the back of the van with Isabelle and Hob. Martina and Skinny Pete jumped on the two open bikes.

"You're driving the van," I said to Holt.

I got in the back with Ginsu, pulled out my phone, and dialed. The phone rang a few times before a woman answered.

"Hey, Doc, it's Obie. If you still want to learn more, I need your help."

CHAPTER 27

Martina was right that the coins hadn't penetrated deeply. Ginsu's injuries didn't appear life threatening in the short term, but I kept a close eye on him just the same. We made it back to the clubhouse, and pulled Ginsu out of the van. Doc Lin pulled in. Her Mercedes, clean and freshly waxed, looked out of place, crawling its way up the dirt road surrounded by the rusted and broken vehicles in the junkyard. By the time she made it to the clubhouse, everyone else had gone inside, carrying Ginsu with them. She parked beside the van, popped the trunk, and got out.

"Where is he?" she asked.

I jabbed a thumb at the door. "They just took him inside."

"I've got a box of supplies in the back," she said. "Can you grab it please?"

I went to the back of the car and pulled out a box with all kinds of medical equipment in it. Some I recognized; most I didn't.

"I'll show you in," I said, holding the box in one hand and closing the trunk with the other.

She followed me to the door where I stopped. She hadn't officially been introduced to the world of ultranaturals. It could be rough the first time. I felt a warning was in order.

"Before we go in, you should know this is a safe place for them. They don't keep up their disguises inside and when I get in there, I am going to change as well," I said. "There aren't a lot of humans that come in here, so when we go in you need to take charge. Don't get hung up on appearances. You're here to do a job and they're just people, when it comes down to it. That being said, they can be a rough bunch and if you show fear or weakness, they're going to notice."

"Would they hurt me?" she asked.

"No," I said. "They would think you were weak, and they wouldn't respect you. If you want to learn more about this world, your best bet is to get on their good side."

Her face scrunched, and she walked past me with stubborn determination. I followed her into the changing room and set the box of equipment on a bench, adjusted my clothing, and made the change to krasis. I became aware that she had moved a couple steps back.

"Are you some kinda ferret?" she asked.

I sighed. "Otter."

"I have so many questions."

"I'll have to answer them later," I said, picking up the box. "You have a life to save, Doctor."

I retrieved the box, pushed the door to the bar open, and held it for her and she walked though.

"Where the hell's the prospect?" Skinny Pete said as we walked through the door. "He should be doing this, not me."

The bodies had been cleaned up, but the blood remained. Skinny Pete was standing by the blood pool in front of the bar with a mop and bucket. He sloshed the mop up and down in the soapy water. Isabelle was sitting at the bar with Holt. Fisheye was behind the bar, putting a glass of something in front of her. The rest of the T.O. were scattered around the room. Everyone stopped what they were doing to stare at Doc Lin and me. She looked around the room, from the bikers staring at her, to the blood pools, to Isabelle, to me, and back to the blood pools. I was more than a little worried she wasn't going to be able to handle it. It was a lot to take in all at once. I was about to lean in to quietly ask if she was all right when she spoke up.

"Well?" she commanded, putting her fists on her hips in a Supergirl-esque pose. "I didn't come here to get stared at. Where the hell is he?"

Everyone turned back to what they were doing. Smirks and chuckles ran through the room. Fisheye dropped a straw into Isabelle's drink and walked from behind the bar.

"He's back here," he said, holding the door to the back open for us. "I'll show you."

We followed him to the back hallway. The door to the kitchen was open and I glanced in as we walked by. I spotted the feet of the shifter I had killed on our raid sticking out from around the corner. The oven had been closed; no doubt the elf was still inside. I don't think Doc Lin noticed; or if she did, she didn't say anything.

She looked back at me with a questioning glance. I gave her a smile and a thumbs-up. We followed Fisheye past the conference room to a bedroom in the back. Ginsu was laid out on the bed with Hank sitting beside him in a chair. Hank stood when we came in and moved the chair out of the way.

"He passed out a few minutes ago," Hank said. "Probably a kindness for the doctor, knowing Ginsu."

Doc Lin retrieved a pair of scissors and cut Ginsu's shirt open to inspect the wounds. He promptly woke up and looked around the room through hazy eyes.

"Who the hell is this?" he mumbled.

"She's a doctor," Hank said. "She's going to fix you up."

Ginsu looked at her and gave the air a couple sniffs. "She's human."

"I am," Doc Lin said.

Ginsu laid his head back on the bed. "Tell me, doc, you a Chink?"

"I'm Chinese-American," she said.

"Good. If I'm stuck with a human doctor, Chinks are the best."

"I'll need some warm water, towels, and an extra pair of hands," she said. "Obie, can you move the chair over here and put my tools on it, please?"

I did as she asked. Hank and Fisheye exchanged a couple of nods, working out that Fisheye would help her with what she needed. Fisheye left the room to get the supplies she asked for.

Hank stepped up to me and whispered, "I need to talk to you."

No more putting it off, I guess. I wasn't looking forward to this conversation, but it would be good to get everything out in the open. I followed him into the conference room. I closed the door behind me. I was just opening my mouth to start my apology when Hank interrupted me.

"We need to come up with a plan for how to handle the Queen," he said. "I'm about to have to tell my plan to the club when we meet in a few minutes. That means I need to have one."

"What about Chisel's plan?" I asked. "Use some bait to lure her out and take care of her?"

Hank scratched his chin. "It's not very original."

"Doesn't have to be original, if it'll work," I said.

"So, we lure the Queen out, ambush, and kill her. Simple, to the point, I like it," Hank said.

"Almost," I said, rubbing my hands together nervously. "The thing is, we can't kill her."

He stared at me blankly before his face contorted with anger. "Maybe you can't kill her, considering how close you are, but I can."

"What's that supposed to mean?"

"It means you turned into the Queen's lapdog," Hank said.

I crossed my arms. "You know that's not true."

"Seems that way," he said. "If it's not true, then why'd I have to hear from the Queen that she had my father killed, right before she tried to kill me, too?"

"I was trying to avoid, well, all this," I said, waving my arms around at everything and nothing. "The confrontation, hurt feelings, not to mention war . . . What did you want me to do?"

"Tell me the truth, maybe? We're supposed to be friends," Hank said.

"If I told you the Queen had your father killed right there on the bridge, you would have killed all the elves there, they would have killed you, or somewhere in between. They brought silver with them. They could have killed the whole T.O. right there," I said. "So, I thought it would best to wait until things calmed down before I told you. That's all."

He raised a clawed hand, stabbing an index finger into my chest emphasizing each word as he spoke. "It's. Not. Your. Decision. To. Make."

Each poke of his finger left a sharp pain in my chest. I looked down to see small dabs of blood soaking into my shirt. I'm sure he didn't mean to make me bleed; sometimes when you're pointy on the ends, stuff like that happens. Regardless of that understanding, when someone makes me bleed, it gets me a little worked up.

"It's not a chance I could take," I said, giving him a hard shove.

He took a step back. His face contorted in anger, baring his teeth, and he charged. He picked me up with his momentum and slammed me into the wall. The whole building seemed to shake with the impact and I yelped as the air was pushed from my lungs.

He definitely didn't have his usual level of strength, being that he was still healing from his injuries. I was glad about that or I might have been hurt. I managed to catch my breath, even with Hank grinding me into the wall with all his might. In his condition, I was pretty sure I could overpower him. I didn't want to. He needed to get some frustration out—and honestly, I had it coming. I braced myself. Not pushing him off, but not letting him pancake me against the wall, either. I could see the realization dawning that he really wasn't crushing me the way he had intended. Hank spun and threw me against the far wall.

I hit hard, but didn't react, opting instead to lean casually against the wall. "Feel better?"

"A little," he said. "You should have told me."

I nodded. "I had worked with Otis for years and we were close, but you're my best friend. I couldn't lose you both on the same night. I should have told you, I meant to, I wanted to, but I just didn't and I'm sorry."

The door to the conference room burst open. I looked over to see Fisheye, Cotton, and Big Ticket standing in the doorway. They must have heard the commotion and come to help. We looked at each other for a few seconds.

Hank asked, "You guys need something?"

"We heard, uh . . ." Cotton said, a little confused. "Just seeing when you're going to be ready for the meeting. Everybody's anxious to hear what you have to say."

"Just a few minutes," Hank answered. "Just wrapping things up here."

They clearly didn't understand, but backed out of the room and closed the door.

Once the sound of their footsteps had retreated down the hall, Hank asked, "So why can't we kill the Queen?"

"Because Isabelle loves her. She can't stay in power, that's clear, but who's going to replace her?" I said. "Isabelle hasn't been corrupted yet. We've got a shot at real lasting peace with her in charge. If we kill her mother, she'll hold it against us and eventually it will come back to haunt us. Maybe not right away, but one day."

Hank nodded. "You're probably right, but that's just not an option. She killed Razor and she shot up our bikes. I can't forgive that. Even if I could, the club won't. There's no getting around it."

"Then when it comes back to bite us, we'll handle it together."

"So, we agree then?" Hank asked. "We use Isabelle as bait, draw out the Queen and kill her?"

"That's the plan," I said. "Except with one correction. We use bait, but not Isabelle."

CHAPTER 28

"Hello?" I said, knocking on the door as I swung it open. "Anybody home?"

While I was sure it would be fine to just walk in, it was an orc's home, and I couldn't help but think of that large, red scimitar Yarwor had and the damage he could do with it. He came from the bedroom, with the scimitar in hand. Isabelle ran past me into the house and he knelt to give her a hug. Holt and I went in, and I closed the door behind us.

"Thank you for bringing her back," Yarwor said.

"How's Livy?

Yarwor stood. "She's the bedroom. I think she's starting to feel better."

I went the bedroom and peered in. She was lying in bed with Harlan sitting at the foot. They were talking. Harlan stood when I walked in.

"Hey, Harlan, I need to talk to you, but I want to check on Livy first, if you can give me a few minutes."

He nodded. "Sure, Obie, no problem. I'll wait outside. Come out whenever you're ready."

Harlan left, and I took his seat at the foot of the bed.

"How you feelin'?" I asked.

"Useless," Livy said. "Everybody's acting like I'm some kind of invalid."

I shook my head. "We're acting like you were attacked by a werewolf, which you were."

"I'm fine." She pouted. "You healed me up. I'm good as new."

"Then why are you still in bed?" I asked.

She wagged a finger in the direction of the door. "That orc won't let me up!"

"He's just lookin' after you," I said.

"Well, he can stop. I'm fine," she said, throwing off the covers and scooching over to the side of the bed. "I'll show you."

I held my hand out and she took it. I helped her to her feet.

She stretched her back. "I've been sittin' too long. I get stiff if I don't move around a little."

"I'm glad to hear you say that," I said. "I was hoping I could get you to take Isabelle and Yarwor up to see Walasi while we take care of the Queen. It would be a big help."

She headed for the kitchen, noticeably happier to be on her feet. "If that's what you need me to do, but first I'm going to have some tea."

"It would," I said. "And you're the only one that can do it."

"All right, all right, no one likes a suck up," she said, waving me off.

I followed her into the kitchen. She fetched a teapot and put water in it. I was concerned she would need help but she seemed to be doing just fine. Yarwor, Isabelle, and Holt were sitting at the table to help her if she needed it. I needed to talk to Harlan. Our whole plan relied on his cooperation. I found him outside, sitting on the tailgate of my truck. The weather was starting to cool. I could tell it was going to be a crisp night. I sat down beside him, but didn't say anything. I wanted him to speak first. I wanted to know where his mind was at, what he was thinking. I didn't have to wait long.

"A few months ago, you had the chance to let me run away. I understand why you didn't, but lately I've been thinking about something," he said. "Do you ever wonder what would have happened if you had?"

I paused for a second before shaking my head. "I'm going to be honest with you, I hadn't considered it."

"I think about it a lot." He sighed. "If you hadn't brought me back, there's no telling what I would be doing right now. I could've had a chance at a life. I could've been somebody."

"You are somebody," I said.

"Somebody else then."

AYAL.** 185

"What's wrong with the person you are?" I asked.

Harlan stood and moved over to lean against the side of Holt's car. "I'm sorry I wasn't here when the Tortured Occult came."

"It's probably best you weren't," I said. "They might have killed you."

"I think I would've been all right," he said.

I didn't want to be contrary, but if the T.O. had Isabelle they probably wouldn't have taken him, too; they wouldn't have needed him. He didn't have a gun, claws, or teeth. He was largely defenseless. He was resourceful, though, maybe he would have come up with something. Either way, it was best not to contradict him. I might have been quiet too long.

When he spoke again, he got right to the point. "So, what did you want to talk to me about?"

"The Queen," I said. "Something has to be done."

He stuck his thumbs in his pockets. "That's what I've been saying."

"I don't want to make any assumptions, but there's a plan in the works to get rid of the Queen," I said. "We could use your help."

Harlan looked down at his foot and shuffled it in the gravel. "Get rid of the Queen could mean a couple things. What sort of 'get rid of' are we talking about?"

"The permanent kind," I said.

"You're going to kill the Queen?" he asked.

"Now I know you got a strained relationship with her, to say the least, but if you don't want to—"

"I'll help," he said before I could get my sentence out. "As long as we keep Isabelle safe, then just let me know what you need me to do."

"I wouldn't risk Isabelle," I said. "The plan's pretty simple, use you as bait to draw her into an ambush."

Harlan tilted his head. "You think she'll stick her head out for me?"

"Wouldn't she?"

Harlan shook his head. "She has to think Isabelle will be there or she won't come."

"Do you feel good about taking Isabelle with us?"

"Not even a little," he said.

I ran a hand through my hair. "So, what do we do?"

"We make her think Isabelle will be there." Harlan smiled.

I shifted around on the tailgate. "Right, okay. I'll just have to plan out what I'm going say when I talk to her."

Harlan laughed. "You talk to her? No offence, Obie, but you aren't that good of a liar. I'll set it up. Besides, I don't think she trusts you that much right now."

"Fair enough," I said.

"Who's watching Isabelle while it's going down?" Harlan asked.

"I'm going to have Yarwor take Isabelle and Livy to Walasi. He's an old Keeper in the mountains. If anyone can protect them, he can."

"The mountains inside the Elven Nation?" Harlan asked.

I shrugged. "Technically. But what are the chances the Queen will be looking for Isabelle inside the Nation?"

"It wouldn't surprise me at all," Harlan said.

"It's either that or we can send her away . . . far away," I said.

"Okay, it'll work." Harlan agreed. "What time should I set the meeting for?"

"Tomorrow morning?" I said. "The sooner the better. I don't want it to drag out."

Harlan held out his hand. "Let me use your phone."

"What good's that going to do?" I asked. "You can't get the Queen on the phone."

"*You* can't get the Queen on the phone, maybe, but I can," he said. "Go get Isabelle real quick, we'll need her."

I slapped my phone into his hand and jogged over to the house. I stuck my head in the door and called Isabelle. When we made it back to the cars, Harlan dialed a number and put it on speakerphone. It rang once before it was answered, but no one spoke on the other end of the line.

"Four . . . delta . . . one . . . India . . . hotel . . . five . . . golf . . . three . . . X-Ray," Harlan said into the phone. He hit the mute button. "Stay quiet. I'll let you know if I need you to say something."

I put Isabelle on the tailgate. There was a click on the phone.

"I need to speak to the Queen immediately," Harlan said.

We waited about thirty seconds. I was starting to wonder if it was going to work at all. The phone clicked again.

"I thought you were dead," the Queen said dispassionately. "What happened to Isabelle?"

"I have her here," Harlan said.

Harlan held the phone for Isabelle and gave her a nod.

"Hello, Mother," she said.

"Are you safe?" the Queen asked.

Isabelle answered. "Yes, Obie saved me from the shifters."

"Did he," the Queen stated. "Don't worry, Isabelle. I'm going to come get you."

Isabelle sniffled a little when she said, "Okay, I'm ready to come home."

"Stop sniveling," the Queen scolded. "I expect you to conduct yourself properly, regardless of the situation."

Isabelle looked as if she'd been struck. Her lip quivered, but she didn't make a sound. Harlan motioned for Isabelle to go inside and she didn't hesitate.

"Obie did save us," Harlan said. "When he heard the Tortured Occult had captured us, he busted into the clubhouse and freed us. He killed a few of them in the process."

"Why would he attack his friends to help me?"

I could hear the skepticism in the Queen's voice.

"You said it yourself, he's weak," Harlan said. "He still thinks he can restore the peace and prevent a war."

"He is rather simple," the Queen said. "Steal his car and bring Isabelle back."

"That's going to be tough," Harlan said. "He's got the keys in his pocket and you know he doesn't sleep."

"So, shoot him in the face and take them," the Queen suggested.

"I don't have a gun and Holt is here, too."

"I forgot about the sidekick," the Queen said.

"He's willing to bring us back. Can I have him drop us off at the southern outpost?" Harlan asked. "Or somewhere else in the Nation?"

There was silence on the other end as the Queen contemplated. She said, "Have him drop you at the Wolf Pen Gap store tomorrow at eight in the morning," the Queen said.

The Queen ended the call. Harlan handed the phone back to me.

"That was easy," I said.

Harlan shook his head. "Not as much as you think. Setting it up, yeah, but you can put money down that she's sending people out right now to watch the roads. The store's at a three-way intersection. We don't know which direction she's coming from, or where she'll go after she leaves. If you think the T.O. is going to ride up on their bikes and surprise her . . . It's just not going to happen."

"I agree," I said. "They aren't going to get the jump on anyone riding around on loud ass hogs. Don't underestimate the T.O., though, they'll surprise you. I'm more worried about the demon aspect."

"What demon aspect?" Harlan asked.

"There's been two large demon attacks recently—"

"That we know about," Harlan interrupted.

"That we know about," I agreed. "I still don't know who's doing it or even how they're doing it."

"So, what do you know?" he asked.

I sighed and rubbed a hand across my forehead. "The demons seem to be after the elves, specifically the Royal Family. It makes me a little worried about bringing you and Isabelle out into the open. Other than that . . . Nothing. I know nothing."

CHAPTER 29

If I did sleep, I wouldn't have that night. There was too much on my mind. I called Hank to tell him about the meeting and the concerns Harlan had with the Queen surveilling the area. He wasn't sleeping either but assured me that he had it under control. We agreed to meet in the parking lot of a church about a mile and a half away from the store. I sent Livy, Yarwor, and Isabelle to Desoto Falls to stay with Walasi. Holt, Harlan, and I piled into my truck. I'd cleaned it out as best I could. The fish smell still lingered a little, but with the windows cracked it was barely noticeable. That made for a chilly ride in the cool Autumn air. It was hardest on Harlan but he wore extra layers. He came prepared with his satchel.

It was still dark when we pulled into the church around seven in the morning. The parking lot was empty. The church was a two-story brick building with a modest paved lot in the front.

Holt stopped the truck horizontal to the lines, taking up a few parking spaces. "I thought they'd be here. You don't think they ran into trouble do you?"

I spotted a small road running to the side of the church. "Let's see where that goes," I said, pointing toward the road. "Maybe they're back there."

Harlan pulled the truck around the building. There was a second smaller parking lot with a large moving van parked behind the church. When the truck's headlights crossed the cab, Hank's head popped up. He must have been lying down in the seat. We parked beside the van and I got out. I met Hank in the headlights.

"Were you followed?" Hank asked.

I shook my head. "Nah, there's no one out right now. Is it just you?"

"We've got a lot of the hogs in the back," Hank said, throwing a thumb toward the moving van. "The club's out in the woods. They couldn't stay cooped up in the truck all night."

"Isn't that a little . . . obvious?" I asked.

"If there were elves around, we'd know it," he said. "And in the middle of the night no one else would even know they're there."

"Fair enough," I said. "So, what's the plan?"

"We have two other trucks watching the other roads. We let her come in and talk to you. On the way out, we use the vehicles to make a roadblock. We just have to stop her long enough for us to get there, four minutes tops," Hank said. "Then we finish her off."

It seemed like a good plan. I had one question. "Once she figures out we don't have Isabelle, what's to keep her from shooting us up?"

Hank thought about it. "You still have thirty minutes. I'm sure you'll come up with something."

Even if the Queen did shoot me, the plan still might work. Harlan would be killed, and I wouldn't be conscious to help out. They could still catch the Queen and kill her on the way out.

"One more thing. Wear this," Hank said, pulling an earbud out of his pocket and handing it to me. "I have one, as well as the other trucks. It's got a two-way mic. If you want to mute it, just press that little button on the outside. Hold the button to turn it on."

I took the device, slid it into my ear, and held down the button. After a few seconds there was a beep.

"Can you hear me?" Hank asked.

I could hear him, both in person and through the earpiece. It made a strange echo with the earpiece being a fraction of a second behind.

"I gotcha," I said, hearing my voice through the mic as well.

I pressed the button on the earpiece, and said, "We're going to head over."

"We'll be ready and let you know when we see anything," Hank said.

This time there wasn't an echo in my ear, confirming that I had my mic muted.

"You got one of these I can give Holt?" I asked, tapping a finger to the earpiece.

Hank went back to the truck and returned with another earbud. I gave him a nod, and climbed back into the truck. I gave Holt the earpiece and told him how to use it. When he had it working and muted we pulled out to meet the Queen. I had Holt park on the side of the Wolf Pen Gap Country Store. It was a plain looking, brick building with a brown roof over-hanging about a third of the building on the front and back. It reminded me of a barn. I checked the clock. We still had a few minutes.

"We should have brought Hob," Holt said, staring out the window. "He could have just blown her up."

"Maybe," I said. "I'll be happy as long as we get through this without getting shot or eaten by demons."

Holt chuckled. "There's no way we get out of this without getting shot."

"You're probably right," I conceded. "This is a big moment. We're a couple minutes away from changing the world."

"Only if our plan works," Holt said. "If we don't kill the Queen today, then nothing really changes."

"Things will change, all right," I said. "She'll come after us. There's been some little altercations but if we don't get her today, it's going to get ugly. We're talkin' Chicago in the late '20s kind of stuff."

"What does that mean?" Holt asked.

"A lotta violence."

"She's late," Harlan said from the seat behind me.

He had been so quiet, I had almost forgotten he was there. I could tell from the look on his face that he was worried.

"She's coming," I said.

"Maybe she's got someone watching," Harlan said. "She might already know Isabelle isn't here."

"You're here," Holt said. "You don't think she'd come for you?"

Harlan's silence was answer enough.

A voice that sounded like Skinny Pete spoke though the mic. "I see her. She's headed your way down Wolf Pen Gap. It's her SUV with a guard truck on either side."

Holt and I shared a look.

"Here we go," I said.

The Queen's SUV, flanked by her guard trucks, pulled into the parking lot slowly and idled on the far side.

I pressed the button on my earpiece. "She's here."

"You have eyes on her?" Hank asked.

"On her caravan," I answered.

"We need to make sure," Hank said.

He was right, of course. I got out of the truck. "Harlan, stand by the door. When we look over at you motion toward the backseat like Isabelle's in it."

I left my mic unmuted and started walking over to the SUV. Harlan got out and made himself visible. The three vehicles idled. The windows of the Queen's car were tinted, preventing me from seeing inside. I stood outside the window and waited. I looked at my reflection in the glass. The scruff on my face was getting long. I would have to remember to shave when I made it back to the house. The window rolled down, pulling me out of my thoughts, to reveal the Queen. She sat with a scowl, anger oozing out the window.

"Your Highness. A pleasure to see you again," I said.

It wasn't, of course, but I wanted Hank to know I had spotted her.

"We're on the way," Hank said.

"Where is she?" the Queen asked.

I motioned toward the truck. Harlan moved from where he was standing to fiddle around in the backseat.

"Bring me Isabelle," the Queen demanded.

"Right away," I said. "Should I bring Harlan as well or did you not want him back?"

If the Queen's eyes were guns, I would have been shot dead on the spot. I held up my hands and began walking backward toward the truck. Just as I was turning around I heard her driver announce that the Tortured Occult had been spotted. The pretense of our meeting would only last a few more seconds. I didn't want to get shot in the back, so I took off running. I waved at Harlan to let him know the jig was up. He climbed back in the truck as tires squealed and an engine roared behind me. I looked over my shoulder to see the lead truck bearing down on me. I dove to the side, avoiding getting run over as the caravan tore out of the parking lot.

"The caravan's headed sixty north," I said, pulling myself up off the ground.

A man stuck his head out of the door of the store. "You all right? They just about ran you down!"

"I'm fine," I assured him, getting to my feet.

"You want I should call the poh-lice?" The man asked.

I jogged to the truck and shouted back, "No thanks."

I got in and closed the truck door. A line of bikes appeared to our left. We pulled out ahead of them, quickly accelerating to close the distance with the Queen's caravan. There were a few miles of road ahead through the mountainside. It was too steep to build houses directly on the sides of the road which gave us some privacy. It was a perfect place for the attack.

"Just keep some pressure on and we'll follow them into the trap," I said.

We gained steadily on the caravan until we were right behind them. The elf on the passenger side of the rear truck rolled down the window. She leaned halfway out the window with her rifle and opened fire on my truck. The bullets ricocheted off the armored hood and fenders and slammed into the bulletproof windshield I'd had Hank put in.

"Hang on," Holt said.

He floored the accelerator, closing in on the guard truck. He slammed into the rear. It jolted forward. The elf hanging out the window of the truck lost her balance and dropped the rifle to keep from falling onto the road. The rifle disappeared under my tires with a *thump-thump.*

A large pickup roared down a side road in front of the caravan. The lead truck had to have seen it coming, but instead of slowing down, the trucks collided at full speed. The Queen's SUV made an evasive maneuver to avoid the crash. The SUV clipped the truck's bumper, ripping it off, and sending it sliding into the ditch. Holt whipped the truck into the other lane, following the guard truck around the wreck.

I watched the line of bikes weave around the crash. "The Queen made it by the roadblock."

"We've got to stop her quick," Hank said. "She's got to have more troops on the way."

I turned to Holt, opening my mouth to speak, but he beat me to it.

"I heard," he said. "I don't know if I'm going to be able to stop both of them."

I was suddenly aware of the scent of something burning. I turned around to check on Harlan. He had his left hand gripping his right wrist. His hands shook as smoke rose from the palm of his right hand, filling the cab with the stench of burning flesh.

"Obie!" Holt shouted.

I turned around to see the largest portal I had ever seen snap open in the road in front of us. The Queen's SUV had no choice but to go through. Holt hit the brakes as the guard truck swerved to avoid the portal. The truck fish-tailed, sliding through the portal sideways. It was cut in half. The back of the truck slid off the road while the cab went through the portal. We began to slide. I put a hand on the ceiling to brace myself, praying to Thera when the truck hit the portal, I wasn't cut in half. Holt let go of the brake and hit the gas, straightening the truck to drive cleanly through.

CHAPTER 30

It felt like we drove over a speedbump as we transitioned from our world into the demon landscape. I didn't get much of a look at it. The cab of the guard truck rolled when it hit the ground, throwing a cloud of rust-colored dust that obscured the windshield. Holt hit the brakes, sending the truck sliding to a stop in the soft earth. Through the back window I could see the blue circle of the portal through the dust shrinking and disappearing completely. Harlan sat in the back seat, still holding his hand. He grimaced in pain, but I had a hard time summoning up any sympathy.

"What the fuck, Harlan," I said. "You're the one doing this?"

Harlan grimaced, his hand still smoking. "I guess my secret's out."

"How?" I asked. "Why?"

"After I was lashed by the Queen, and you stood by and let it happen, I decided that running away wasn't an option any more. If I just left, she'd continue her reign of oppression and tyranny. The Queen had to be stopped. When you fought that demon on the bridge, I found an opportunity. You and Cearbhall went over the side with the demon into the water, so I drove down to see if you were okay. In the center of the bridge was a leather satchel with a book in it. I had just taken the book out to look at when an athol flew down and grabbed the book with one foot and the satchel with the other. I wrestled to hold onto it and the demon only got away with a few pages and the satchel. I intended to give you the book, at first, but after Otis's assassination we didn't end up sticking around to chat. When I got back, I looked at it and I had an idea—maybe there was something in it I could use to put the Queen in her place."

"I'm going to need that book," I said.

Harlan nodded. "Of course, Obie. I have no problem giving it to you. You see, what I found in the book changed everything. It turns out that I am a magical adept. I'm one of few that can do small bits of magic without dust. I think people like me don't even realize they're performing magic most of the time. Things just work out for them. It really makes me question why things haven't worked out better for me, but that's neither here nor there. When I found the book, I learned how to use that ability to open a portal. Just a sliver of a portal, barely even a pinprick. I had a plan to get my hands on some dust and summon enough demons to kill the Queen. That, in itself, wasn't enough though. I had to ensure the throne would pass to someone . . . different."

"Isabelle," I said.

"She hasn't been corrupted like my other sisters were. She was the only option," Harlan said.

"Where'd you get all the dust from?" Holt asked. "And where are you keeping it."

"There's no dust," Harlan said, a little pleased with himself. "I would open those tiny portals as practice for when I got my hands on enough dust. One day someone spoke to me. He said he could help me. I was skeptical at first, but we talked and over time I agreed to let him. He taught me how to create a link that lets me pull power directly from this world. I can use it to open portals and summon creatures. Pretty impressive, if I do say so myself."

I put my arm on the back of the seat and twisted around to look at Harlan directly. "Harlan, please tell me you don't think anything from this place is going to help you out of the kindness of its sludge-pumping heart."

"Oh, there's a price," Harlan said. "Lord Belial isn't kind, gentle, or understanding, which makes him similar to the Queen. They are very different in one aspect, though."

"What's that?" Holt asked.

"He respects me, which is more than I can say for anyone back on Earth," Harlan said.

"You know that's not true."

A breeze picked up, moving the dust, and giving us a clear view of the landscape for the first time. The terrain was mountainous and barren with two suns beating down. We looked to be in a holler; the ground here was mostly flat. I wasn't sure if Harlan put us here on purpose or if it was just a happy accident. Either way, I was glad we hadn't come out on the top of one of the mountains, we'd probably still be crashing down the side of it. The Queen's black SUV stood in stark contrast to the orange terrain. It had stopped thirty yards in front of us. The cab of the guard truck was much closer, only five yards. It rested upside down in the dirt. I could see the driver hanging motionless, strapped in with her seatbelt. The elf that had been shooting at us right before we went through the portal was missing. We had driven by the truck before we stopped, and I was glad we hadn't hit it. A car wreck my first time off Earth was the last thing I needed.

"We better get some weapons," Harlan said, opening the rear door and getting out.

Dust, heat, and the sulfuric stick of the demon world rushed in. He walked over to the disconnected cab and bent to look through the window.

"What are we going to do now?" Holt asked.

"Let's change to krasis," I said. "Harlan's right, we need weapons."

I started my change, but nothing happened. I remained in my human form. I looked over at Holt who hadn't changed either and now had a confused look on his face.

"Obie," he said. "We got a problem."

"We're not in Kansas anymore." I agreed. "We're cut off from Thera here."

"So, we can't change?" Holt asked.

"I'd be willing to bet we can't heal either," I said. "Here, we're human."

"By the Mother," Holt gasped. "What are we gonna do? How are we going to get home?"

"One step at a time," I said. "If we can't change to krasis, I might be able to get us some guns from that wreck."

"What about Harlan?" Holt shouted. "We should be ripping his throat out!"

I shrugged. "Hard to do without claws or teeth."

"To hell with him and the Queen," Holt shouted. "We need to get home."

I looked at Holt freaking out in the driver's seat. "Harlan got us here, so he should be able to get us home. Stay calm and think. We're in a bad spot, but we ain't dead yet," I said, opening my door. "Stay in the truck."

I got out and walked over to Harlan. As soon as my foot hit the ground, I broke into a sweat from the intense heat. I squinted involuntarily to keep my eyes from shriveling up in my head. The heat didn't seem to bother Harlan. I didn't know why he wasn't affected the same way I was.

"I got no problem with you handling the Queen, but how are we going to get home?" I asked.

"We?" he asked. "Are you including me in that?"

I put an arm over my eyes to give them some shade. "Sure, why wouldn't I?"

"You haven't been paying attention for the past few minutes, have you?" Harlan asked. "Do you believe in forgiveness, Obie? Do you think I can come back from the horrible things I've done? Forgive and forget, just like that?"

"I'm saying, I understand why you did it. What's done is done, though, right?" I asked. "You can come back and start over."

"Don't be naïve," Harlan said, smirking. "You couldn't let me come back to a normal life."

"If you're not summoning demons, then we don't have a problem," I said.

"How would you know what I'm doing?" he asked. "I could do whatever I want. I guess that means I'd have to stay where you could keep an eye on me, right? So, I wouldn't really be free. That's beside the point, though, because if I need to summon a demon, for whatever reason, then I will. I'm not going to give up my power. I'm not going back to being Harlan the servant, ignored doormat extraordinaire. I won't be ruled anymore."

What was I supposed to do with that? He might as well wear a T-shirt that says, *Kill me as soon as it's convenient.* I had tried to give Harlan the benefit of the doubt. It didn't sound like I could work with him. He was still my ticket home, though, so for the time being I wasn't going to piss him off.

"You didn't answer the question," I said. "Can you get us home?"

Harlan gave me a gentle smile. "Yes, Obie, I can get us home."

"Great, can you send me and Holt home now?"

"Don't worry, I'm going to make sure you get home," he said. "But I'm not going to open a portal until the Queen is dead. The sooner we finish up that loose end, the sooner you get home."

I sighed. "Fine."

I walked around to the driver's side of the cab and tried to open the door. The frame had been warped when the cab rolled. The door wouldn't budge. The window had broken out in the crash. I knelt and stuck my head in, avoiding the few shards of broken glass that remained in the cab. Harlan was pulling a rifle out the opposite window. The elf driver was suspended by her seatbelt and wheezed as she struggled to breathe. She had a pistol on her belt, but I didn't think I could get it without unbuckling her seatbelt. I slid in under her, supporting her neck with one hand, and with the other reached up to the buckle. When I undid the latch, she fell into my lap. I did my best to slide her out without killing her.

"You can't save everyone," Harlan said, from the other window.

"Isabelle's going to need guards," I said.

One I got her outside the cab, I picked her up and took her to my truck.

Holt got out when he saw me coming and put down the tailgate. "It's hot as balls here. How the hell are we gonna get home?"

"Harlan says he will send us home once the Queen's dead," I said.

"You think he will?" Holt asked.

"We'll see, I guess," I said, laying the injured elf in the back of the truck as gently as I could.

I slid her up into the truck bed and put a rolled-up shirt from my clothes stash under her head. I took the gun belt from around her waist. She might not make it, but if she could hang on until we got home I could heal her.

I handed her gun belt to Harlan. "You take this, I'll find another one."

I went back to the cab and looked inside. I didn't see any other weapons. I could probably find another pistol on the guard that had been thrown from the cab—if I knew where she ended up. I looked around. I spotted the black uniform through the heat haze rising from the ground. As I was looking, a hellhound seemed to come up out of the ground and move over to the elf.

"They live under the ground," Harlan said, stepping up beside me. "The whole place is full of caves, like Swiss cheese."

"How do you know that?" I asked.

He met my gaze. "It's not my first time here," he said. "Stay here, I'll check her for a gun."

The hellhound started chewing on the elf as Harlan handed me the rifle and walked toward the beast. He looked like he was strolling through a park instead of walking on the roasting surface of the demon world. He walked right up to the demon and scratched it on its back. The hellhound gave him a sniff as Harlan bent down and pulled a belt off the body.

"You seeing this?" Holt asked. "How is that even possible?"

"I have no idea, but it's not a good sign," I said.

The demon went back to chewing on the guard as Harlan walked back to where we were standing.

"Harlan, assuming we get back, I'm going to need the grimoire," I said.

"What's a grimoire?" Harlan asked.

"The book you got from the demon on the bridge," Holt said.

Harlan smiled. "Oh, it's right here," he said.

Harlan opened the back door of the truck and fished around in his satchel. He pulled out a leather-bound book. He held it out to me and I took it. I felt reassured that he was willing to hand it over. Then again, he didn't appear to need it anymore.

Harlan looked genuinely happy for the first time in a long time. "All right, let's kill the Queen."

CHAPTER 31

Harlan sounded downright chipper when he suggested we kill his mother. Holt gave me a look I took as *How can you be okay with this?* I wasn't okay with it, of course. Harlan was on a dark path. I just didn't have any way to stop him. I gave Holt a shrug and we got in the truck. I wedged the grimoire between the seat and center console.

My relationship with Thera was tedious at times, and I wouldn't really consider her evil, so much as self-absorbed. I knew next to nothing about this Belial. If a deity can be judged by its creation, I had all the information I needed. This place was harsh and unforgiving, damn near inhospitable. Harlan was right in that he couldn't come back to a normal life. His admission that he intended to summon demons in the future put us at odds. I didn't want a conflict with Harlan, but it seemed inevitable. That problem could wait until later. It didn't make sense to get into it now; as long as we weren't even on Earth, it didn't really make a difference. I was off the clock, so to speak. My entire focus was living long enough to get home. If that meant working with a demon-summoner then so be it.

Holt drove us to where the Queen's SUV had stopped. The Queen and two guards got out as we pulled up. When we got out of the truck, the two guards raised their rifles and opened fire. We dove to the ground as, for the second time today, elven bullets slammed into my truck. They weren't actually trying to shoot us; if they had, we would have been shot. Just the Queen sending a message in her less than subtle way.

"Do I have your attention?" the Queen asked, stepping out from behind the SUV.

I sighed, pulling myself to my feet as the gunfire echoed off the mountains.

"If you want someone's attention, did it ever occur to you that you could just talk to them?" I asked, brushing the red dust off my clothes. "The answer to everything doesn't have to be to 'Open fire.'"

"Watch how you speak to me, Obie. I'm still the Queen, despite our situation," she said.

"That's where you're wrong," Harlan said, getting to his feet. "The second you went through the portal you stopped being Queen. Not that you ever deserved to be in the first place."

"You're lucky I haven't given you what you've deserved," the Queen spat.

"I'd be lucky if you did," Harlan said. "A child deserves, at the very least, to be safe. Forget attention, or even love. The best thing you've even done for me was ignore me. At least when you did, I didn't have to worry that you were going to hurt me."

"Harlan, if I didn't know better, I'd think you weren't grateful for what I've done for you," the Queen said coldly.

"That is all you've ever given me," Harlan said, pulling his shirt down to show a scar from when she had him lashed. "Pain."

"You don't want to feel pain anymore?" the Queen asked.

With a flash of her hand, she drew her revolver, fanned it with her left hand, firing a single shot, and spun it back into her holster. Harlan's body went rigid as if he were hit by lightning and fell backward with a *thud*. I looked down at him. He had a bullet hole in the center of his forehead. His eyes were still open, staring off into nothing with a blank expression.

"Maybe he's happy now," the Queen said. "And if not, who cares. At least I don't have to listen to him whine."

"You just killed our ride home," I said.

Holt bent over, putting his hands on his knees. He appeared to be having trouble breathing. His chest heaved. I couldn't tell if he was having a panic attack or if the heat was getting to him. He complained about the summers in Georgia. They were hot, but nothing like this place.

"You all right?" I said under my breath.

Holt nodded and waved a hand.

The Queen gave me a suspicious glance. "What do you mean?"

"Harlan's the one that's been opening portals and attacking the Nation," I said.

"Impossible," the Queen said.

"I realize you've never thought much of him, but you were wrong to underestimate and abuse him," I said.

"Don't lecture me," the Queen ordered, her hand sliding back to her revolver. "I'm not in the mood."

I started figuring what the odds were that I could shoot her without getting shot by either the Queen or her guards. It only took a quarter of a second to determine it was impossible. That didn't mean it wasn't a risk worth taking. We had gone to a lot of trouble to remove the Queen from the picture and while things didn't go according to plan, the objective was achieved. Harlan was right; we couldn't let the Queen get back to Earth. Until she was dead we weren't going anywhere—not that we had a way back in the first place. A shootout with the Queen and two of her guards was suicide, but it was better than roasting to death in this stink of a world or being torn apart by demons. I looked over at Holt. He seemed to know what I was thinking. He stood up straight and gave me a nod. I didn't see that we had any other choice.

I was preparing myself for what would most likely be my last minute when I noticed an orange light coming from the hole in Harlan's forehead. Then he sat up. Holt and I moved a few steps away. Harlan sat still with a blank expression. I wasn't surprised by that, considering bits of his brain were cooking on the ground behind him. He still had the hole in his head where he had been shot. I wouldn't say it healed so much as filled in . . . with fire. I could see into his head through the hole and it looked like coals glowing orange. What looked like burning veins began to spread from the hole over his bald head and down his cheeks. Harlan got to his feet and turned toward the Queen, taking a few steps forward.

"Harlan?" I said, coming up behind him and touching him on the shoulder.

It was as if I touched a hot stove. I jerked my hand back and shook it in a vain attempt to cool it. He turned to face me. Not his body, mind you, just his head, turning slowly around past normal limits until it was facing backward. His eyes looked strange and they bulged. I moved back to put some distance between us. His eyes popped, splattering and burning on his cheeks. His sockets now showed the same embers as the hole in his forehead, making the corners of a triangle. Smoke began to pour upward from his body as his flesh burned. His head continued around, still going in the wrong direction, until it was oriented correctly again. His attention was back on the Queen and I was glad for it. This was devolving into an every-man-for-himself kind of situation and I think everyone knew it.

"Let's get in the truck," I said.

Holt didn't waste time and sprinted for the driver's seat.

The Queen unloaded the remaining five shots in her revolver into Harlan's chest. His body jostled slightly from the impact. The holes seemed to let more heat out. His shirt caught fire from the impact points and began to burn.

"Shoot it!" the Queen shouted.

Harlan walked past her two guards.

They looked at each and looked over in my direction, but didn't start shooting.

"If you want a ride, we're leaving now," I said.

They climbed into the back of the truck.

"Traitors!" the Queen shouted, pulling her other revolver. "Treasonous, backstabbing, disloyal—"

The Queen was still talking, but her words were drowned out by the roar of her revolver as she unloaded it into Harlan. The new volley didn't affect him any more than the last, and with a sudden burst of speed, he lurched and grabbed her arm. I could hear her flesh searing from Harlan's touch as he pulled her to the ground and bit into her. I got in the passenger seat.

"Get us out of here," I said.

"Three problems," Holt said. "The truck's overheating, we have nowhere to go, and the gunfire's attracting demons."

I looked out the window to see a few demons here and there coming up out of the ground. We were surrounded. A few athol had taken off from the mountains and were headed in our direction. Hellhounds popped up from the ground all around. I saw one demon that looked to be half-person, half-snake. The snake demon hung back and watched as the others headed toward us. It was a sign of intelligence not to run blindly in our direction and if it was intelligent, I was glad it was staying away from us.

Harlan rose from his attack on the Queen, and then she stood with a blank expression and bulging eyes.

"If the truck'll drive, put some distance between us and them," I said, pointing a finger at Harlan and the Queen.

Holt threw it into reverse, executing a J-turn to get us facing the other direction, and hit the gas. He sat up on the edge of his seat, getting as high a view as he could at the terrain to avoid holes. While we left Harlan and the Queen behind pretty quickly, the demons were another matter. The truck suddenly jolted as if the back wheels fell into a ditch. An athol had landed in the back. It grabbed the elf I had laid there and took off, carrying her away.

"Can you keep them off of us?" I asked the guards in the back.

"Until we're out of bullets," one of them responded.

They rolled down the back windows and hung out each side. Sporadic gunfire rang out as they opened fire on demons that approached the truck. I grabbed the pistol off Holt's belt, tossing it and the rifle I had in the back seat for the elves to use. I pulled my gear bag from the back floorboard.

"We're going to blow a gasket soon," Holt said. "Truck's getting real hot."

"I got an idea," I said. "Just keep us going for a few minutes."

"We may not have a few minutes."

I rummaged through my bag, grabbing my stash of emergency dust.

I took the grimoire I'd wedged beside the seat and flipped through it. If Harlan had been here before, like he said, and I believed he had, then he had to get home. When he opened the portal that brought us here, he did it without the normal chanting. There's no way the first time he came here and went home he did it that way. It's an advanced technique to *think* the incantation and have it work. A few pages in I saw notes someone had made in the book. I stopped flipping when the notes at the top of the page said, "to Earth."

There was a picture of a circle. It looked a lot like the circles I has seen before, but some of the symbols were different. There was a language I didn't recognize as well as a phonetic reference scribbled beside it. I pulled a utility knife from my gear bag, and started carving the circle from the book onto the dash of my truck.

"Try to hold it steady," I said.

"Oh sure, avoid giant holes in the ground and dodge incoming demons with a truck that's about to burst into flames, but do it gently." Holt scoffed.

"I'd appreciate it," I said, concentrating on the circle I was carving.

I finished it up and it looked all right, considering. I dropped the knife into the floorboard, opened the dust, and read the incantation in the book. When I finished, the circle started to glow on the dash. I could feel a tingle in my brain as the magic worked; I held onto that feeling to keep the circle growing.

"It's working," I shouted, feeling hope for the first time since we got here.

I saw a portal opening ahead of us. It was still too small for us to fit through by the time we passed it, but it was still growing.

"We'll have to turn around," I said.

I could hear the panic in Holt's voice as he spoke. "Turn around into the demon's chasing us?"

"It's either that or look for timeshares."

"Hold on!" Holt shouted, pulling the wheel to the right.

The truck turned. I could see a number of demons flying and running toward us. Hounds and athol, as well as some other demons that reminded me of snake and dragons. The portal continued to grow. The elves fired on the demons, sending many crashing to the ground. Holt swerved to avoid a hound that made it through the gunfire. It bit at the truck. Its teeth scraped the side of the truck, ripping the bumper off, and jolting the truck hard to the right. Holt maintained control and steered us back toward the portal.

"Uh, Obie?" Holt questioned. "There's no sky."

I looked through the portal and he was right. The portal had opened in-side a building. I had no idea which building it was, but at this point in time it just didn't matter as long as it wasn't *here*.

"Buckle up!" I shouted.

The elves stopped shooting, dropped into their seats, and fastened their seatbelts. We didn't have time to put up the windows before driving through the portal.

CHAPTER 32

I braced my hand against the dash as we exited the portal into a living room, through the wall into a bathroom, then through another wall to the outside. Holt slammed the brakes, bringing the truck to a stop. A bumpy ride, to say the least. We weren't moving, but the truck was shaking. A demon thrashed around in the bed of the truck. I threw the door open and was hit by a cold that felt as if I jumped into an ice bath. It was normal fall temperatures, of course, but the sudden transition from the heat of the other world to this was a shock to my system. As I stepped out of the truck the second thing I noticed was the familiar tingle of healing. I made the change to krasis and draw my blade just as something that reminded me of a pterodactyl with two sets of wings like a dragonfly popped out from under the building debris that had collected in the truck bed. I gave it a swift strike to the head and it collapsed lifeless.

I breathed a huge sigh of relief. Holt and the two guards got out of the truck.

"Hey, Holt," I said.

"Yeah?"

I smiled at him. "You owe somebody a house."

"It was your portal," he countered.

He and the elves laughed. It was surprising and nice to see. I hadn't ever seen one of the Queen's guards so much as smile before.

"Great job, you two. It was nice to be working together for a change," I said.

"I'm Tori and this is Meghan," Tori said. "I can't believe we made it back."

"How's the truck?" I asked.

Holt stuck his head in to look at the temperature gauge in the dash. "Still hot. It'll cool down pretty quick. There might be some damage, but it should get us where we need to go."

I tucked the wings of the demon that were hanging over the side of the truck back in the bed and threw debris from the house on top of it. "Can you all check the house, make sure we didn't run over anyone?"

Holt, Tori, and Meghan went into the wreckage, calling out for survivors and looking under collapsed walls. They finished their search by the time I got the demon covered.

"Looks like no one was home," Meghan said.

"Let's hope they have good insurance then."

We climbed into the truck and left. I flipped through the grimoire as we drove. It wasn't a very big book to have caused so many problems.

"What are you going to do with that?" Tori asked.

"Thera has ordered it be destroyed," I said, closing the book and putting it back between the seat and the center console. "Let me ask you, with the Queen gone, what will you do now?"

"We have a Queen," Meghan said. "It's just not the same one it was twenty minutes ago."

"You'll both stay with the Guard and work for Isabelle?" Holt asked.

Tori leaned forward. "We're soldiers of the Elven Nation. If there's a Queen to protect, then that's what we'll do."

"We're going to drop you at the Southern Outpost and then go get Isabelle," I said. "Can you get it ready for her?"

Tori nodded. "Leave it to us."

~⌒~

I picked up Isabelle from Desoto Falls. I didn't enjoy telling her that the Queen and Harlan were both dead. She took the news with the muted emotionality that the Queen would have expected from her. She nodded and we didn't say anything else about it. I wanted her to have a stable, caring figure, so I asked Livy to stay with her for a bit. I hadn't planned on taking Yarwor, but Isabelle wanted him to go and he wouldn't have taken no for an answer, so we piled into the truck and headed to the Southern Outpost.

Tori and Meghan were true to their word. When we arrived I didn't even have to stop at the checkpoint. They had a new guard detail and staff for the outpost. Holt and I hung out for a bit, just to make sure everything was kosher and there wasn't anything to worry about. All the angst with the Nation had come from the Queen's leadership and that was gone. For the first time, in as long as I could remember, we had a chance for a real lasting peace.

I reported to Thera that I had the grimoire that caused so much trouble and would be destroying it. She was as pleased as I had ever seen her—which is to say, no discernable amount. I took the book out to a burn barrel in my back yard, with a little gas and some matches. Standing in front of the barrel, I flipped through the book for one last time.

A couple weeks had passed since the Queen was killed; things were slowly returning to normal. I had Morrison Salvage replace the bumper and windshield on my truck, as well as give the engine an overhaul. Livy had stayed with Isabelle while the management of the Elven Nation was put in order. Now she was ready to go home, and I was giving her a ride. I pulled into the little road winding its way up the mountain to the checkpoint. When I got there Meghan came outside. I rolled down the window as she crossed over to the driver's side.

"Hey, Obie," Meghan said. "One sec, we'll get you through."

"Thanks," I said with a smile.

Meghan rolled a finger in the air as she walked back to the checkpoint. The barricade rose, and I gave them a wave as I pulled through. I had never gotten through the checkpoint so easily. No metal detectors, cavity searches, or bomb sniffing dogs. I wasn't sure if it was because of policy changes since Isabelle took over the Nation, or because I knew Meghan and she was making exceptions. Whatever the cause, I hope it continued. I pulled up to the Southern

Outpost and didn't have to wait long. Tori escorted Livy outside, opened the passenger door and helped her inside.

I put my arm on the seat and ducked my head, so I could see Tori. "I hope she wasn't too much trouble."

"Oh, stop it, Obie," Livy said.

"You're welcome here any time," Tori said, leaning in and giving Livy a hug.

Tori closed the door and waved as we turned around to leave.

"Did you have a good time?" I asked.

"They're good people, Obie," Livy said. "They're on a hard road, but they'll get there."

I put the truck in drive and headed down the mountain. "Seems like they're doing pretty well to me. I haven't seen them this happy in . . . well, never."

"Isabelle and the elves will be fine," Livy said. "How's everyone else doing?"

"The Tortured Occult's still figuring things out and Holt's the same old Holt," I said.

Livy looked out the window. "What about Naylet?"

I sighed, but didn't say anything. Livy caught on right away.

"What's the matter, hon?" she asked.

"We have a meeting at the clubhouse after I drop you off," I said. "I haven't seen Naylet in a couple weeks, but I arranged to meet her there. It's going to be tough."

"Ah, to be young and in love," she said with a smile.

"We're the same age!"

"So, what's the problem? You never had a problem talking to her before," she said.

"She's my first love. She found my heart and we broke it in together," I said. "I guess I'm afraid of the outcome."

Livy sighed and cocked her head. "Listen, Obie . . . people come and go in our lives. Sometimes they go and come back, sometimes they don't. I don't know what's gonna happen. Whatever happens don't change what you meant to each other. The best you can do is appreciate the time you had together. If you're meant to come back together, then you will when the time's right."

"You're right, of course," I said. "Doesn't make it easier."

"There's only one thing that does that," she said. "Time."

"I just have one question," I said.

"What's that, hon?"

I couldn't help but smirk as I spoke. "Is it a burden being so wise?"

"You're mean as a snake."

I dropped Livy off at her house and made sure she was settled before heading to the clubhouse.

People were starting to hang out at there again, although it wasn't as busy as it had been before Chisel had taken over. Arriving early, I parked the truck out front and found myself sitting outside, dreading going inside. I showed up early to speak to Adin. I'd asked him to find someone for me. Laying my head back on the seat, I closed my eyes, and took a few deep breaths.

I was jarred by the sound of slurping and squeaking glass. I opened my eyes to find Holt standing outside the door. He had pressed his mouth against the driver's side window and was blowing to inflate his cheeks. His tongue flickered around on the glass. I thought about putting my fist through it, but I would just have to fix it if I did. Not worth it. Instead I turned the ignition and rolled down the window.

"What are you doing out here?" he asked, wiping his mouth on his sleeve.

"Just sitting. I'm about to come in," I said, getting a whiff of alcohol off him. "Are you drunk?"

He staggered back toward the clubhouse and shouted, "I'm not *not* drunk!"

I rolled up the window and followed him inside. I made the change to krasis and went to the bar. Adan was sitting in his normal table and came to greet me when he saw me.

"Were you able to find someone for the job I asked you about?"

"It took some looking but I found someone that I think will be a great match," he said, pointing to a honey badger sitting at a table alone. "There she is. Her name's Awiti. I wouldn't keep her waiting."

Even at its busiest, a honey badger in the clubhouse would have been an unusual sight. She had black fur, head to toe, with a wide silver stripe starting at her forehead and running all the way down her back. She wore plain comfortable clothes: khaki pants and a blue T-shirt that reminded me of someone hiking the Appalachian Trail. Her expression was the epitome of resting bitch face.

I thanked Adan and walked over. On the way, I passed a table with Holt, Skinny Pete, and Ginsu having a nice time, judging from the number of empty bottles and glasses on the table.

"You're over thinkin' this whole Martina thing," Ginsu said. "If you want to know how she feels about you, all you gotta do is bite her on the neck and growl a little. If she likes you, you'll know it pretty quick."

"And what if she doesn't like me?" Holt asked.

"You'll know that pretty quick, too," Skinny Pete said.

"You might want to wear a cup," Ginsu conceded. "Either way, your junk's going to get some attention."

I opted to ignore their conversation and went to meet Awiti.

"Hey, Awiti, I'm Obie. I appreciate you coming. Mind if I sit down?"

She waved a hand at the empty chair across from her.

"Did Adan explain the situation to you?" I asked, taking a seat.

"He said you wanted to hire me for a job. I came as a courtesy, but I'm not the type that stays in one place for too long, so this is probably a waste of time," she said.

"That's why you'll be perfect for the job," I said. "Why don't I get you a drink and you can tell me about yourself?"

"You can get me a drink, but if you think there's going to be something between us, I'll go ahead and tell you that you're a little too pretty for my taste," she said.

I smiled. "I'll take that as a compliment."

"You do that."

I signaled Tico for a drink. "So tell me about yourself. Where have you been? Where are you going? How many languages do you speak? All that kind of stuff."

"I've been to every continent, but only to Antarctica once. There's not a lot down there. I don't know where I'm going next. Sometimes I just start walking and see where I end up. I speak eight languages fluently and know bits and pieces of a few more."

Tico placed a couple of beers on the table and headed back behind the bar. Awiti took a glass and sniffed it before taking a long gulp.

"I suppose you've seen a fair share of trouble then?" I asked.

"Nothing I couldn't handle," she replied. "Why don't you tell me what you are looking for?"

"Basically, I need a tour guide. I'm looking for someone to take . . . a friend around," I said. "Her name is Naylet. She has amnesia and has had some trouble settling back into a life here. I want someone to travel with her, let her rediscover the world, and herself, and keep her safe."

"You want a babysitter," she said, not sounding excited by the prospect. "What are the terms?"

"I can give you a salary and I will cover all the expenses for your travels. You keep her safe and take her wherever she wants to go. Simple as that," I said.

"Is she prissy?" Awiti asked. "I don't do prissy. I travel cheap, sleep outside, and eat whatever I can find or hunt."

"That may be fine some of the time, but this is about Naylet. She needs to be exposed to a variety of experiences. If she wants to do that for a while, that's fine, but she needs to be exposed to art and culture as well."

Awiti looked down at her beer and slid it around in a circle on the table, swirling the beer inside the bottle. "I don't do culture. Doesn't sound like a good fit."

"You say you've been all over and travel cheap," I said. "Have you ever stayed in a nice hotel, taken a cruise or a train ride? Things that cost money."

"I stowed away on the top of a train in India once," she said.

I smiled. "It sounds to me like there's a bunch of things around the world you haven't done yet. If you take this job, it will open up a whole new world of experiences to you, as well. You can try another kind of life on for a while."

"How long would this arrangement be for?" Awiti asked.

"As long as she wants to travel. Whenever she wants to stop, or you want to quit just make sure she gets back here safe and sound. I've asked her to meet us here and she should be here soon. The two of you can get acquainted and see what you think. You can have this, too," I said, pushing my beer across the table to her. "If you accept, Adan has a package for you to get started. Anything else you want while you wait is on me."

She nodded. She leaned back in her chair and drank her beer. I saw Naylet walk in.

"Actually, there she is now," I said, getting up from the table.

I moved across the room and passed Holt's table again.

"Bullshit," Skinny Pete said.

Holt raised his right hand. "I swear by the Mother, lava zombies. Came back to life full of fire. Where's Obie? He can tell ya."

I walked a little faster toward Naylet. I wanted to be involved in that conversation even less than the last one. Naylet saw me coming and gave me a sheepish smile.

"Hey," she said.

"Hey, I'm glad you could make it," I said. "No Zaria this evening?"

"I didn't tell her I was coming," Naylet said. "She gave me my diary . . . I'm sorry I don't remember you. I wish I did."

"It's okay," I said. "I asked you to come because there's someone I want you to meet. She's sitting over there."

"Who is it?"

I pointed the table out. "Her name is Awiti and she is a traveler."

"Do I know her?" Naylet asked.

"No, you've never met her before. I was thinking about what you told me about how everyone knows more about you than you do. I figured the best way to fix that would be to take a trip. To go where no one knows you, get out and have some adventures, see the sights, try a bunch of stuff. Really get to know yourself."

She stuck her hands in the back pockets of her jeans and looked at the floor. "I don't know."

I knew this pose. I'd seen her make it many times before, but I wasn't going to tell her that.

"Why don't you meet her and see what you think. If you don't feel good about it, then don't go. Simple as that," I said. "There's no pressure."

"I like the idea," Naylet said. She looked up into my eyes. "If I was going to go with someone shouldn't it be—"

I interrupted her. "You can't ask me to go. If you ask me I won't be able to say no. The thing is, Thera won't stand for it. I have a job to do and that job's here."

She took my hand, stood on her tiptoes, and kissed me. "Okay, why don't you introduce me."

Naylet followed me to the table where Awiti was just starting on the second beer. She glanced up, put the glass down, and licked the foam away that had stuck to the fur above her mouth.

I started to choke up and had to clear my throat before I spoke. "Naylet, this is Awiti. I'll let you two get acquainted."

Naylet sat down and I went to join Adan at his table. I sure as hell didn't want to talk about lava zombies or Holt's love life. Turning the chair around, I took a seat without waiting to be invited. He was busy scribbling some notes on a scrap of paper the way he always did. I sat quietly, taking the opportunity to compose myself as I waited for him to finish. With the council meeting coming up as soon as Isabelle arrived, he had to wrap it up soon. He scribbled a bit more, raised the pen, and brought it down with a decisive tap on the paper.

"That's it for today," he said.

He closed his binder and put it, along with the rest of his papers, into the filing cabinet.

"Do you have everything ready for Naylet?" I asked.

"Assuming she decides to go you mean? Yes, right here," he said pulling a manila envelope out of the filing cabinet.

He returned it and locked everything with a key from his pocket before sitting back down.

"Identification, passport, cash, a credit card, it's all sorted out. Do you think she'll go?" he asked.

I didn't answer.

CHAPTER 33

The clubhouse went quiet. Everyone turned to see Isabelle walk in. While she hadn't been crowned yet, she would be the first queen to ever set foot in the clubhouse. The grandiose nature of the event hadn't been lost on anyone, except for Naylet and Awiti. While Naylet didn't know the significance and Awiti didn't care, they both paused their conversation, aware that something unusual was happening.

Isabelle looked a little different than I was used to. She was dressed reminiscent of the Queen with combat boots and jeans. Where the Queen wore flannels, Isabelle opted for a spaghetti strap tank top. She wore a gray, short-brimmed, military-style cap. Instead of a pair of six shooters, Isabelle carried a nasty looking SMG on a two-point harness. Yarwor stood to her right. He wore plain clothes and had his scimitar on his belt. Tori stood to her left, wearing the uniform and carrying the accompanying weaponry of the Queen's Guard. I was surprised to see Hob walk in with them. I hadn't seen or spoken to him in the past couple weeks. Isabelle looked around the room and when she spotted me, I gave her a smile and motioned for her to join us.

The room was still silent with all eyes following as they crossed the room. When Isabelle got to the table, she took a deep breath before turning around to face the crowd. Everyone immediately went back to their own business. With the gentle rustle of conversation restored, she took a seat. Tori, Yarwor, and Hob remained standing.

"Your coronation's tomorrow," I said. "Are you nervous?"

Isabelle shrugged. "A little."

"No six-shooters?" I asked.

"I was advised to get something a little more modern," Isabelle said, presenting her gun. "It's a Sig MPX."

The submachine gun was compact and fit her better than a rifle would have, although not as well as a smaller pistol. A small pistol may not have been *royal* enough to be considered, though.

I motioned a hand across the table. "Let me introduce you to Adan. He's the emissary for the rats of Atlanta," I said.

"A pleasure," Adan said. "Should we get back there?"

"Yes. I'm getting more attention than I am comfortable with," Isabelle replied. "I need to bring Tori and Hob with me to the meeting. Is that all right?"

"If you want them there, then it will be fine," I said.

We went into the back room. Hank and Hambone were already seated when we walked in. Hambone had a small pile of candy bars on the table in front of him.

"Well! The new Queen," Hambone said. "Come sit by me, Your Majesty."

"I'm not the Queen until tomorrow," Isabelle said, moving around the table to the vacant chair beside Hambone.

"A technicality. Feel free to help yourself to some of my candy," he offered.

"Thanks," she said. "I might have one."

As we took our usual seats around the table, Hambone eyeballed the candy bars. He subtly picked one from the pile and moved it to the other side of the table, away from Isabelle. Then he moved another one.

"You wouldn't like this one, it has peanuts," he said, taking a third candy bar.

"Let's get this meeting started," Hank said. "Isabelle, I don't want to put you on the spot at your first meeting, but I think we need to clear the air. I assure you the Tortured Occult has no ill will for the Elven Nation. Otis, my father, along with members of my club have been killed in this conflict as well as your mother, sisters, and brother. I think enough is enough and I hope you feel the same way."

Isabelle sat her cap farther back on her head, showing more of her face.

"I want to make it clear that I don't blame the Tortured Occult for any of the deaths in my family. My understanding is that my brother killed my sisters, and then my mother and brother killed each other. I should be apologizing to you. It was my family that was responsible for the trouble."

"If you don't want trouble, then there won't be any. We've seen enough blood over the years," Hank said.

"I'm glad to hear that," Isabelle said. "Actually, that's something else I wanted to talk about. In the past two weeks, I've named advisors. It's customary for the Queen to have a council. My mother disbanded hers before I was born, but I think it's a good idea. Hob is one of those advisors. I've asked him to be my magical council and he agreed. He wanted to come earlier to speak to you about it, but he hasn't been able to get away. I thought I should tell you. He will be living in the Elven Nation, and for the foreseeable future, won't be available to resume your dust operation."

"If we can't make dust, it's going to dangerous for a lot of people around here," Hank said.

"I agree," Hambone said, snagging another two candy bars. "If the dust runs out, it's going to be a big problem. Stores are already low."

"How long would it take to rebuild the facility?" I asked.

"Hob?" Hank asked.

"Three months, give or take," Hob said. "But you would need someone to oversee it."

"What about Wilix?" I asked. "Could he set up and run a dust operation?"

"*Ja*, it is possible," Hob said. "If he is willing, I could give assistance. With Isabelle's permission of course."

"It doesn't appear we have much of a choice," Hank said. "Does anyone know what happened to Wilix?"

"We'll have to track him down," I said.

"If it's going to take three months or more to get a facility up and running, what are we going to do with the bodies that we should be dusting in the meantime?" Adan asked.

"I took the demons I had to the copper mines," I said. "It's fenced off and cold enough in there to mute the stink. It's a fine place to store them in the short term."

"Does it even make sense to have this meeting if we can't make dust?" Hank asked.

Hambone grabbed his chest like he was struck by a heart attack. "Disband?"

Adan leaned forward. "Good point. If we're all at peace and can't make dust, then what are we really doing?"

"I don't like this one bit," Hambone said, standing up in his chair for emphasis. "I think you're forgetting people that would be perpetually damaged by the dissolution of this organization. We protect numerous ultranaturals all over North Georgia. We shouldn't forget them." Hambone sat down and then stood right back up. "And what about me? I'm a politician. If I lose this job, what will I do? I don't have any skills. It's like you're all just thinking of yourselves."

"There he is," I mumbled to myself as Hambone sat back down. "If we can get Wilix on board, we can get another operation up and running, or we may be able to find another duster. They're out there."

"All right," Hank said. "We'll give it a few months and see how it plays out. Isabelle, do you have anything to bring up?"

"Yes," Isabelle replied. "You had an agreement with Mother to do pack runs inside the Elven Nation. I wanted you to know that I intend to honor that agreement, but I will need time. I am already planning changes that may take a while to gain acceptance. Too much change at once will cause problems. I hope you can be patient."

"How much time are we talking about?" Hank asked.

"Can we revisit it in six months?" she replied. "I really would like to make it sooner, but I feel that's already moving quickly."

Hank leaned back in his chair and tapped the fingers of his right hand on the table. "Speaking of revisiting, who will be representing the Elven Nation at our meetings?"

"I'll attend them myself, with a couple of my council," Isabelle replied, holding a hand toward Tori and Hob. "I believe the relations with our neighbors are essential for our security and deserve my attention."

"You're shaping up to be a competent Queen already," Adan said. "There's a lot of business that we can do, now that we are going to be good friends."

"Speaking of friends," Isabelle said. "I hope that you will all come to the coronation tomorrow. It would be nice for people to see us getting along with the Tortured Occult."

"And maybe make your enemies think twice about crossing you, hmm?" Hambone said, swapping candy bars between piles.

"Closer to showing we don't have any enemies anymore," she said.

Our meeting lasted about thirty more minutes. By the time it was over the pile of candy bars Isabelle had to choose from was a Snickers with a bite out of it. It didn't seem to bother her, or if it did, she didn't show it, but she also didn't take the candy bar.

CHAPTER 34

I had never seen so many elves in one place. Not only soldiers, of which there were many, but regular looking folks. Elves that could have been farmers or accountants. Children ran through the trees and the crowd. What looked like teenagers, but were probably closer to centenarians, hung out in groups, doing their best to look uninterested in the proceedings. I caught them, and many of the other elves, giving us sideways glances. No doubt we were the first shifters many of them had ever seen. Only the oldest elves here had a chance of remembering a time when the borders weren't closed, and shifters were allowed into the Elven Nation.

There was a stage with a podium in the center, a shooting bench beside it, and tables on either side. A long row of tables with green tablecloths ran out in front of the stage, looking like the elvish version of the Hogwarts dining hall. Tucked away in the woods were multiple trucks catering the event. They loaded tables along the sides with a selection of food and drinks. Holt and I were shown to the table to the right of the podium. We watched the crowd grow and waited for the ceremony to start.

Holt eyeballed the tables of food. "You think they have anything to drink?"

"Don't you think you had enough last night?" I asked.

Our natural healing ability prevented the more unpleasant effects of alcohol, namely hangovers.

"Oh yeah, I had way too much last night," he answered. "But it's a new day."

"Maybe we should just sit here, show our support, and not attract too much attention to ourselves?"

"All right. Fine," he said, bobbing his knee up and down. "I'm going to look at the food and get some water. I'm feeling parched."

I didn't want to argue with him in front of a few hundred elves. If I thought it would do any good, I might have. Hank, Adan, and Hambone walked up to the table as he was leaving.

Holt shook their hands as he passed them and said, "Obie's grumpy again."

They took their seats beside me at the table.

"Are you grumpy, Obie?" Hank asked.

I shook my head. "Don't listen to him, he's an idiot."

"Sounds pretty grumpy, to me," Adan mumbled.

Hambone nodded in agreement, but froze like a deer in headlights, when he realized I saw him.

"There is something I wanted to talk to you about," Hank said, leaning in for what little privacy we could get. "My son's missing."

"Wasn't Lugnut locked up?" I asked.

Hank shook his head. "Not Lugnut, he should be getting out soon. Torch. He stepped away from the club when he saw what Chisel was doing with it. The last time anyone talked to him was right before we ambushed the Queen. We don't know where he was staying exactly, but it shouldn't have been too far away. He was just laying low."

"Any idea what happened to him?"

Hank sighed. "I think the most likely thing is the elves got him."

That hadn't occurred to me and the line of thinking worried me a little. "You don't think Isabelle—"

"I don't," he said. "But she wasn't in charge then."

"Have you asked her? That seems like something she would know, or be able to find out," I said.

Hank shook his head. "Not yet. It's too early for any kind of tension with the elves. If he hasn't shown up by the next meeting, I'll ask."

"If you need me to help look just say the word," I said. "I'll keep an eye open in the meantime."

Holt sat down on the bench beside me with a turkey leg in one hand. He put a stein on the table in front of him. I could smell it wasn't water.

"Did you find any water?" I asked.

"Forgot to look," he said. "They do have a ton of wine, though. It was like pulling teeth to get anything besides those tiny wine glasses they're passing out. Once it was brought to their attention I was sitting at the Queen's table, they shut up pretty quick."

"You couldn't just stick to water for the ceremony?"

"How bad could a little wine be?" he asked. "Jesus turned water to wine. If it's good enough for him, it's good enough for me."

"So, get some water and if Jesus turns it to wine for you, I won't argue," I said.

"Nah, I'll just skip the middleman."

"There's turkey legs?" Hambone asked, lust dripping from his words.

"Oh, yeah," Holt said. "They still have turkeys attached to them, but they just pull right off."

"Gentlemen, if you will excuse me," Hambone said, disappearing under the table.

He popped out the far side and made a beeline for the food.

"I don't think I've ever seen him move that fast before," Adan said.

Hank nodded. "Something tells me we won't see him again today."

The guests continued to pile in. Hob showed two wererats we didn't recognize to our table. They sat on the end.

"Thank you all for coming," Hob said. "We're going to be getting started soon, so if you would not mind changing to krasis? We have a private area if you wish."

We all looked at each other, no one willing to hide their abilities. We made the change to krasis. Gasps rose from the assembled elves. It was one thing to know about shifters, it was something else entirely to witness a change for the first time. I wasn't concerned about their shock. We were building a new world and they'd have to get acclimated to people different from them.

"I will have to go up to be introduced, but after I will come back to explain the ceremony to you," Hob said.

A forest green, four-door Jeep Wrangler with a matching escort truck on either side parked in the back. A group of elves got out of the truck; had to be Royal Guard. They still had the weaponry and surly disposition of the Guard, but no longer wore the black uniforms. Now they wore khaki tops and dark green pants. It took me a minute to figure out where I had seen the color scheme before; it matched the forestry service uniform.

Three elves took positions on either side of the Jeep. The door opened, and Isabelle jumped out, landing between them. She wore matching colors, but with shorts and a tank top and a khaki cap.

Yarwor, with his scimitar, got out of the Jeep behind her. He was dressed similarly, except wearing all green and no khaki. They formed a procession with Isabelle in the center and made their way through the crowd. The crowd parted for them. The movement of the crowd combined with Yarwor's bald gray head bobbing up and down through the crowd like a buoy in the ocean gave away their position. When they made it to the stage, the guards stood in front at ground level while Isabelle and Yarwor came up onto the stage. Isabelle stood beside the podium with Yarwor standing behind her to her right.

A woman in a flowing robe the color of fresh pine needles stood up from the table on the other side of the stage and walked to the podium. She held up her hands to quiet the murmur of the crowd.

"Who is this?" I asked Hob.

"She is the sharpshooter. A kind of priest. For an elf, the highest ideal is one who never misses. This is true in both word and action. The sharpshooter is said to never miss."

The sharpshooter addressed the crowd. "Before we begin the ceremony, Isabelle would like to say something."

The sharpshooter stepped aside, and Isabelle took a step stool from inside the podium and placed it to grant her the clearance to be seen by the crowd. She stepped onto it and paused for a moment, inspecting the crowd.

"It's customary for a family member to hold the target during the ceremony. As you all know, my family has been killed. The right of revenge is mine, and mine alone, to claim."

I could feel everyone on the bench tense up at this statement and I couldn't blame them. If Isabelle had been holding a grudge this whole time, this would be the perfect opportunity to execute us in a very public way. If it were the Queen, I would be diving for cover right now, but we sat still, exchanged some nervous glances, and I made a note to ask Hob about what the *right of revenge* meant to elves. Isabelle looked at us and I felt my feet digging into the ground, ready to propel myself away as soon as the signal was given.

"I choose to reject that right," she said, turning back to face the crowd. "There is another right I will claim though. The right of the blood bond."

The table gave a coordinated sigh of relief as a new wave of murmurs rose from the audience. Isabelle gave Yarwor a nod. He drew his scimitar and held it between them, blade up. Isabelle went first, running her hand over the blade. Aside from a slight clenching of her mouth, she gave no indication that it hurt.

Yarwor did the same and they clasped hands, symbolically mixing their blood as it flowed from their hands and dripped onto the stage. They held up their hands to the crowd, showing the cuts. Then she motioned to our bench.

"She needs you now," Hob whispered in my ear.

I didn't know I was going to be part of the ceremony. I stood and joined them on the stage.

"Could you heal us?" Isabelle asked.

I nodded, and they held out their hands. I made quick work of the cuts. They wiped the blood from their hands and again held them up for the crowd. I returned to my seat.

"Yarwor is now my family and I choose him to be my target bearer," she said.

Hob whispered to us, "Now she will introduce us and tell everyone her plans for the Nation."

She introduced everyone at the tables. The only elves I knew were Hob and Tori. There were two others I didn't know. She then introduced us, giving explanations of who we were. The two wererats that joined us were representatives of Charlotte and Knoxville. Rat populations bordering the north side of the Elven Nation. Everyone went through a customary stand and wave as we were introduced. When the introductions were finished, Isabelle began to speak in a tongue I hadn't heard in hundreds of years. I knew it as elvish, but I hadn't known they still used it or taught it to the younger generations.

"Hob," I whispered. "you want to translate for us?"

"*Ja*, Obie," he said.

"My grandmother founded the Elven Nation in 1753 as a place for elves to find peace and protection away from the persecutions of the Old World. It's in this nation that many elves, some of you included, found refuge in isolation. Far removed from our enemies, the Nation grew strong, building new friendships and conducting trade for the good of elven kind. And so, when treachery ended my grandmother's rule, my mother stepped up to take her place. My mother was a great Queen. She fought relentlessly for the good of the Nation. She made controversial, difficult decisions, but she always did what she believed was right. She pushed the Nation forward into a new area of firearms and military superiority. But for the second time, our nation was isolated. As new challenges arose we had no friends, no support, to help us. The result was destruction.

"Now, as the last living descendant of the royal bloodline, it is my duty to take the throne. It is a great responsibility, one that cannot be taken lightly. With much consideration and council, I have decided to take the Nation in a new direction. We move forward, no longer isolated, relying only on ourselves. The Nation was made strong by the actions by my foremothers. We will honor them with continued strength in a new age of cooperation. One with few enemies and many friends, where we don't face every obstacle alone. It will be a challenging transition. One that will test us in ways we have never been tested before. The Nation will not only survive, it will prosper. The Nation is strong, and we are strong through it."

The crowd repeated the last line.

Isabelle said, "So I speak the truth, so shall I shoot true."

Isabelle stepped down from the podium and to the shooting bench. The sharpshooter produced a rifle from a chest behind the stage. It was a pristine Sharps rifle—I hadn't seen one in a long time—and after holding it up to the crowd for inspection, the sharpshooter presented the rifle to Isabelle. A Sharps was a hunting rifle from the 1800s that was known to be accurate at long ranges. As Isabelle loaded the rifle, Yarwor took a circular target attached to a piece of plywood and followed the sharpshooter through the crowd. We all stood as they walked through the woods into the distance. By the time they stopped, and Yarwor held the target up over his head, the orange circle in the center was barely visible.

Isabelle positioned the rifle on the bench and readied herself for the shot. It was much too large a gun for someone her size, but the only option she had was to shoot it. She cocked the hammer and sat perfectly still, taking aim down the barrel. The slow rise and fall of her breathing was the only sign of movement, and then that stopped. Hob stuck his hand discreetly in his pocket. I could see a faint light coming from it and the wisps of burning dust coming out. The gun fired. The recoil nearly pushed Isabelle off the bench altogether. Everyone was perfectly silent as Yarwor lowered the target and presented it to the sharpshooter. They walked back to the crowd, anticipation growing.

The sharpshooter held up the target. "Bull's-eye!" she shouted.

The crowd erupted with cheering.

Isabelle picked up the rifle and carried it behind the podium. She used the podium to shield her from the eyes of the crowd. I could tell her shoulder hurt, but she seemed all right. She breathed a sigh of relief.

I caught Hob's eye and he knew I had seen what he'd done. He gave me a wink. I was sure I was the only one that knew he had used magic to aid Isabelle's shot. I wasn't about to tell anyone about it.

Isabelle waited patiently as Yarwor and the sharpshooter made their way back through the crowd. They moved slowly, showing off the target as proof of Isabelle's right to the throne. When they made it back onto the stage she waved to the crowd, presenting herself for the first time as the Queen of the Elven Nation.